G000241549

Feeling Alienated

Lauryne Wright

BookLocker
Saint Petersburg, Florida

Copyright © 2020 Lauryne Wright

PRINT ISBN: 978-1-64718-776-7
EPUB ISBN: 978-1-64718-777-4
MOBI ISBN: 978-1-64718-778-1

All rights reserved. No part of this publication may be reproduced, stored in a retrieval system, or transmitted in any form or by any means, electronic, mechanical, recording or otherwise, without the prior written permission of the author.

Published by BookLocker.com, Inc., St. Petersburg, Florida.

Printed on acid-free paper.

The characters and events in this book are fictitious. Any similarity to real persons, living or dead, is coincidental and not intended by the author.

BookLocker.com, Inc.
2020

First Edition

For my sister. Test reader, sounding board, friend.

The further society drifts from the truth, the
more it will hate those that speak it.
George Orwell

Chapter 1

Our Uber driver taking us back to the Aria hotel was Latino but might have also been alien or a government agent because he was looking at me intently in his rearview mirror.

"You're that lady that hangs out with Red Orbiters? Am I right? I've seen aliens," he said, "but a different kind."

"Where?"

"Up at Mount Charleston while camping, and it was wild, dude. There was a spaceship too!"

"Did they have red hair?" I asked.

"It was hard to see anything but a shape. They looked small, skinny but with a belly bulge."

"You said there was a spacecraft?"

"It was dark, and I saw trees that looked all lit up down this trail. I walked towards the light and saw something oval shaped with two green lights over an opening. The lights went out, and it disappeared."

"Did you hear anything?"

"Just a whoosh of air like it zoomed away. But I felt something. It reminded me of *duendes*, but more like a fairy. *Hada malvada*. It was like they could hold you back, keep you from getting too close. I couldn't move. Not all fairies are good. Some are evil."

My sister couldn't move fast enough to get out of his car when we reached the Strip, and I was left with unanswered questions, such as, what's a *duende*, and how do you spell it?

My name is Rowan Layne, soon to be a former local newspaper columnist once I relocate from rural central Nevada. I hear aliens with my overly sensitive ears or, more specifically, I hear Red Orbiters and their observers can hear me when I speak out loud. But I wasn't hearing a darn thing at the moment.

As G—that's what I call my sister, Gwynne—stood in line for fancy coffee to help her not wig out about evil fairies in Las Vegas while she was helping me find a rental house, I did a search on my phone for "Latino fairy name."

Up popped *"mediocris,"* Latin word for "fairy" and not what I aimed for. But the picture of a cloud labeled *Cumulus mediocris* looked familiar, so I clicked on it.

"A low- to mid-level cloud exhibiting small protuberances from the top."

Protuberances shaped suspiciously like a dome atop a flying saucer with little green men inside, like on one of my coffee mugs. Or like clouds my pals Rauc and Rowdy routinely created to camouflage their flying red orb.

I tried searching "Mexican mythology." Jackpot.

Duendes were little elves similar to trolls or leprechauns. About twenty inches tall, and they ran around naked. Yikes.

Someone posted, "Today, we merely sense them in the wind, sometimes we catch an unfamiliar smell or hear them whispering. But duende language is different from ours, so we cannot understand what they are saying."

OMG, if I was going to hear elves too, I was done for.

"How did we reach this point where you're the go-to girl for everything alien? My little sister? How did this happen?" said G, handing me a caramel macchiato.

After three sips through voluminous whipped cream, I was totally shaky from a sugar high, but I searched "evil fairy in Spanish."

The answer: *Hada malvada.*

Holy guacamole.

I forged ahead, looking up Mount Charleston, which I'd visited twenty years ago. Wikipedia said it was an unincorporated town in Clark County with an elevation of 7,510 feet and a population of 357. It was also the eighth highest US city by altitude.

I didn't realize Mount Charleston was known as Spring Mountains National Recreation Area, which touted, "Hiking, camping, and much more!"

Our Uber driver seemed to think so.

It was time for a chat with the Red Orbiter brothers about what they weren't telling me. As observers from the planet we know as Jupiter but they call Cumulus, as well as keepers of all known data about the universe, they were bound to have answers. If only I could reach them.

"Raucous and Rowdy Wilde, why can't you hear me? I really need you to come back from wherever you went! I have questions, damn it! And the government is on my case again! Because of you and your mysterious disappearance!"

Chapter 2

Okay, so I shouldn't have shouted out my missive to Rauc and Rowdy in public, but we were in a crowded Las Vegas casino, so no one paid any attention. Except my sister, who glared at me and stalked off.

I chased after her, feeling too-sweet coffee sloshing in my stomach.

"Where's the spa? I'm scheduling pedicures and massages," G said over her shoulder. "We need to chill."

"You know I can't get a massage here!" I said, waving my arms. "If I get too relaxed, I'll hear every freaking Red Orbiter voice out there and lose it! Plus I didn't bring the right sandals for a pedicure." My sister probably had plenty of open-toed shoes at the ready. She's a chip off the octogenarian block known as Mom in that regard.

"We'll have cocktails then," said G, frown-pouting.

"But we just had coffee, and it's only three o'clock…" I sounded ridiculous. This was Vegas, baby! Soon to be my new home.

Speaking of Mom, her timing was uncanny as always with an incoming text.

"Thinking of our dear Doodles and Peaches and hoping house search is going well!!! How is weather??? Cloudy here. Ugh. Enjoy your special dinner reservations tonight!!! (kissing hearts, cloud, dinner plate emoji)"

It didn't matter that my age was fifty-seven and my sister's sixty-one—Mom and Dad used our childhood nicknames as much as Mom used emoji and excessive punctuation in texts. Shamelessly. And in public.

It was mid-May, so the weather was warm and sunny, not having revved up to summertime extremes.

"What do you say, Peaches?" I smirked after we responded to Mom. "Shall we call a truce and shower and change for dinner so you can meet the latest most popular chef in Vegas?"

"I can't believe Rose Bergin's an alien," said G. "All those years of watching her show, and I have all her cookbooks. Her latest is called *Galaxy Table*, same as her new restaurant!"

Unlike me, my sister received the gourmet cooking gene. I was likely to lop off a finger while chopping with kitchen knives. But I was all in when it came to fine dining, especially if my sister was buying. My bank account wouldn't be flush until I sold my house in Yearntown.

I was able to get coveted restaurant reservations in the newest and most insanely devised casino on the Strip, Planet Wynne, due to my Red Orbiter connections. Or perhaps because of my auditory abilities, because the minute I arrived in Vegas, a voice in my ear invited me to dine at Galaxy Table, the voice being celebrity chef Rose Bergin.

It was good to know my Red Orbiter clout remained despite the fact that my communication with Rauc had been cut off when he vanished soon after our trip to Monterey for my birthday last month. Had this happened *before* a grandly publicized announcement about me writing an unprecedented book on Red Orbiters, I would not be in the spotlighted pickle I was now.

People titillated by all things otherworldly knew my name and my face, but my personal and professional futures were on hold, at best.

And if significant others in my life did not stop disappearing on me without a word, I might just take my dog and cat and move to the moonship to commune with Labyrinthians from Mars. Government agents presumably couldn't hound me with calls there.

Arriving at Planet Wynne early, we got that cocktail after all in the newest desert watering hole known as Galaxy Grog. Inside, it looked kind of like a planetarium, which reminded me of the interior of Rauc's orb.

"Rauc spoke to me from this bar when I was in Portland with you back in March. He said, 'Oops,' and had to run off because Rowdy won a bundle gambling again, drawing attention." I moped and sipped my handcrafted concoction with botanicals from Saturn, the extraterrestrial version of a gin and tonic.

"I know you're worried about him, but don't you think his sister would get word if something bad happened?" said G.

"It was Ophelia who told me I should just keep on with my plans and all would be okay," I sighed.

Rauc's sister was busy with plans of her own, to wed fellow Red Orbiter and scientist Bruce Robertson, the acoustical engineer who'd tested my ears and Dad's for extraordinary ability. Would her brothers return in time for the couple's nuptials in October?

"See? You're doing just that," said G. "Let's have a toast. To finding you a great place to start a new life in this fabulous foodie city."

Our glasses pinged as they touched, just as my phone pinged an incoming text message. Mom. It always was.

"Forgot to tell you!!! Your horoscope said not to take any unscheduled excursions this week and beware of strangers! Love you oodles, Doodles! (scary face, kissy face, heart emoji)"

I made a face, showed my sister, and downed the rest of my drink.

"Gee thanks, Mom," said G. "Let's go have dinner. You'll feel better once you eat something. But first, make me feel better by explaining to me one more time the difference between being OW and alien?"

"We're otherworldly, or OW, because we're human hybrids with more than 50 percent extraterrestrial DNA. But actual percentages aren't important—it's just a benchmark the Other Worldly Coalition came up with. Also, they rejected the term *alien* because of its historically bad connotation among racist bigots, but everyone pretty much still uses it anyway." I snorted.

"There's also those who have less than 1 percent human DNA, so they're an alien even if they were born here. Martians, Venetians, etc. And of course we have Red Orbiters, total aliens from another planet and pretty much gorgeous," I said, grinning. "And now, according to at least one Uber driver, there's another little alien running around as well."

"Let's not talk about that," said G with a Gigi pout. At least she didn't demand I call her by that French name she'd come up with months ago.

It was fun to watch my sister's beaming face as our first, second, third, and fourth dinner courses were served—all galaxy-to-table marvels of culinary wonder, including a cheese fondue invented in

Earth's moonship by galactic gastronomes. It came with apples from Jupiter for dipping, as delectable as Honeycrisps, my favorite.

"Who knew our moon had a culinary school? It's still hard to think of it as a spaceship," said G.

I thought she might spontaneously combust when her chef idol arrived at our table sporting short dark hair and merry green eyes, bearing the finale to our dining experience. I already knew about it because she'd spoken to me before emerging from the kitchen.

"Rowan, it's me, Rose Bergin," her charming Red Orbiter voice resonated in my ear as if she were right next to me. "Don't be alarmed. I'm bringing dessert, and yours has a special message inside. Be ready to make something up about what it says to read aloud at the table."

I smiled and nodded as she approached to greet my sister and me. G was on cloud nine because the famous chef bent down to hug us both.

"This creation from a distant star might remind you of a cannoli in taste and texture, but it has a message inside, like a fortune cookie, although the paper is edible and the 'ink' is flavored with pomegranate juice, which is also otherworldly." Rose winked.

"Pomegranates and cannoli! Two of my favorite things, Rose! Thank you so much!" I said, probably too effusively as we dove into the sweet surprise.

"Mine says, 'You will soon be rewarded for your efforts in helping others,'" read G. "Does that mean I'll hit a slot machine jackpot for helping you find a place to live?"

I rapidly scanned my message with a frozen smile. It said: "Copper, it's me. I'm okay and will contact you as soon as possible. For now, do not under any circumstances go to Mount Charleston.

And you should stop researching it on your phone. I'll explain when I can, and I miss you, my queen of hearts."

My smile was no longer fake, but I struggled to hold back tears. Rauc finally found a way to communicate with me in the sweetest way possible. And I could eat his words.

"What does it say, Sis?"

"Well, it's rather uncanny because it sounds like the horoscope Mom sent," I said before pretending to read aloud, "Avoid strange places that may beckon. You will soon have answers." Not bad for drafting rapidly in my head while my ears rang up a raging storm.

The universe was undoubtedly speaking directly to me, even if my alien lover couldn't.

Chapter 3

As we departed the restaurant, two millennials in dark-blue suits approached us.

"Well, if it isn't Tim Rider and Bart Reynolds from Homeland *In*security!" I snarked. "Am I supposed to be grateful you waited to ambush me until I finished eating?"

"They wouldn't let us in the restaurant," muttered Bart.

"Why? No reservation? Or no probable cause to harass patrons? You must be racking up frequent flyer miles stalking me. Should I be on the lookout for your rental car chasing me again on my drive north?"

"Ms. Layne," said Tim. "We're sorry to approach you this way, having been unsuccessful reaching you by phone, but we are once again concerned for your safety. We think your friends Raucous and Rowdy Wilde were abducted, and if they're in danger, you very well could be too."

My sister grabbed my arm and emitted a squeak.

"Abducted?" I smirked. "How? By whom? Little green men?"

Bart's pronounced Adam's apple bobbed as his eyes bulged.

"Rowan. Ms. Layne," Tim Rider implored, "we just want to warn you. Truly. We're in Las Vegas for the indefinite future. This is a number where you can reach us." He handed me a white business card with the Department of Homeland Security logo.

"I appreciate that," I said. "But how do I know it isn't you who snatched them? Funny how you haven't asked me if I've heard from them. Why is that?"

"Have you heard from them?" blurted Bart Reynolds, and I silently congratulated myself for refraining yet again from chuckling at his name.

Instead I narrowed my eyes. "Sure, every day. With texts full of weather reports and emoji. They send them through my mother. No ransom note, though."

My sister snorted.

"Ms. Layne, we would greatly appreciate any information you have, including whether you've received communication from them on their whereabouts," said Tim.

"Because you're so very concerned for their safety? And mine? Or because you want to stick your nose into their nonsubversive business?" I said, hands on hips. "What if I told you I received an edible message from them moments ago in my dinner?"

G's nails dug into my wrist as she emitted an eek.

Tim smiled tightly. "We won't take up any more of your time tonight. Call me if you hear anything, or if you need anything at all."

"Ms. Layne, are these gentlemen harassing you in my establishment? Do you need assistance? Shall I call security?" asked an unfamiliar yet pleasingly vibrant voice.

A tall auburn-haired man dressed in elegant black designer togs Mom would approve of reached out a manicured hand laden with rings. Emeralds flashed glowing green amidst one huge, spectacularly faceted red gemstone. Was it a diamond?

"Octavius Wynne, at your service. I trust you ladies enjoyed your dinner at Galaxy Table?" He grasped my hand with a flourish.

"Thank you, Mr. Wynne. Dinner was delightful. We love Rose. My sister, Gwynne, is a big fan."

"Gentlemen." He turned to Tim and Bart. "Surely you are aware Las Vegas casinos do not look with favor upon law enforcement pursuing law-abiding patrons inside our establishments? But if you're interested in gambling at Planet Wynne, where winning is out of this world, I will be honored to comp you each five hundred dollars at a game of your choice."

"I could go for some blackjack," said Bart Reynolds.

"Thank you, Mr. Wynne. But we'll be leaving now. Enjoy the rest of your evening, ladies." Tim Rider nodded to me, unsmiling.

"Rowan—may I call you Rowan?" said Octavius Wynne once Homeland Security departed. "Next time you must stay with us. I can arrange suites for your family. Is this your sister? Charmed to meet you, Gwynne. Love your name!" the Vegas mogul shook her hand.

"Thanks, Mr. Wynne," we said in unison. I added, "But next time, I'll be staying in the home I'm renting. Although my family might take you up on that offer when they visit."

I didn't have the heart to tell him no way could I stay in his hotel because I'd never make it to my room via elevators moving in a circular motion, like an amusement park ride, around the circumference of Planet Wynne, including the bottom designed to resemble a ringed planet with two upper portions depicting a flying saucer and Earth's moon—correction, moonship. An indoor escalator to the second floor was the only reason I'd reached the restaurant without getting queasy.

"Please call me O.W.," he said. "I trust that you especially enjoyed"—he looked over his shoulder—"dessert?"

How had I not known Octavius Wynne was a Red Orbiter? One more bit of information Rauc had neglected to impart before darting off to who knows where.

"Yes, I did. Very much." I nodded, smiling.

"Good. Please call on me if you need anything once you're settled, and come back to see us. Rose is full of culinary surprises!" O.W. pressed his business card, with its shiny red-orb logo, into my hand.

We exchanged air kisses to both cheeks, and G and I tottered off toward the escalator.

"I can't believe he goes by O.W.," I muttered. "I hope this won't mean I have to explain the difference between OW and alien to you again. This dude is just going to confuse matters."

"I can't believe you told those government guys about dessert! And what did your message really say? Is Rauc okay?" asked G, eyes growing wide. "And was that a big honking sphere of a red diamond on his finger?"

"I suppose it's symbolic for Red Orbiter."

"Seriously? Is *everybody* who's famous going to turn out to be a Red Orbiter?"

Chapter 4

I awoke with a small scream, strangled in my throat and pulling me out of deep sleep. It also awakened my sister occupying the hotel bed next to mine.

"Jeez, your snoring is bad enough, but now you have to scream? Are you okay?" said G.

I reached to turn on the bedside lamp, uneasy with unfamiliar shadows in the dark room. "I heard strange beeping, or I dreamt I heard it. What time is it?"

My sister checked her phone. "Three thirty-three."

All I heard now was a roaring rush of blood from my heart pumping. My ears rang, my go-to self-defense mechanism to avoid alien voices. Rauc disappeared before he could help me manage my auditory abilities from hairless cochlea, that spiral-shaped thing in your inner ear.

I felt as if I were spiraling, struggling to remember my dream or why I'd screamed.

"Sorry," I said. "Let's try to get more sleep. But I'll turn on the bathroom light and crack the door so we have a nightlight."

"I did that already, before we went to bed," said G. "Maybe the bulbs burned out."

No, the bulbs hadn't burned out. The light switch was flipped off.

I looked at the hotel room door, but both the deadbolt and U-bar locks were in place, and windows on the sixteenth floor did not open. "One of us must have hit the light switch," I said.

I tossed in bed, wanting to speak out loud to Rauc in hopes I'd reach him, given our shared abilities to hear from afar, but it would freak my sister out. And Rauc probably couldn't answer even if he did hear me. If only I knew why.

Roughly three hours later, I woke to voices.

"Who the hell put the little shits in charge, and why's it up to us to protect their identities?" said a male.

"Right now we need to work with them on this and keep a low profile," answered a female. "Let the Wilde brothers do their thing, what they're good at, and we will help them if they need it."

"That's a laugh. They don't need my help financially. Rowdy's so damned lucky, he has the Gaming Board breathing down my neck with all his gambling winnings. And now Homeland Security is sniffing around Rowan Layne. In my casino."

"I know, but she's good at stringing them along. I'll get with her as soon as I can."

The woman speaking to Octavius Wynne was Senator Cassandra Rojas-Ortiz of Las Vegas, when she wasn't in Washington, DC. I was supposed to meet with her because she approved of my pro-alien stance in my newspaper column.

She was a Red Orbiter. I knew that because I inadvertently heard her talking about announcing her run for president months ago. So far that candidacy had not materialized any more than our meeting had. The senator also had not publicly revealed she was an alien, even if she was born in the US, which she had to be if she wanted to run for president. But the Constitution says nothing whatsoever about having to be born *human*.

My sister stirred. "Are you awake again?"

"I'm going to get us coffee," I said, pulling on clothing. "Be right back."

She mumbled her thanks.

I was alone in the elevator due to the early hour, so I let it rip. "Damn it, Rauc! What's going on? I'm moving to Vegas, and you aren't here. But it sure seems to be Red Orbiter central. And I think someone or something was in my room last night."

When I'd left for coffee the bathroom light was turned off—again—and the U-bar lock was unlatched.

No answer from Rauc, and once I hit the casino cacophony of pinging slot machines, I might not have heard him anyway. There were plenty of new games with alien themes and no shortage of swooshing and whooping noises that were in no way stealthy like extraterrestrial crafts the world had actually observed, including red orbs. One machine had flying saucers piloted by cows, complete with ringing cowbells and galactic mooing. I wish I was kidding, but no. My ears especially wished I was.

When I returned to the room, my sister was showering and I planned to relax to open myself up to auditory messages from afar, or potential sleuthing. But I couldn't.

My notes were missing. I'd compiled lists of available houses for rent, including addresses and notations on amenities and neighborhoods, and they weren't on the desk. Had I left them in my car the day before?

As I sipped dark coffee, free of sugar or foam even if it wasn't flavored, I pondered this. "Damn it, Rowdy, you better not be playing a prank on me. This is not fun." No answer from either of the brothers Wilde.

After G blow-dried her hair, I said, "Do you have my rental house notes?"

"No, but I took notes too. Do you want them?"

"Sure." I was not going to tell her something creepy was going on.

Because I knew I hadn't left my notes in my car. When I'd researched Mount Charleston yesterday, I wrote down my findings. On the same pages. While I was out in the open in the casino.

Chapter 5

Two months later

It was a two-bag morning, as in two poop bags on my walk with Bodie in our new neighborhood. And that about summed it up.

The dog had rarely if ever pooped on walks in Yearntown, where my house was on mostly undeveloped acreage dotted with sagebrush and few manicured yards to befoul. Here in North Las Vegas, Bodie was intimidated by palm tree bark and barrel cactus, but not enough to wait to poop in our own backyard.

A yard I had chosen for its patch of grass for the dog despite misgivings about wasting water on it. Instead, Bodie lay about in the section predominated by sandy dirt, as that's what the scrappy border collie/Queensland heeler pup was used to.

I thought the two bags of poop indicated agitated nerves. I knew mine were jangled.

Last night was the Fourth of July hoopla, including insanity on the Las Vegas Strip, which morning news said required the National Guard due to "skirmishes," but not divulging details. This left my paranoid brain to speculate, and I had enough to obsess about. Not only had nearby neighbors celebrated their independence by shattering my existence and Bodie's and Morris the kitty's with excessively loud fireworks for seven hours straight, but at three a.m. I awoke screaming again.

It didn't help that Morris, orange tabby tail swishing, had sat next to my head on full alert, staring down the dark hallway leading from my bedroom to the front of the house. Bodie was curled at the foot of the bed trembling like he'd done the entire maniacal fireworks-plagued evening, but it could have been because I screamed.

I did what all lame-brained females in horror movies do when alone in the dead of the night. I got up to investigate. It was three in the morning. What could go wrong?

But…nothing. No weird shadows or sounds. Other than the fridge, which hummed periodically like a distant foghorn. It was good I didn't have a basement or attic to consider—scary places for someone who thought her childhood home was haunted.

The grown-up me now realized it was likely aliens and not ghosts I'd heard as a kid.

I let Bodie out the back sliding door to pee, noting the air hung thick with the fog of gunpowder. Fireworks—an annoyingly selfish way to celebrate these days, with too many not feeling all that patriotic.

As I had walked Bodie, fighter jets from Nellis Air Force Base flew over low and loud. When I'd worked for the military as an environmental attorney, we spun this as "the sound of freedom."

The sound of paranoia was a stronger case to make lately. My subdivision already felt like a war zone after the "bombs bursting in air" last night. As if people weren't on edge enough, what with the president Twitter-fueling fear and outrage that aliens were coming to take guns and everything else. This morning's national headlines:

"PRESIDENT DEMANDS US DECLARE INDEPENDENCE FROM ALIENS"

"ALIENS ARE DANGEROUS, MUST BE ANNIHILATED, SAYS PRESIDENT"

"PRESIDENT SAYS ALIENS OUT TO GET HIM AND HIS MONEY"

There were also egomaniacal excerpts from his Independence Day speech at the Lincoln Memorial. All of which reinforced an intense desire to remain home, snuggling with my critters, and blocking out a world gone mad.

If only I could. Instead I had to meet a United States senator from Nevada on the Strip for a late lunch. At least we'd be dining privately on a meal prepared by Red Orbiter chef Rose Bergin. Maybe I'd get another edible message from Rauc.

My phone rang, and it was my physicist friend George in Washington State and not Tim Rider or another government prober in Washington, DC, so I answered.

"Hi, Rowan! How's it going in Vegas so far?"

"Two weeks here and still no word from Rauc and Rowdy. Have you guys heard anything at OUTWARD?"

"Bruce said to tell you he can't say anything yet, but he and Owen wanted me to thank you for the work you did for us. And you know we can always use your skills."

When I hadn't been packing to move over the past couple months, I'd been writing promotional materials for their new company OUTWARD, which stood for Other Universal Transport, Weather, Acoustics, and Research & Development.

"I appreciate that, George. At this point I'd hoped to be hard at work on the Red Orbiter book, which is impossible with Rauc gone.

But I'm really feeling the need for creative writing pursuits these days."

"Are you going to keep doing your newspaper column?"

"They decided their budget had to remain local, so no. The good news is I sold my house up there at a profit, so that buys freedom to decide what to do. What about you? Doing anything exciting in the physics world with your new company?"

"Several things, including upgrading Red Orbiter technology. We're using Rauc and Rowdy's orb as the prototype, and I'm learning new things every day."

"Great, that means they're not in their orb. No wonder the government thinks they were abducted. I myself feel like I'm in *The Twilight Zone*, hearing nothing after one big brain dump about Red Orbiters. But I meet with Senator Rojas-Ortiz this afternoon, though I really hope it's not about working for her." I sighed. "You know I'm in a funk when I'm prepared to turn down perfectly good writing jobs."

"You'll find your way, Rowan. You never know what awaits in Sin City!"

***

As I drove out of my garage, my neighbor pulled into his driveway in his county public works truck. I cut my engine and walked over to chat.

"Weren't you working downtown last night? What happened that required the National Guard?"

"What didn't happen?" said Darius. "The fireworks were going off without a hitch when there was a big one shaped like a cylinder with all sorts of flashing lights spewing from it, so it seemed like fireworks falling to the ground in reverse. People were drunk and might not have noticed except someone screamed we were under attack by aliens."

See, this was precisely why I avoided crowds.

"And you remember those little 'snake' fireworks that always left black burn marks on the sidewalk back in the day?" asked Darius.

"I remember." And as Mom would say, I had a sneaky feeling about what was coming.

"Well, the next thing you know, a bunch of guys in HUMANS FIRST! ballcaps started bullying anyone who wouldn't sing their version of 'God Bless America and Not Aliens' with them, so the ground started smoking at their feet, burning a message like those firework snakes."

"What did it say?"

"It said, 'Don't be stupid!' and had a big red ring around it. But those boys went right back at it, and fists started flying and then the gunfire." Darius shook his head.

"Please tell me no one was shot."

"Only the guy who tried to shoot the words on the ground and shot his own foot."

"And I'd hoped to get away from those cretins in the big city," I murmured.

"Crazy is everywhere," said Darius.

"You guys talking about last night?" said Eddie, our approaching neighbor from across the street. "My son, Julio, was downtown and said that before fireworks, there was a group having a rally about making America an alien-free zone. A couple of them got arrested for waving guns around."

"Let me guess—they said it was their Second Amendment right to kill aliens," I said.

"Probably. But what was weird was a couple of the guys were freaked out, claiming a few of their buddies disappeared on Fremont Street during a light show," said Eddie. "Julio said they were hollering about alien abductions."

Maybe it was Rauc and Rowdy doing the abducting as opposed to being abducted. Because that "Don't be stupid" message had Rowdy Wilde written all over it.

Chapter 6

Las Vegas Strip hotels were really pushing it by charging for parking. The garages weren't even air-conditioned. Perhaps I should mention this to my new pal O.W.

But Octavius Wynne was nowhere to be seen in his Planet Wynne parking garage or Galaxy Table restaurant, closed this afternoon for a "private party." Did I feel important, or what?

I nodded to two Secret Service guys, wondering if their presence signaled an impending announcement regarding the senator's presidential run.

"You look very nice today," said one, making me pause.

Did the startlingly handsome Secret Service agent know me? Or did he just like my new turquoise boots as much as I did? Plus, I was wearing a dress!

"Rowan Layne. How is it we've never met before?" said Senator Cassandra Rojas-Ortiz with a flash of green eyes and her notorious red-lipped grin.

"Perhaps because I tend to avoid the nation's capital region, having grown up there."

"Too many old ghosts? Or buried bodies?" she teased in her smoothly coaxing voice.

"Something like that." I grinned, thinking of ex-boyfriends in clandestine areas of work while noting the similarity in our hair color. Although now my red mostly came from a bottle, and my hair was tangle-curly, not sleek like the senator's.

"I appreciate your meeting with me today, and I'll get right to it before lunch," she said.

I sat, thinking her eyes now looked more blue than green.

"One of your columns from last month is stirring up notice in Washington," said Rojas-Ortiz. "You hit a nerve, asking what members of Congress have historically known about aliens, and what they might still be hiding."

"You mean former Nevada senators scoffing references to little green men despite one claiming not to believe in UFOs and cutting SETI funding?" I snorted. "Meanwhile the other championed studying UFOs with the surprising help of a Wyoming senator who claimed he saw one while in the military."

"That's the one. You've even got the president tweeting about it, although his attacks are more about women in relationships with aliens, which also puts you square in his sights." She rolled her eyes.

Were they blue or green?

"Look," she continued, "I know Raucous and Rowdy Wilde aren't around right now, so you might want to lay low in terms of what you write."

"But I'm not doing my column anymore. And do you know where Rauc and Rowdy are? I guess you probably can't tell me." I sighed.

"You're right, I can't. Tensions are high on the alien-citizenship issue—that much we both know. People tend to vilify what they don't understand, or don't want to understand. It's an age-old story.

31

But I have a suggestion on a writing project, or more like a request for your help."

"Your eyes are two different colors!" I blurted.

The senator smiled. "One blue and one green right now?"

"I'm sorry for being rude. It just took me by surprise because they keep changing."

"They do that. I wear green contacts in front of the camera so they don't draw attention. Another alien anomaly people might demonize. We may appear human, but we're not."

"Greetings, dear ladies!" said Rose Bergin, brandishing plates of colorful fare. "It's hotter than blazes outside, so I made a nice chilled salad plate with some of your favorites, Rowan. Shrimp, artichoke, and avocado tossed with lime-cilantro dressing. All otherworldly and out of this world!" She laughed. "And red potato salad especially for you, Senator!"

"Uh, thank you, Rose," I stammered. "But how did you—"

"Oh, not to worry," the chef patted my arm. "I read your column on otherworldly foods to learn your favorites."

I smiled, but inside I was bummed there was no mention of another secret message from Rauc in my salad.

Senator Rojas-Ortiz leaned toward me and said, "I know you realize I'm a Red Orbiter, Rowan. But surely you can understand why I've chosen to not yet reveal it. Given rampant rage against anything alien by certain constituency groups, people you've written about in your column."

"At least in Las Vegas it's not every public official," I said, biting into a succulent shrimp. "In the town I used to live, too many folks wouldn't like you simply for being a powerful female. But the journalist in me has to ask: Is this why you haven't announced a run for president? And were you once an observer?"

"I know what you're asking, Rowan. And no, I don't possess the ability that you do to hear others speaking from a distance, which is how I presume you knew about my plans to run for president?"

I nodded. "What I heard was entirely by accident. If it's any consolation, I thought it was a great idea."

"At this point timing is everything. And right now we're in such a chaotic state when it comes to all things alien, it's better I remain incognito and in the Senate." She leaned towards me. "But I do require your help, as I don't have your gift for writing, but with your words I can make a provocatively persuasive speech."

"You want me to write speeches?" I asked, thinking that wily former spy Oswald Winslow was right on the money.

"Not for campaigning. It's specific issues I need to address the Senate on. Think back to when you studied property law. Remember that concept called first in time?"

"You mean the utterly ridiculous notion that Anglo Pilgrims were somehow first in time on American soil, so might makes right when it comes to who owns commandeered land?"

"Exactly." She smiled. "I need you to write about hypocrisy of the origin of property rights. I'm co-drafting legislation to counter the senseless argument that the otherworldly cannot be US property owners. And I'm supporting legislation to create an Indigenous Peoples' Day in place of Columbus Day, so I suspect you have some choice words to write about that."

"Because as too many can't quite comprehend," I smacked my forehead, "Columbus was never first in time in North America, nor did he ever set foot on what is now American soil!"

"No kidding. At least cities like Las Vegas were named by Spaniards who did actually venture into this valley," said the senator. "And Nevada was inhabited by the Paiute, Shoshone, and Washoe long before Europeans showed up and named it for snow-capped mountains."

"Boy howdy!" I said. "And count me in on writing about it."

Chapter 7

I had a rubber stamp that said, "I know I came into this room for a reason," and it was appropriate these days as I roamed about, unpacking boxes, and getting sidetracked while deciding where to place stuff in my new home.

I found the scrapbook of my newspaper columns in my not-yet-unpacked craft room and flipped to the recent one in June mentioned by Senator Rojas-Ortiz. There it was with the headline "WHAT IS IT ABOUT LITTLE GREEN MEN?"

Morris the kitty, thrilled to find an open door to an unexplored space, promptly hopped into the box and crouched down, his extra-long tail swishing in the air like a furry question mark. He protested loudly when I lifted and carried him from the room.

As I sat down to reread what I'd written last month, Morris leapt up to knead his too-long claws into my thigh.

"Ow!" I howled, making Bodie look worried where he lay curled in his spot at the opposite end of our new couch, which Morris proceeded to claw.

It was one of those cantankerous-cat days.

My column started with how, in 1992, NASA began observing potential alien transmissions but stopped a year later when Congress cut their funding, thanks to Nevada Senator Rick Brandt. His rationale? "The Great Alien Chase will finally meet its end," Brandt crowed in 1993. "Millions were spent, and we did not discover a single little green fellow. No Martian said, 'Take me to your leader,' and no flying saucer applied for FAA approval."

In my column, I espoused:

> Aside from the questionable presumption that aliens need FAA permission to fly their own aircraft, given what we know now about alien life and technology and what we continue to learn, it begs the question of what Congress may have long known and is hiding. Why the references to "little green fellows" and "Martians"? It's curious this is a chosen benchmark for determinations of alien existence. Plus, given our current "leader" and his attitude about aliens, it's not surprising they wouldn't be lining up to be taken to him.

Bodie was barking his fool head off in the backyard, so I let him back inside. Too many new noises here in North Las Vegas for a skittish dog. Not to mention neighbor pets, one of whom yapped enough for two dogs, ostensibly to make up for his scrawny stature. It did not blend well with my annoying ear-ringing. I went back to reading my column:

> And even more suspect is how many use this specific reference, even those claiming to believe. Former Senate Majority Leader Jerry Meade defended $25 million earmarked for studying UFOs. Yet when

interviewed by media, the senator said, "I am happy to discuss it but will not talk about little green men. If you want to talk science, I'm all for that."

This despite a zealous pursuit of funding from Congress for UFO research in the name of "national security." To protect us from what? Science?

One ponders why public officials would validate existence of UFOs, yet adamantly refuse to speculate on who's flying them. Why did our government spend taxpayer millions to investigate potential alien spacecraft but not pilots? It seems either naively shortsighted or protectionist, and reeks of prescient paranoia.

We now know humans are genetic alien hybrids, and some of these otherworldly human hybrids pilot flying saucers. We know actual aliens exist among us called Red Orbiters, who fly orbs. We know our moon is a spaceship inhabited by aliens including actual Martians, Labyrinthians. Our cats and dogs and a whole host of other animals and plants are not originally from Earth. What else and who else of extraterrestrial origin resides among us, and how long have government leaders known of their existence?

Senator Meade grew up in a Nevada town called Searchlight, a lonely enclave in the saddle of two mountain ranges. What did he see there that led him to enlist fellow members of Congress to research UFOs? Do he and others scoff at "little green men" to avert our attention? And if we consider ourselves superior

intelligent life forms, perhaps it's time we start acting
like it.

Once done reading, I looked up Searchlight again online. Sure
enough, like Mount Charleston, it was in Clark County, roughly fifty
miles from Vegas. Maybe I should check it out. After all, Rauc
warned me not to go Mount Charleston, but he didn't mention
anywhere else nearby with higher altitude and minimal population.

Morris was crashing into things and wailing like he hadn't eaten
for days, so I fed the critters dinner and decided to help myself to
leftovers that Rose Bergin had sent me home with.

I poured a glass of Chardonnay and pulled the restaurant box
from the fridge, flipping open the lid. On top of my shrimp salad was
a wrapped cannoli. The message inside, in pomegranate ink, said,
"Go to V of F ASAP."

Valley of Fire. Nevada's oldest state park. And Red Orbiter
headquarters.

"Damn it to hell. It's more than a hundred degrees outside, and
you want me to go to Valley of Fire!" I screeched, making Bodie
look up from his food bowl, so I softened my tone. "And yet I can't
go to Mount Charleston, which would be infinitely cooler despite no
snow this time of year."

No answer, and now I wasn't hungry and Morris's tail swished
around my arm, poised to take a furry dip into my wine.

I moved to the couch with my glass and willed myself not to yell,
but only for sake of the critters.

"And am I to assume it's tomorrow you expect me to hightail it
out into open desert? Or was I supposed to see the message in my
leftovers earlier today, or another day? And did you presume I'd be

totally available on a whim, that I have no life because I was supposed to move to be here with you and write a book about you, and what on earth am I doing?"

I drank too much wine, took a cool shower before bed, and refused to cry myself to sleep.

Chapter 8

I awoke feeling trepidation at what to expect at Valley of Fire, and I knew better than to hope it was actually Rauc I'd see, because if he was nearby he'd be speaking to me out loud right now to stop this silly subterfuge.

I slapped on a wide-brimmed straw hat after pulling my too-long hair into a ponytail and walked Bodie before heat could permeate sidewalks. No ominous clouds today, though those would have been nice to block out the blistering sun.

Stuffing two Hydro Flasks in a backpack, I headed out to reach Valley of Fire as it opened. No way was I up for a high-noon meeting like the time I first met Rauc and Rowdy in a canyon.

The park was forty-two miles from my front door, the last eleven of which were on a ribbon-candy-looped, two-lane road that might as well have been dirt, it was so crumbled and cracked. But it led to a red-rock paradise and hopefully to some answers for me, making it challenging to maintain the 45 mph speed limit.

The sign just before the entrance warning "No Fireworks" was a good omen.

I paid the ten-dollar fee and made it through the gate and then spoke aloud, figuring a Red Orbiter would hear me or I wouldn't have been directed to come.

"Okay, I'm here. What now?"

I knew their headquarters was nestled in the staggering red range of mountainous rock in the distance, but I was pretty sure that wasn't where I was headed. It wasn't accessible by road and not visible to the human eye from any park vantage point. Not much to see anyway, according to Rauc. I hadn't actually been there.

After our April trip to Monterey and before he vanished, we came here to tour the area at night from his orb, but its state park status meant tooling around in a vehicle on the ground after dark was trespassing. Campers had to remain in designated campsites. And I apparently had to remain in the orb and not be privy to Red Orbiter headquarters activity.

A voice spoke quite clearly from the ether, yet directly into my ear, "Hi, Rowan, it's Oz Walden. Thanks for coming. Drive up to the lot next to the beehive formations. We'll come get you after making sure you haven't been followed into the park."

Well alrighty then. I was meeting Rauc and Rowdy's uncle, a former NASA astronaut. But who was the "we" in the equation? And did they think Homeland was still on my tail?

It didn't matter. I was happy to be swooning over colorful and calming—at least for me—sandstone formations worn down by wind and rain over millions of years.

I didn't want to leave my engine running with the AC on, and I wasn't going to sit in a car that would rapidly turn to sizzle city. So I grabbed my backpack and left my SUV, slapping on a straw hat to head for rocks that did indeed resemble giant red-and-orange-streaked beehives.

Oz said, "We'll be there in five."

"Okay, I'm paying homage to the sandstone."

I figured it wouldn't be an orb that swooped down to collect me, and I was right. A Jeep with two men I recognized pulled into the parking lot. I'd met one at the OUTWARD facility in Washington State. I'd also seen them both on television.

Oswald Winslow, aka "Win" and former American spy, hopped from the Jeep before it came to a stop and swept me up into a strong hug, surprisingly not unwelcome. "Hiya, Rowan," he said. "It's damn good to see you again."

"Good to see you too, I think. Is everything okay?"

"Yes and no. But you weren't followed, so that's good. We don't need Homeland or anyone else sniffing around," he said, taking my arm and depositing me in the front seat before leaping in back.

Oz, short for Olin Zachary, grinned from the driver's seat, his turquoise-blue eyes twinkling when he raised sunglasses to greet me. I remembered his silver flattop and oversize ears from his stint on *60 Minutes* discussing Red Orbiters. Back when we didn't know he himself was one—or I didn't know back then. He still hadn't come out to the rest of the world as far as I knew.

As Oz drove to Arch Rock Campground on Scenic Loop Road, he glanced at me and said, "Sorry about all the secrecy with the cannoli message. I didn't want to pop in your ear and startle you when we hadn't met, so Rauc suggested it. Plus, we never know who's listening these days in public places."

"Are you going to tell me where Rauc is?" I tried not to sound too testy.

"We'll talk in my RV," said Win. "I'm staying here while I consult with Red Orbiters for OUTWARD and work on other issues."

Other issues? Cagey and vague, tricks of his former trade. Plus, he was one of a dozen aboard the spaceship as a human-hybrid member of the Other Worldly—or OW—Coalition that shocked the world when it landed in Monterey Bay while I was there with my folks last November.

We entered a surprisingly spacious and unstuffy RV, which I was relieved to discover wasn't chock-full of an arsenal like it belonged to some doomsday prepper.

"Are you thirsty? I've got bottled iced tea. Peach flavored," said Win.

I narrowed my eyes at him.

"Let's just accept I know pretty much every detail about you that could be gleaned from various sources." Win handed me a chilled bottle of my favorite summertime tea, which I immediately pressed against my sweltering neck.

"I presume I don't need to worry about potential interrogation then?" I snarked after taking a gulp of tea, and we sat at the table. "So what am I doing here? And it's nice to finally see you, Oz. I've never met an astronaut. And where the hell are your nephews?"

"Rauc and Rowdy are in the moonship working issues of intergalactic diplomacy," said Oz. "But that's not why they initially disappeared. They were abducted but not anymore."

"So Homeland was actually right about something?"

"I wouldn't go that far," said Win, who was seated next to me. His lean-muscled arm brushed mine as he took a sip of his drink. Was the ex-CIA clandestine officer left-handed?

"Rowan, dear," said Oz. "When Rauc announced you would write about what Red Orbiters do and know, certain entities objected."

"Other Red Orbiters?"

"No, another species entirely. And these little dudes don't necessarily play nice in the sandbox," said Win.

Chapter 9

"Please tell me I don't have to be concerned about evil elves in addition to aliens?" I said.

Both men burst out laughing. When the sound of their mirth died down, I realized my ears were bleeping in a strange, though not unprecedented, manner.

"Why's your head cocked, Rowan? What are you listening too?" asked Win.

"I'm not sure, but it sounds like an electronic transmission."

"They tracked you here," said Oz as something slammed against the side of the RV, or onto the roof. I couldn't tell, and it didn't matter because I hit the floor and scrambled under the table while everything was shaking.

We got slammed again, and the RV shook back and forth like an earthquake was underway. Win was now on the floor with me, inexplicably laughing as he held me in his arms.

"Dust devils," he whispered in my ear. "They're pissed they can't get ears inside."

"They're pushing it," said Oz. But he, too, grinned.

"This is nuts." I panted.

"A temper tantrum," assured Oz. "It'll be over soon, once they realize we aren't going to run outside screaming."

Another roaring slam nearly teetered the RV on its side, or felt like it did.

"It sounds like we're under mortar attack," I muttered, clenching my teeth.

"Good thing it's not hail, which they wouldn't dare attempt in July. Too suspect."

"Hail? What are they? Some sort of weather wizards?" I asked Win, whose face was pressed next to mine, arms gripping me tightly because I was shaking. And I didn't know if it was due to dust devil mania or him and the way he felt, up close and far too personal. Not to mention I could see something under the skin of his arm that looked disturbingly like a bullet.

"They tend to use weather tricks to screw with humans," said Oz. "I'm done with this."

He staggered to the couch while the RV swayed and ricocheted, pulling a small, slim device from his pocket resembling the phone Rauc had given me for contacting him privately, of no use once he disappeared.

"Red Orbiter Oz Walden here! Cease fire! Cut it out, right now!" he shouted into it.

A peaceful pause, and then another wham!

"Okay, fine!" Oz roared. "Keep it up, and the lady here will do a press conference this afternoon on the origins of dust devils!"

Immediate and total calm. Silence too, except for Win laughing.

My blood pressure shot up. "So this is funny? I'm supposed to be amused?"

"It's hilarious," gasped Win. "The little cretins throw one hell of a hissy fit when they can't just snatch someone. Control freaks to the max."

"Hey, Oz," said Win, catching his breath. "Tell them they better be glad I've got insurance on this thing."

"You okay, hon?" Oz offered me a hand so I could get up from the floor.

"I don't entirely know," I said, sinking to the couch. "What's going on? What on earth are they?"

"Little green men!" said Win before collapsing in another chuckling heap.

"More like menaces," I grumped, which only made him laugh louder.

Oz toed him with his hiking boot. "Come on, man. She deserves some answers."

"Okay, so they're not actually men and are only green in natural light," said Win, sitting up but still grinning, which was disconcerting. "In artificial light, they are…wait for it...gray!"

"I'm in *The Twilight Zone*," I murmured, cocking my head. "So, what's with the beeping?" I still heard it, rapid-fire.

"That's how they communicate from a distance," explained Oz. "It's high frequency so most humans can't hear it, and it resembles Morse code, though it's their language. The guy who invented Morse code likely had hearing capabilities like you and your dad, Rowan."

"But they communicate in person through mental telepathy, and we don't know that language," said Win, now snuggled next to me on the couch. "They can also really mess with your mind if you're in their direct presence."

Kind of like the ex-spy was messing with mine by sitting too close?

"And they really do abduct people?" I asked.

"People, other species, whatever yanks their chain at any given moment. They nabbed Rauc and Rowdy after getting twisted around the axle that your book would be a tell-all of their activities as documented by Red Orbiters."

"I'm fairly sure they were in my hotel room snooping around months ago and, more recently, in my house in the middle of the night. Why didn't they abduct me? And they better leave my critters alone." I frowned, wrapping my arms across my stomach.

"Greens won't mess with Bodie and Morris," said Win, "because they're afraid of cats, and dogs often think they're something to chase. Neither is susceptible to their mind manipulation."

"You even know my pets' names?" I swatted Win's leg and wished I hadn't. It felt like hard cheese. Very hard.

"As for you," said Oz, "Rauc and Rowdy told them if you were abducted, you would absolutely write about it. And if they messed with your mind so you couldn't remember, they'd end up plastered across every front page. You'd go on every TV and radio program, spreading the word about them."

"And unlike their other victims," added Win, "the world would believe you because Red Orbiters would confirm every word you spoke."

"Yikes," I said. "So the only way I'm protected is by not writing about them?"

"Pretty much." Win shrugged. "But they're stubborn, apparently not convinced you won't blow their cover."

"Do they have some connection to Mount Charleston?"

"It's their regional headquarters. A western hub, like Valley of Fire is for us," said Oz.

"Well, no wonder. I researched it on my phone. Do they think I'm stalking them?"

"Likely so. They also don't want you leading Homeland to their whereabouts," said Win.

"How much do the feds actually know? And don't give me some mumbo-jumbo spook answer." I glared at Win but didn't swat his leg again. Mostly because his hand was now on my leg, feeling way too strong and capable. Alarming, yet protective.

"Certain factions of the government know of their existence. Some have more intel than others, but the information is not disseminated far and wide," said Win.

I snorted. "Ya think?"

Chapter 10

"The problem is," explained Oz, "Greens don't like attention drawn to them. If word gets out in the current political climate, can you imagine what the president would say about them, or blame them for? Not to mention his cronies in Congress."

"Boy howdy," I said. "And not to mention Mr. Superspy here finding them a source of mocking amusement."

Win tweaked my thigh above the knee, making me twitch.

I shot him my best steely eye, which was no match for his, and said, "So how do I convince them I mean no harm and will not out them to Homeland or anyone else? Can't I just meet with them to tell them I'm only writing about Red Orbiters?"

"Negative on that," said Win.

"You do not want to approach Greens if you don't have to," said Oz. "And they likely wouldn't let you."

"Then what do you suggest?" I waved my hand around. "I want to explore Vegas, and it shouldn't be up to little green...whatever's to determine where I go. Do you really call them Greens? Like they're salad or veggies? No wonder they're grumpy."

"Don't you want to hear why my nephews are in the moonship? Perhaps it will persuade you as to a course of action," said Oz.

"Of course." I sighed, frowning. "I kind of got sidetracked, what with maniacal dust devils wrought by little green dudes."

Oz stood his tall, gangly frame and approached me on the couch. "Clear out, scamp," he said to Win. "Go get the lady more tea."

Win slid away from me but not before giving me a piercing glance, the implication being, *You and I aren't done yet. Not by a long shot.*

My mouth went dry, and I thought of Mom—which, given her timing, is why my phone pinged.

"Excuse me," I said. "My mom's texting me, and if I don't answer right away, she'll think I've been abducted."

"Sure," said Oz. "Do you look like your mom? Is she single?"

"Somewhat, but more like my dad's mom. And Dad's still in the picture."

"Bummer," said Oz.

I stifled a chuckle at a retired NASA astronaut alien saying "bummer" and wanting to date my mother.

Mom texted, "Your father keeps expecting me to tell him what he was doing before he came to ask me what he was doing. And he was supposed to fix us lunch. Now he's cooking bacon for BLTs, and I have to make sure the bacon is crisp the way I like it. But I can't have tomato anymore because it gives me hives. (frowny face, tomato, bacon emoji)"

Holy cow, there's a bacon emoji.

As I typed a quick emoji-less reply to Mom, Oz's phone also beeped with a text.

"I need to step outside. Headquarters wants to know why they're being bombarded with dust devils," said Oz, chuckling.

I was suddenly alone with a former James Bond who looked way too tasty in his tight white t-shirt. Lean, hard muscles that didn't bulge. They didn't need to. And that was definitely a bullet embedded under his skin.

"It just occurred to me that Greens won't be thrilled about a column I wrote, which repeatedly referenced little green men and what Congress might know about them. Do they read?"

"Probably not firsthand, but they'd likely hear of it," nodded Win, eyes narrowing. "And they do tend to get tweaked about anyone else reading about them, or suggesting they exist."

"Well then, I'm toast."

"Not necessarily. Maybe there's a way to deflect the spotlight— to another alien species."

"What other aliens?" I glared at Win. "Lizards? Hummingbirds? What are you not telling me?"

Chapter 11

"Have dinner with me, and I'll reveal all," said Win, flashing a dangerous grin.

"Fine. Why don't we eat in Searchlight? I want to do a little reconnoitering."

Win snorted. "To begin with, there's nothing there. And only one chain diner. Not exactly what I had in mind for wining and dining Rowan Layne."

"What do you mean, nothing's there? What if it's a hotbed of alien activity?"

Another snort, and I itched to swat his arm.

I said instead, "It is, after all, where Senator Meade grew up, and I suspect his interest in UFOs and little green men was hatched long before he entered Congress."

No more snorting. But I did get a raised brow followed by a gaze that I'd be lying if I said it wasn't intimidating. And titillating.

"What are you after, Rowan? If you want a *hotbed* of alien activity"—his light-blue eyes pierced my smirk— "you might as well stay here tonight. Valley of Fire won't disappoint. Neither will I."

"I'm tired of everyone diverting me from here, there, everywhere. I've got a Red Orbiter senator concerned for me about what I write, albeit legitimately, and a bunch of fellas herding me like I'm cattle.

This Texas Longhorn's about had it." I scowled, hands on hips. "Wait? Did you just proposition me?"

"Maybe we're just looking out for you. And yes, I did."

"Is this about concern for my safety? Like Homeland Security? Please!" I scoffed. "Maybe all y'all could use your influence to prevent the president and his cult-member thugs from attacking women on Twitter. *That* might be helpful."

"Did you just ignore my proposition?"

"No," I snapped. "I'm still trying to process it." And still confused by my potential attraction to his cool-eyed, slick persona.

"All right." He held up his hands in surrender. "If you don't want help, I'll butt out."

"Win, it's not that I don't appreciate you having my back." I put my hand on his shoulder. "But I spent years after 9/11 feeling like I needed personal bodyguards from the bad guys. Guys who were supposedly foreign, but who've turned out to be domestic Twitter terrorists and demented, trigger-happy homeboys way too emboldened these days. By comparison, aliens seem like an invigorating, enlightened challenge."

"I get where you're coming from." Win laid his hand on top of mine. "But you can't fault those of us who deem courageous people worthy of protecting."

I took a step back. "That's why you want me to have dinner with you? To protect me?"

He smiled, and it was unnerving because it made him frighteningly attractive. Win was a man deceptively unremarkable in size and appearance, but that smile…so similar to the sinuous way he moved—as if stalking prey.

"Look, I moved too quickly after my last disastrous relationship, which I also jumped into hastily and with blinders on. But I gave it another go, only to have Rauc disappear without a word. I am too old for this. I have enough to deal with making sure my dog likes me, not to mention my crazy cat."

"I saw you, you know. Sitting on a bench, talking to otters and seals in Monterey Bay when you lived there."

"What on earth?" I gaped.

"I remember being struck by how absurdly beautiful you were, so utterly unselfconscious, and beguiling. Then I noticed the wedding ring, and my heart plummeted."

"You were *spying on me* thirty years ago?" I screeched.

"No. I was out for a run. And a student at the Defense Language Institute."

"You were in the military? Please tell me not the Marines."

"No." That smile again. Was it just another skill born of his tradecraft?

"So how many languages do you know, Mr. CIA Slickster?"

"A few." He all-out grinned.

"Are you an Aggie?" I frown-squinted. "I know the agency loves to recruit from there."

"Yes, but not Texas. My undergrad degree is from New Mexico State."

"Physics?"

"Behavioral psychology."

"Ouch. Okay, I'll have dinner with you." I slapped my thighs. "But please not Galaxy Table or anywhere near Planet Wynne. I need a breather from all things Red Orbiter."

"Glad to hear it," he said, this time unsmiling. A sizzling and oh-so-lecherous gaze.

I gulp-swallowed. Damn it, was I now afflicted with dry mouth like Mom?

"Do I have to wait until our dinner date to learn why you've got a bullet embedded in your bicep?" I nodded towards his arm.

"No. It's a work-related injury, too tricky to remove." His eyes didn't waver any more than his tone.

"Can I touch it?" *Did I just say that out loud?*

Win smiled slowly. "The very words every teenaged male longs to hear."

Chapter 12

That was the problem with the raw-silk Win. He made me feel like I was in high school again. Or my libido was.

I was not in any way confident this was a good thing.

So it was a relief to have Oz return, muttering about wanting to make mincemeat out of Greens.

"Pain in my ass," he said. "Give me a beer, Win, and let's talk counterintelligence."

"Where should I start? With the CCS Block?"

"Sounds as good a place as any other."

Win turned to me. "Space Force is using an updated CCS Block to deny communications capabilities of others. It essentially jams an adversary's satellite transmission, and right now they're using this so-called nondestructive electronic weapon against the moonship. Which is why Rauc can't communicate with you directly."

"So I have Space Farce and its galaxy domination fetish to thank," I smirked.

"As you may know, Rowan, the moonship has already been under attack by the Pentagon," said Oz. "It started when the president got frustrated over not being invited to visit. He ordered F-35s to stage a forced entry because he thought no one could see them."

"And someone had to explain to him that they couldn't fly all the way to the moon nor does stealth capability mean invisibility?"

"That, and find a way to appease him. Hence, deployment of the CCS Block—that is, once an April Fools' Day attack was foiled by a magnetic force from Red Orbiters. It protects spacecraft from things like missiles and other forms of sabotage."

"Did that ignoramus really give an order to launch a missile at the moon? And on my birthday?"

"Something like that," said Win.

"My nephews are there to stave off a nasty confrontation between Earth and its moon. Comical, but not really." Oz shook his head. "The US is on track to alienate everyone on Earth, including Greens, but also every living entity on the moonship and beyond."

"The Founding Fathers were right to be worried about people too stupid to entrust with a vote. Look what we've come to." I snorted in disgust.

"At this point, we need a diversion to shift focus from the moonship, Red Orbiters, and Greens. Anything deemed a threat by the government or citizens stirred into a frenzy over alien invasions," said Oz.

"We're going to create a fictitious alien species, complete with accompanying spacecraft, at which all of this misplaced paranoia can be directed. Orchestrate a new target," said Win.

"But isn't that deceptive and potentially dangerous?"

"This administration already decrees everything real to be fake, everything dire to be a hoax, and everything alien as the enemy," said Win.

"Yes, but two wrongs don't make a right," I said, realizing I sounded like my third grade teacher.

"The key is to pull this off for as long as necessary to prevent galactic war while these idiots are in power," said Oz.

"Maybe it will help if you hear details about the plan from your friend George," said Win. "I'll get that teleconference going." He pulled a screen down over a window and said, "You there, OUTWARD?"

George's smiling face popped into view on the screen, complete with wire-rimmed glasses and blond dreadlocks.

"Hi, Rowan! Surprise! Remember when I told you we'd been working on new technology for orbs? Turns out that wasn't the whole story," he said.

A picture replaced him on the screen, colorful. Kind of like a rainbow shimmering on the surface of a soap bubble but shaped more like a peach pit.

"This is a design of a spacecraft for Red Orbiters," he said. "They require new transportation for long-distance and space travel, and this benefits from concealment by color."

"Concealment?" I said. "Looks pretty flashy to me."

"Funny thing," said George. "It's based on the colored shell of what's known as the iridescent jewel beetle. Scientists determined it produces visual signs that confuse predators, making it a form of camouflage."

"No kidding?"

"The changeable, metallic colors create an illusion of inconsistent features and depths in landscapes, making it difficult to identify a target shape, helping to elude detection or attack. Also, the iridescence doesn't shine as brightly in dappled sunlight, making it difficult to see against certain backdrops. It works for the beetle, so we think it will help Red Orbiters avoid undue notice in daylight."

"But it's not an orb," I said.

"Yes, well, this shape—kind of like a pistachio nut—blends better. It's not as distinctive as a sphere or a flying saucer, which are also less aerodynamic than this more cylindrical craft."

"If you say so." I shook my head in wonder. "Does it open like a pistachio shell splits in half?"

George chuckled. "Actually, it does."

"So your idea" —I turned to Win— "is that some sort of alien flies about in this craft that looks like a jewel beetle and is gearing up to attack Earth?"

"Earth, other alien species, anything as long as it's deemed hostile for purposes of diversion from entities well on their way to being extremely ticked off at the US under its present leadership."

"Question," I said. "Was one of these beetle crafts out and about in Las Vegas on the Fourth of July? Shooting fireworks at spectators and lasering messages onto the ground?"

"What was the message?" said Oz.

"My neighbor told me it said, 'Don't be stupid.' And you know exactly who that sounds like." I stared at Oz. "Was it Rowdy?"

"No, Rauc and Rowdy were already at the moonship, and it wasn't a Red Orbiter craft."

"Then who?"

Oz sighed. "Greens. They fly in cylindrical crafts, and they're still peeved with Rowdy for putting their likeness on a sign in Yearntown next to the same message on the ground. So they persist in making it look like Red Orbiters are causing trouble. Vindictive little bastards."

Chapter 13

"Where do I fit into this end-justifies-the-means beetle scheme?"

"Rowan," said Dr. Bruce Robertson, appearing in place of George onscreen in all his handsome, redheaded glory, "we hope you understand why the Red Orbiter book is delayed. We can't have attention on us any more than Greens due to current social and political upheaval. But that doesn't mean you can't participate in our plans."

I looked at Win. "You want me to spy with you?"

"In a manner of speaking. It's more like adapting the situation to our advantage. Homeland is already watching you. We can use that to make them useful in perpetuating this idea of an Iridescent Insect War."

"Insect War? That's seriously where we're headed?"

"It may sound bizarre," said George from off-screen. "But think how outlandish the whole concept of aliens was for many when the news broke this time last year."

"Speaking of aliens, where's Owen the Martian Marine? Is he visiting his homeland?"

"No, he's aboard the moonship with Rauc and Rowdy, trying to keep his fellow Labyrinthians not only from destroying US satellite communications blocking capability but also from obliterating Space

Force in its entirety. Tensions are high, and folks are fed up with suffering fools."

"I honestly do not know how to feel about that." I bit my lip. "But this whole insect thing might work. I for one know many Marines are terrified of bugs."

"No comment," said former Marine Bruce, chuckling. "With your auditory ability at the forefront of government focus, Rowan, they're already predisposed to believe you're in on alien secrets by hearing communications."

"So we build a scenario," Win chimed in, "wherein you feed them intel about the Iridescents and how it *sounds like* they might be planning attacks on America."

"Okay, but you know the president is never going to be able to spell *iridescent*," I said. "And do you also want me to write about this? Through a blog or something?"

"Negative on that for now," said Win. "We need to be concerned for your safety and keep you out of the social media spotlight. And also not have you take the fall for the ultimate misconception."

"But that doesn't mean you can't write about it in another capacity." George popped back on-screen with his happy-go-lucky Pollyannaism, dreadlocks swaying. "As you know, Las Vegas has an active writers community. Join up and share your work for feedback. Write about UFO sightings. Weave real-life experiences into a fictional series. You get the picture?"

"It's your chance to launch the adventures of Luna Moth Woman upon the literary world!" crowed Win.

"How'd you know I want to write about Luna Moth Woman?" I asked, giving Win my best stink eye, but he merely grinned.

"We think once you start reading aloud at meetings, certain entities will show up to learn more—and to secretly corroborate what you've told Homeland. And I'll be working behind the scenes to facilitate this," said Win.

"Of course you will," I snarked. "So where are these bug creatures supposed to be from?"

"Uranus!" Oz grinned. "The planet humans like to make fun of due to its Earthling name, which is actually a derivative of Greek god Ouranos, father of Saturn. Humans and their obsession with Greek gods. Don't get me started."

"What are their real names?" I asked the Red Orbiter-turned-NASA-astronaut.

"Saturn is Cultura, and Uranus is Glacies."

"Did you know that Uranus, or *Glacies*, wasn't discovered until modern history because it was too dim to be seen by ancient civilizations?" said Win. "And did you know our equally dim leader of late decries having alien DNA, but what little he possesses comes from…Uranus!"

"That's going to make it extra special when he attacks the origin of Iridescents, because you know he will," I said.

"We're counting on it," said Win, looking up from his phone. "But we might be a tad late in keeping you out of the spotlight, because he's attacking you on Twitter as we speak."

He handed me his phone so I could read: "Nasty alien lover and writter Rowen Lane met with sneeky sen. R-O in Nevaduh. Helping aliuns take your guns and steel my money and I don't have sex with aliuns. Red Orbitoors lie. Ploting against me. Coused 2008 market crash."

Unholy crap, the president tweeted about me, although he couldn't spell my name or anything else correctly. No wonder he didn't attempt *Rojas-Ortiz*.

Win read what it said for the others.

"Painful," said George.

"I'll handle this," said Win. "Rowan, it's best if you don't respond."

"I've learned the only way to deal with a narcissistic sociopathic is not to engage. They want you to do so, *need* you to feed their sickness so they can twist your words and ultimately accuse you of that which they are culpable and guilty. A vile form of projection, and it's toxic." I sighed and pressed a hand to my forehead. "So no, I won't respond. And I don't follow the president, or any of his followers, on Twitter. But I do plan to honor Senator Rojas-Ortiz's request to write something about property rights in support of legislation."

"Capital idea," said Oz. "The senator's on track to have you writing things that won't trigger Greens, even if anything and everything a smart woman does yanks this White House wanker's chain."

"You've got quite a way with words yourself, Oz." I smiled.

"Thanks," he said, winking. "I've got to head out for a meeting, filling in for my nephews with an update on OUTWARD progress. Thanks, everybody. I'll see you soon, Rowan."

I was alone in the RV with Win, but at least George and Bruce were still on screen.

"Good to see you, Rowan," said George. "Work with Win on next steps, as we won't be sending anything via email or text on this plan. And happy writing, Luna Moth Woman!"

The screen went dark, and I was out of peach tea again.

"So what time should I pick you up tonight?" said Win, looking far too pleased with himself.

Chapter 14

Going out to dinner, even if it was a working date, was tricky in hundred-plus temperatures. I unearthed a black sundress Mom sent the week I moved here and paired it with espadrilles she got me last year. Thankfully, they weren't open-toed, as I'd been too busy for a pedicure but no way was I attempting boots again in July. My hair hadn't been trimmed in eons, and it smothered me when down—but I wasn't a bun woman either, so, ponytail.

I was anxious to observe how Bodie reacted to Win. Would he like him? Was that a realistic indicator? After all, the dog had seemed to worship my ex live-in, Lucas, when he ought to have been wary. Although I couldn't rationally fault Bodie because I damn well should have been more discerning too.

Bodie barked before whimpering, which he always did when someone was outside. I looked out to see Win's Jeep, all zipped up so at least I could count on AC for the ride. I also watched him walk to my door, which I shouldn't have. The man moved like syrup oozing over pancakes. Pure, maple, potent. Well-fitting khakis and tight black t-shirt did not help.

"This is a great house," he said, stepping inside. "You look wonderful."

"Thanks. I'm still unpacking."

"Hi, Bodie," Win said, petting him as if they'd done this every day for years.

Bodie did the lean thing before rolling on his back for a belly rub.

"That answers that," I murmured.

Win looked up, knowing. Damn it.

No secrets from this dude.

Morris, who usually hid at least temporarily from a human invasion, strolled right up, tail swirling with an air of insouciance, his deep purr resonating in the clay-tile-floored room.

"And here's Morris the kitty," Win said, stroking his white-furred chin. "So nice to meet a champion mouser."

"Are you an alien?" I asked. "Perhaps even a Red Orbiter observer who's listened to my every utterance?"

"No." He laughed. "But I am 83 percent OW."

"You are not—I am!"

"See? We're practically twins, we're so compatible."

That smile had even the backs of my knees perspiring, and we weren't outside yet. He'd probably unearthed innumerable state secrets from unsuspecting women of the world.

I gave Bodie a dog cookie and walked with Win to the Jeep.

Watching him drive, I admit I fixated on his hands. What were they capable of, what had they done in his past life? Was it all in the past? And could a man have sexy fingers?

"So you know my DNA breakdown because your Origins company did my spit analysis, actually everyone in my family's. What's yours?" I asked.

"Forty-six percent Mercury, 12 Mars, 6 Sirius, and the rest from stars and planets in Pleiades."

"My dad is mostly Mercury too, and one of Jupiter's moons, like me."

"Did you know Pleiades is a cluster of middle-aged, hot stars?"

"No way you're middle-aged, unless you plan to live to well over a hundred."

"Who knows? And Mercury's actually called Cinereus, which is 'gray' in Latin."

"So where are we headed, Mr. Grey?"

This time his look was so penetrating, I shifted in my seat. "You haven't eaten beef in six months, so I thought seafood, and there's a good new place in Caesars Forum, Water Grill."

"Are you a water sign in addition to being disturbingly knowledgeable about my habits?"

"Are you asking me my birthday? I'm a Libra. Air sign. October seventeenth."

"How smooth of you not to have added the year."

"I'm sixty-one. Same as your sister." He shot me a cheeky grin and exited for the Las Vegas Strip.

We were seated elbow-to-elbow at a four-top in a part of the restaurant where tables jutted out to the Forum shopping area. The Fendi shoe and handbag boutique was just across the way; G and Mom would love this place.

Over oysters that really did originate from the Chesapeake Bay and not another planet, I probed deeper. "Which side of your family did your light-red hair come from?"

"You can still see some red through the white? From my Uncle Angus. My mom's got good Scottish stock. My first name, Oswald, is actually her family name."

"That was my next question, how you go that name."

"Maybe I should be the one worried about interrogation."

"Hey, I have to catch up," I said, sipping a handcrafted cocktail with mint and cucumber.

"Why don't I give you a quick rundown so we can focus on a plan? I'm from Alamogordo, New Mexico, population just over thirty thousand and too small for me, though humans have lived there for at least eleven thousand years," he smiled. "It's known for its connection with the Trinity test, site of the first atomic bomb explosion. My folks raised Appaloosa horses, but they're gone now. The best thing about the area might be the commercial pistachio business."

"I've been there once, and I love pistachios. You weren't a cowboy were you? Because that fantasy's pretty much wrecked for me on many levels."

I expected him to smile, but he didn't. His gaze was all-knowing.

"No, but I was a Rhodes Scholar, and I speak nine languages, not all of them human."

I choked on a halibut bite with mango relish. "Maybe I should have another cocktail."

"Would you like a sip of mine?" He leaned close to offer me his icy copper mug.

I sipped and took a few deep breaths. "I bet this means you could decipher if I'm hearing other alien languages amidst occasional Red Orbiter conversation? And help me translate?"

"That could be negotiated. Would you like dessert?"

I hesitated to answer, not certain what he might be offering, asking a question instead. "I watched you hold a fork with each hand. Are you left- or right-handed?"

"Ambidextrous."

"Yikes. Is that a recessive gene?" I pondered implications of him being adept with both hands.

"Why are you tilting your head? Are you hearing voices?"

"Mostly I think I'm hearing the sound of my heart beating too fast," I said.

He smiled. My heart accelerated.

"This spot is great for people watching. Look out at the crowd. What do you see?"

I watched tourists, mostly in shorts, flip-flops, and shirts with goofy slogans or sports teams. Women in heels so high, I didn't know how they remained upright. No DHS dudes in suits or little green men.

"Was I supposed to detect something sinister?" I turned to Win.

"Not really. I wanted you to realize it would not be easy for anything to approach us without notice. I'm always going to be looking out for you."

Chapter 15

While I tried to enjoy my pecan praline coffee in a Three Rivers Petroglyphs mug from visiting White Sands with ex-CIA-beau Jason Braxton—not far from where Win was from—Morris attacked the sliding-glass door to the back yard.

He pounded and scratched, mewling at high volume. Was it birds? I looked. No birds. A stray cat perhaps? Nada. Maybe minuscule aliens of the green variety?

I stood, looking out, only to realize he was likely reacting to his kitty reflection in the glass. So yes, an alien. But the orange tabby kind.

During my second cup of coffee while I bravely scrolled through Twitter, Bodie let it be known he wanted out, for the third bleeping time that morning. After checking my news feed and growing monumentally irritated with clickbait headlines like "THIS PILL WILL REMOVE ALL ALIEN DNA," I finally huffed and let Bodie out before switching to email.

I was in a group for former Department of Defense lawyers that shared job announcements via email. Today's was a newly established position as an attorney-advisor for none other than Space Force with the job description: "Performs legal research and analysis in solving legal problems pertaining to matters of interest of the Air

Force on space law, intelligence, security, cyber law issues. Expertise in Space Law highly desirable."

Chalk one up for a legal opportunity teeming with potential for professional and personal ethics violations. The secretary of the Air Force all but assured this by gloating about "space domination" months ago. The whole endeavor was one massive exercise in projecting nefarious intent. And what the hell was "space law"? To boldly seek out new life and annihilate it? To travel to other planets and claim we were first in time so now America owns the universe?

Huh. I might have a good start to my assignment from Senator Rojas-Ortiz. And maybe this Iridescent Insect War plan wasn't such a bad idea. Writing about it offered diversion of the cathartic kind. Luna Moth Woman battles bugs—and bullies! Take that, Space Force!

After all, I remained inactive in terms of my status with the Nevada State Bar, and not only because I still had anxiety from working with the Air Force JAG and Pentagon. A featured article on the cover of this month's *Nevada Lawyer* magazine offered why: "CHRONIC STRESS AND THE PRACTICE OF LAW." And on the very same cover: "MALPRACTICE OR NEGLIGENCE?" How about neither?

Time to walk Bodie, as he was now back inside with half his body pressing down on my arm so I couldn't hold my phone or coffee cup without risk.

A large cloud resembling the giant evil-alien spaceship in the movie *Independence Day* dominated the sky at the end of the street. Surely not a good thing.

I braved on with Bodie obliviously sniffing and peeing on every bush, lamppost, fire hydrant, and cement wall edge. Peering over my shoulder as we rounded each corner, I tried to convince myself all was fine due to no orbs, flying saucers, or cylindrical crafts.

But that cloud was huge and oddly, impossibly shaped. And it hung static in the sky, not drifting as clouds are wont to do. Creepy.

Most times on walks there were dogs behind gates erupting into barking fits. How dare anyone use the sidewalk in front of their abodes! Today it was Bodie that let loose with a tirade of barks and growls, twisting on the leash. He focused on a group of cars in a driveway.

I wrangled for control of the leash, trying unsuccessfully to corral or calm him. No people, other dogs, or stray cats. Nothing but empty vehicles. What could I not see?

Dragging Bodie away took all my focus and strained my arm muscles. He kept barking and twisting, and I kept hollering at him to stop—until I realized *I* needed to stop.

Heading back the way we'd come, I held tight to the leash.

We didn't make it far before I knew what that Uber driver meant when he said it was as if they could keep you from getting too close. A force pressed inside my chest and screamed in my head to come no further, a foreboding mix of mental and physical onslaught that was daunting and draining.

I stopped but did not retreat.

Kneeling down to my now-silent pup, I stroked his fur and spoke softly to him, taking deep, calming breaths.

Bodie whimpered, but his tail thumped on the sidewalk where we lingered and I breathed until I could hear the distinct sound of electronic communication. Were they talking about me?

I spoke, in a quiet, even tone, as if still soothing my dog.

"You want to engage me? Fine. But harassing my dog or cat is off-limits and will get you nowhere but outed. I'll only write about you if you make it necessary. And it's not a good idea to mess with my mind. I've had enough of that with humans. I'm living in a new place, which can be scary. So please, cut me some slack and back off."

My voice was sort of shaky there at the end, but at least I refrained from threatening to let Bodie off his leash and lead chase. Plus, my chest no longer hurt.

I scooped up two loads of poop before we reached home. Another two-bag day.

Chapter 16

Once home, I got busy writing the first-in-time speech to keep my mind from running rampant about Greens. It wasn't as if I was going to haul off and text anyone. Ears and eyes were everywhere. And I didn't feel like jumping on the burner phone Win had given me. I needed time to process.

My initial angle involved DNA, of course:

> Well before the alien revelation and Other Worldly Coalition, millions of Americans had their DNA tested to learn where they came from. Not one single person received results identifying them as being from the United States. Why? Because DNA doesn't work that way, and neither should property rights. You're an American if you were born here, live here, or hold citizenship status. All of which entitle you to own property if you so desire and have the means, irrespective of where you might hail from or how long you've called America home. The inalienable right to pursue life, liberty, happiness, real estate. As a human, an alien, or some combination of both.

Holding tight to this outdated and outlandish concept of first-in-time property rights renders all immigrant-owned property dating back prior to Pilgrims null and void. If being here first means you hold dominion over land, then it's those who are 100 percent American Indian, as in original Americans, who qualify. European settlers unquestionably were not first in time to this continent, with aliens arriving millions of years prior. And unlike Christopher Columbus, they actually set foot on that now claimed as American soil. Everyone else, including every member of Congress, is a trespassing foreigner if we persist with an antiquated fallacy of property rights.

Facts matter. And the truth is, every single human in this nation and on this planet possesses extraterrestrial DNA. If aliens can't own property, no one can. Think about it. It's alien DNA and any modicum of American Indian ancestry you might possess that best qualifies you for landowner status under the hypocritical and convenient first-in-time rationalization of previous centuries. Anglo humans are newcomers, interlopers who deign to declare others have none of the rights they sanctimoniously claim for themselves. It's an age-old story of greed and treachery greatly needing a new, enlightened ending. Aliens are among us, and we are them. Now, as in the beginning.

A voice in my ear said, "Rowan, did you just engage with Greens?"

"Yes, Oz, I'm fairly sure I did. They stalked me on my walk with Bodie, so it was kind of unavoidable."

"They're persistent creatures."

"So am I, but not to worry. I simply asked them to leave me alone because I'm not writing about them. And now my burner phone from Win is ringing. Hang tight while I answer."

"Hello, Win, and yes, I did have a close encounter with Greens."

"Their electronic circuitry is all lit up about it. They're in a frantic flap because you didn't act properly terrified of their presence."

"What presence? They never showed their faces."

"Correction. It's the alarming reality that you weren't susceptible to mind manipulation. You stood your ground. They're poleaxed."

I giggled.

"You think this is funny?" said Win.

"You're the one who could do nothing but howl with laughter when they let loose with dust devils. Why are you bent out of shape when I manage to laugh over something that was actually intimidating? You'd think you'd be pleased with me, you butthead."

"*Butthead?* Is this our first fight?"

"Rowan," interjected Oz, "don't listen to him. He's just jealous. I myself am beaming with pride over how much your Red Orbiter DNA is coming through. We can't be messed with by Greens either. You do me proud, as if you were my own daughter."

"Ha! You hear that, Mr. Spook Man? Luna Moth Woman soars!"

"Who else are you talking to, crazy lady?" said Win.

"Oz. He was in my ear before you rang. And he's *proud of me*!"

"Tell him howdy. And to shut up so I can tell you what's going on. I'll call him in a minute."

"Oz? Win says he'll be in touch. He wants to be the boss of this conversation right now."

Oz's laughter roared in my ear before he said, "Roger that, catch you later."

"Okay, Win, ready for interrogation."

"Hold on a sec. Translating. Good stuff."

"So now you want me to wait when I could be talking to Oz about how wonderful he thinks I am?"

"You know, I really like watching you breathe in a tight-fitting bodice, Luna Moth Woman, but right now I'm picturing you without one while I listen to little green men have a meltdown."

Oh. My. Gosh.

"I'm going to get some water now," I said, gripping the phone so tightly my fingers hurt.

"Whoa, wild woman? What did you just finish writing?" said Win after I gulped water.

"The stuff about first-in-time property rights Senator Rojas-Ortiz asked for. Why? Did those green meanies hack my laptop too?"

"They like it. They really, really like it."

Chapter 17

"How is it you hear Greens communicating in high frequency?" I asked Win over a late lunch. I was wearing a shirt I'd made sure was not clinging or lowcut.

"Special equipment OUTWARD is currently upgrading for me. With the potential to be almost as good as your ears, but not quite." He grinned.

I swallowed some tequila-lime marinated shrimp, but it got stuck in my throat and required a few hasty gulps of margarita to get past that grin.

"So how'd you learn about Greens? The CIA? Red Orbiters?"

"All of the above, in terms of learning their language and other details. But I knew of them long before. Close encounters of my own as a kid."

"Don't tell me you were abducted?"

"No, but I saw them, many times. Apparently I have an uncanny ability to sniff them out, likely due to my Pleiades DNA, which I share with a great deal of natives to this land, and others. Not to mention canines." He smiled.

"What do you mean, natives?"

"You don't know about the legends of the star cluster Pleiades? From Aboriginals in Australia, to Native Hawaiians, Mayans,

Cherokee, and a whole host of others claiming ancestry from Pleiades visitors to Earth eons ago? People who consider themselves hybrid Pleiadeans?"

"How'd I miss that? I need to bone up, as it fits with what I've written for the senator. So you've seen Greens? What are they like? Are they from Pleiades?"

"Small and skinny, maybe three feet tall. No mouths. Hairless. Large black eyes and sort of oblong-oval bald heads. And like I said, glowing green in natural light, otherwise gray."

"Well, this is a bummer." I sulked.

"How so?"

"If they know they can't screw with my mind, they won't ever abduct me, and I won't see them up close."

"You like to play with fire. Must be the hair." He reached out to tug on my curls. "Have you signed up for a writers group meeting yet? We need to get cracking."

"Next week, but I haven't written anything to read yet. And I still want to talk about Greens." I pulled away from him "How and what do they eat?"

Win set down his fork and looked at me with a slow smile. I quivered, damn it.

"Veggies?" He chuckled. "Do you want to get out of here so we can do some of that sightseeing you're hell-bent on?"

I swallowed the last of my margarita, and refrained from stating I knew damn well he was chauffeuring me to points of interest so I wouldn't go off on my own.

He paid the bill, and we left the restaurant in Summerlin. It was 112 degrees, so Win cranked the AC in the Jeep, and I pulled my hair up and held it atop my head until I didn't feel lightheaded and smothered.

Win made a disappointed sound.

"What?"

"I like your hair down. Like a curly, molten lavafall."

"More like a smoldering sauna, but thanks."

Red Rock Canyon National Conservation Area wasn't far, and Win had us winding along the scenic drive as I drank in the sight of sandstone vistas like it was a cool glass of water.

"There's a hiking path I want to take Bodie on called Ice Box Canyon. It used to have a Ponderosa pine growing at the lowest altitude they exist in the US. I wonder if it's still there? But it's too hot for that today! And the visitor's center has a desert tortoise preserve. Now there's a creature as ancient as aliens. Positively prehistoric."

"We have to focus on our plan anyway," said killjoy Win. "In a few weeks, you need to be ready to reach out to your pals at Homeland about the Iridescents. We'll have some flashy pistachio crafts buzzing around so sightings can go viral on social media. You ready to do your part?"

"Yes." I looked out the window trying not to get queasy from the winding road. "Did you know pistachio shells were dyed red back in the day to hide flaws? They stopped doing that in the eighties. I bet pistachios nuts are alien, what with their bright-green color. Where do you think they're from?"

"Why are you diverting the conversation?" Win snapped as he whipped the Jeep into a hiking trail parking area but kept the motor running.

"The AC won't feel cool for long if we don't keep moving," I said, turning towards him.

Win shot me a look that made me contemplate every possible facet of his CIA training. I literally shivered. And he saw it—damn his slow, satisfied smile.

He let me squirm in silence under his gaze.

"I looked up the meaning of Oswald online," I blurted.

"Oh yeah? What'd you find out?" Win hit the release on his seatbelt and shifted toward me. I could see the bullet in his bicep, and my eyes locked onto it.

"Well, um, it's an ancient name, chiefly from northern England and Scotland." My throat felt like sandpaper; my ears rang like public safety sirens.

"And?" Win leaned closer, forcing me to look into steely-blue eyes.

"The, uh, *Os-* part means 'god.'" I breathed the words softly. "And -*wald* means 'powerful.'"

That grin again, blasting my senses just as his lips took possession of mine.

Oswald Winslow kissed like he moved. As if his tongue pushed me slowly down a cool, dark hallway. Like I was sprawled naked on crisp cotton sheets and—

He let me come up for air.

"Who's diverting the conversation now?" I panted.

He kissed me again, thrusting his left hand into my hair, wrapping traitorous curls in his fist and drowning me in desire I did not want to contemplate—or resist.

His right hand stroked the side of my face, leaving little shocks in its wake. I grew lightheaded. I never wanted it to stop.

"We need to keep driving for the AC. Your cheeks are looking way too flushed." Win pulled away, smiling.

Chapter 18

"You didn't answer my question earlier about whether Greens are from Pleiades," I called out to Win while wrapped in sheets in his RV at Valley of Fire.

And I felt guilty enough about kissing him, but now this?

Win walked back into the bedroom, naked and not at all self-conscious about it. He handed me a frosty bottle of peach tea.

"Man, can you talk a blue streak. And your brain is like a steel trap—or pit bull jaws latching on to something."

"And still no answer to my question," I said.

"You know, that mind of yours is truly wonderous, as is your mouth."

Win slid into bed beside me, and I stayed put, even though I kind of wanted to run away in mortification of what we'd just done. And how much I enjoyed it.

"Greens?" I persisted.

Win sighed. "Their origins are shrouded in mystery, but they're not from Pleiades as far as I can tell. I have theories about them, but nothing definitive."

"Care to share?"

"There's something else I'd rather share right now." Win's hand slipped underneath the covers, and electricity seemed to shoot between my legs. Heat radiated outward, making me glad I lay prone or I might have grown faint like a virgin in a historical romance novel.

"Um, I kind of need a breather or, you know—"

"Don't worry," he said, voice as smooth as his sheets. "I brought olive oil from the kitchen. Excellent lubricant. All natural."

***

"What...to do about...Rowan?"

"She cannot be...stopping...this."

I awoke with a yelp after hearing squelched voices in my sleep.

As I sat up in bed, utterly confused, Win walked in, now fully clothed.

"Were you dreaming? Or did you hear something?" he asked.

He sat on the bed, and I hurried to cover my boobs but not before he grinned lecherously.

"I think Red Orbiters are talking about me. What happened? Did I fall asleep? Did you do something to me?" I glared at him.

That smile again. "Of course I did, and you were exhausted so I thought I'd let you nap."

OMG, was I snoring?

"What time is it? I have to get home to take care of my critters. I need to make sure they're okay! Where are my clothes?" I looked around the room.

Once in the Jeep and on our way, I tried to decipher what I'd heard just before waking.

"I can see that mind of yours going a mile a minute," said Win. "Do you want to talk about what you heard?"

"It was spliced up, but I heard my name. And I'm peeved I was asleep because I can't be sure if it was familiar voices or not. You didn't drug me, did you? Give me some sort of CIA concoction to get me to talk?"

Win laughed, and it made me want to smack him.

"Like you need to be drugged to talk!"

My face burned. I wanted to make his face burn.

"Rowan, sweetheart"—

"I'm not your sweetheart!"

"Is that what this is about? You're feeling conflicted? Because of Rauc?"

I felt my face squinch unattractively.

"Well, I'm not going to apologize," said Win. "Nor will I bash the other guy, except to say I saw you first."

"Oh, for crap's sake! Is this like the whole first-in-time thing? You claiming me as yours because you saw me first? Well, you didn't *have* me first! So there!"

"Don't remind me, woman. And I meant I lost my heart first. A long time ago. When I finally saw you again twenty years later, you were with Jason Braxton. I came around a corner at Langley, and there you were. Felt like I'd been shot."

"Oh." I felt like I might swallow my tongue.

"Is it possible Rowan Layne is speechless?"

"That must have been the time I was there for family day, but I'd been there before," I said, remembering. "For an interagency meeting when the CIA had a hissy fit about having to comply with environmental laws at Area 51. Jerks."

I snuck a peek at Win, and he was smiling, so that was a plus. Wouldn't want to piss off a dude who knew fifty ways to slay your lover.

"Good to see you smiling again," said Win.

Okay, so I needed to stop thinking about his hands. Both of them. Doing anything and everything…

"Hmm," he said. "What's got that grin going?"

I should not have looked at his hands, because his smile already had me squirming in my seat.

A rainbow-bright craft flashed across the windshield with an annoying buzz-roar, like a mosquito whizzing around your ear in the dead of night. It was in full-blown glow at dusk—no bright sunshine to trick the eye.

"Here we go, hold on tight!" said Win, jerking the steering wheel to the right, bringing us onto the shoulder of I-15.

Win slammed on the brakes, slipped into reverse, and sent us sailing backward to reach the last exit we'd passed, for Highway 93. All the while the pistachio-shaped iridescent menace swooped around us, creating enough of a spectacle for the few others on the highway to pull over, phones at the ready to film the latest UFO to frequent the skies.

We drove onto Highway 93 past the large sign for Great Basin National Park with an arrow pointing like it was just up the hill, neglecting to mention it was three hundred miles away. When Win executed a few donut spins just for grins on the road—lonely but for the demon beetle divebombing us—I was glad I hadn't eaten in hours.

"Is this really necessary?" I said through gritted teeth, gripping my seatbelt, which was locked up and threatening to strangle me.

"Oh, I'm sorry," said Win. "I somehow didn't get a chance to mention this plan while I dealt with accusations of drugging and your consternation at how great your sex life is now."

I did it. I hauled off and whacked him on the arm, making sure not to land my blow on the bullet. Then I smacked his thigh and drew a breath, fixing to scream.

Win stopped the car after a triple tailspin, taking one hand off the wheel and reaching for my shoulder.

Uh-oh.

When I came to, we were still on the side of the road, and my head felt funny.

OMG there really was such a thing as a Vulcan grip.

"You were either going to puke or pass out anyway, so it seemed the best way to get you through this," said Win, pulling back onto the road.

No fluorescent beetle craft was in sight.

"I would like to learn how to do that, whatever it is you just did to me." I peered at him.

"Not a chance," said Win, unsmiling.

"Who was flying that thing?"

"Oz. Crazy-ass astronaut."

"Look who's talking? You drove like a maniac."

"Thank you," said Win, tweaking my nose.

I sat there remembering what Jason Braxton had told me about the CIA evasive-driving course and how he'd failed it numerous times. I didn't think Win failed it. Ever.

Chapter 19

We pulled into my driveway, and Win cut the engine. "I'm going in with you to secure the house, and it's not negotiable. I'll make sure you and the critters are settled, then I'll leave you be—for tonight."

I felt huffy, but not overly so, and anyway I could hear Bodie barking and crying. "I'm here! It's okay," I soothed as I rushed to open my front door.

I knew I'd been gone too long because it smelled bad inside. The evidence: a load of poop on the tile just outside the kitchen.

"I'll grab some paper towel," said Win.

Morris sidled over, noisy but kind of plaintive, like he might have missed me, so I squatted down to pet them both. Poor Bodie was still having a rough time being left alone.

"There's small plastic bags in the cupboard by the fridge," I told Win, who was picking up the dog poop—and pretty much ensuring I'd never want to smack him again.

While I fed the critters, Win did a sweep of the house and the backyard, so I'd probably never yell at him again either.

As I watched my fur babies eat, he took me in his arms. "I very much enjoyed our time together today. Even the part where you got aggressive." He grinned before touching my chin and leaving with a stealthy grace that made me continue to stand there, admiring his ability to exit a room in total command of himself and his abilities.

My phone pinged me out of my reverie. It wasn't Mom—it was about her.

"Your mother just texted that she wants to try out some false eyelashes. OMG." My sister had a tendency to claim Mom was only *my* mother when it suited. I was concerned this eyelash thing meant Mom had watched a Kardashian show.

I texted G, "Heaven help us if she starts in about butt implants."

My phone rang, and I answered to hear hysterical laughter. When G stopped chortling, she asked, "So, what's up with you?"

"Funny you should ask," I said, heading for the fridge to pour myself a glass of chilled wine. Or three or four or eight.

"I didn't want to talk out loud over the phone in fear of being heard, but I don't think Rauc or Rowdy can hear me from where they are, though their uncle Oz probably knows everything," I said, sitting down and trying not to gulp Pinot Gris.

"Knows what? What happened? And where are Rauc and Rowdy?"

"In the moonship, but don't broadcast that. And I'm a terrible person."

"What did you do?"

"Oh, just had the best sex of my post-middle-aged life, no biggie. With a former spy."

"What is it with you and badass men? Who is this guy? Is he a Red Orbiter too?"

"No, he's the ex-CIA guy who started Origins.com, and he got us our DNA test results early, remember? Oswald Winslow. Goes by Win. He's doing consulting work for George's company,

OUTWARD, and he saw me once when I was twenty-seven years old in Monterey, and I don't know if that's the appeal. That he knew what I looked like when I was young and is still attracted to me now. What the hell am I gonna do? I don't want to hurt Rauc."

"Hey, you're not married, and you are not a bad person. There's still so much you don't know about Rauc, as sweet as he is. You told me yourself you weren't sure how a relationship with an alien who flies around with his kooky brother twenty-four seven was going to work."

"Yes, but I could at least give him a chance to come back from outer space and give it a try. After how good he was to me?" I paced my living room. "He's probably the nicest, handsomest alien in the galaxy."

"That might be the problem right there."

"That's he an alien?" I screeched.

"No, that he's too nice for you."

"Oh my gosh," I wailed. "Have I not progressed at all in forty years of relationships?"

"It's okay, sis. Breathe."

"Easy for you to say." I plopped onto my couch next to Bodie. "You've been married forever to a guy who's the only person in the universe who can tease Mom and get away with it."

"True," she said. "But sometimes if he chews in my ear, the sound makes me want to hurt him."

I laughed, knowing she was sporting that Gigi pout.

"Let's review the situation," she said. "Is he heavily armed at all times?"

"No, never seen him with a gun, but he does have a bullet embedded in his arm."

"Seriously? How is that possible? Oh, his job. Yes, you might be following a pattern."

"Damn it!" I leapt to my feet.

"I'm kidding. Was he in the military? A cowboy?"

"No and hell no."

"Is he super intelligent?"

"Rhodes Scholar and speaks nine languages."

"See, that's a good pattern. Brainiac. What's his politics?"

"Actively working to thwart the current administration from destroying our democracy."

"Well, no wonder you hopped in bed with him."

Chapter 20

As I got ready for bed, I noticed my hair was more tangled than usual, and if I were thirty years younger, I might have blushed.

My phone pinged as I tried to repair the matted mess. "Your spy guy's one of the people on the spacecraft that landed in Monterey Bay when you and Mom and Dad were there, wasn't he? I just googled him. Seriously sexy."

I replied to my sister's text, "You got all that from a photo of him at that briefing? He's pretty much ordinary looking."

"Are you kidding me? Those eyes. And that smile. Like he knows all your secrets."

"He does know all mine, it seems. Probably knows all yours too."

G replied with a snarky laughing-face emoji, not realizing I wasn't kidding.

I crawled in bed thinking I hadn't gotten around to asking Win what the moonship was like. When I'd asked Rauc, he said it was similar to a giant, multideck version of his orb with the population of a midsize city.

Needing a diversion from thinking about Rauc—and Win—I checked social media.

There it was on Twitter, the beetle craft, glowing like a rainbow on a bubble, buzzing in the Las Vegas early evening sky. A giant glittering pistachio stalking Earth.

"It's piloted by some sort of bug-like alien! And they're nasty, dude!" said one guy.

"I think it's kind of pretty," said a woman. "Like a sparkling jewel."

"You wouldn't think that if they were after you!" replied the guy.

I refrained from commenting as I'd been advised by the bug-scheme team, though it was hard not to wade in with snark. I had to be up early for my annual physical, requiring fasting for the blood test. At least I could still have coffee.

***

Once I finished voluminous paperwork on my entire health history in the medical center waiting room, I scrolled through social media. Folks were upping the ante on bug aliens:

"It's the same UFO that abducted me and my buddies on the Fourth of July! Mean, weird little green creatures!"

"Like praying mantises? I've seen them!" replied one person.

"No they're not!" replied another. "They're tall with bulging bug eyes and antenna!"

If someone thought Greens looked like praying mantises, this alien-insect plan could backfire on us. We also needed to do better at distinguishing the sparkly nut from crafts flown by Greens. And that last reply was suspicious, so I looked at the Twitter handle behind it. "Alamogordo61."

"Rowan Layne?" It wasn't a Red Orbiter voice in my ear—it was a nurse calling me for my appointment.

Once they recorded my weight—so sadistic that they always weigh you—and painfully squeezed my arm to test blood pressure, I peed in a cup and was subjected to a gazillion questions I'd already answered in writing. I particularly enjoyed being asked if I was pregnant, which would be a medical miracle at my age. And how was I supposed to know an exact timeframe when menopause began? Or the date of my last period? Can one magically determine when menopause is over? By the time they finished asking questions, they should've taken my blood pressure again.

When I finally met with the nurse practitioner, she asked if I was sexually active, and I reflexively almost said no before realizing that was no longer true. She asked if I was in a monogamous relationship, and I said, "Define relationship." Next she grilled me on whether anyone in my family had issues like cholesterol, cancer, you name it.

"I'm not totally up on the entire medical history of my late grandparents, my parents, or my sister," I said. "I tried to check as many boxes as I could recall about that on those forms you had me fill out." I didn't add, *Forms you're holding in your hands and haven't looked at.*

"I only ask," she said, "because sometimes with things like high cholesterol, your diet doesn't matter if you're genetically predisposed to it. If your parents have a medical issue, you could too. You can't get away from your DNA!"

I left the office thinking maybe I should add her rhyming phrase to the write-up I'd already sent Senator Rojas-Ortiz. And someone ought to tell the president because he kept insisting he had no extraterrestrial DNA. And tell his HUMANS FIRST! cult members too, because they kept getting stirred into anti-alien frenzies by bigots like Ian (Calamity) Cassidy on Fox News.

Sitting in my car waiting for the air to get cool enough to breathe, I pulled out the burner phone and called Win.

"Hey there, Alamogordo61!" I said when he answered.

"Why are you scrolling Twitter when you should be busy writing about Luna Moth Woman?"

"I had my annual physical, and I don't feel like writing yet," I grumped. "So, should I start calling you Gordo?"

"I wouldn't recommend it, sweet pea." He sounded lethal.

"Sweet pea? Well, it is my zodiac flower, but these days I'm more like a sour pea. And I probably have cholesterol issues because both my parents do."

"You *taste* sweet."

My mouth went dry, and my brain did a somersault.

"You still there, Rowan?" Win asked, sounding on the verge of laughter.

"You're smirking aren't you? I can hear it."

"Wow, you really do have hearing like a moth."

I hung up because he was laughing, and I hadn't eaten and was liable to get snippy.

My intention was to head home, but I turned the wrong way onto Martin Luther King Boulevard. I knew this because after a couple miles, I could see the Strat in the distance. And thank goodness for that sky-high landmark or every newcomer to Vegas would be forever lost, wandering in the wrong direction, starving to death.

There was, however, a bonus to my lacking navigational skills today. Buzzing above and around the Strat was a rainbow-glow UFO.

"Is that you up there, Oz?" I said aloud.

"Roger that, Rowan! I'm headed over to the Luxor next. Gonna do some touch-and-go's off the pyramid!"

The former astronaut's whooping glee rang in my ears all the way home, in concert with the high-pitched whizzing-whine of the pistachio craft.

Chapter 21

Tuesday night I sat in a meeting room at an off-Strip casino pub. I felt out of place, not only because this was a writers group and I didn't bring written material to read for critique. You had to sign up ahead of time for that anyway, and there were no open slots. Besides, I wanted to get the lay of the land, see how it was done. Nonwriters like Win or George would not understand this need to acclimate, even if our purpose was to draw out bad guys.

After hearing three people read excerpts from their novels for ten minutes each, followed by five minutes of feedback, I realized this might be more difficult than anticipated. It's tricky to follow a plot when you aren't privy to the backstory, only receiving a snippet from any given scene.

Plus, these were far from dramatic readers, and I was simultaneously dealing with my overly active ears picking up bleeping and ringing. Everything but a certain Red Orbiter telling me he was coming back to me so I should stop all this nonsense and get busy writing about him and what he does as an observer.

Once again, a little voice in my head raised an issue I didn't want to address. How was I to go zipping about in an orb, gleaning knowledge to write this book, when I had a dog and kitty at home who need me? Creatures who were nurtured by routine and normalcy and a human who wasn't going batshit crazy over the machinations of the universe. They'd dealt with enough already.

What was weird was when I introduced myself as a former newspaper columnist and new member of the OW Coalition, there was not a scintilla of recognition—or interest. Not even when I revealed I was working on a series about aliens. It was like I was trapped in an alternate universe, or perhaps I'd gone back in time before the great revelation.

The next two who read excerpts were also writing series, elaborate tales of other worlds in the ancient past or distant future with strangely impossible-to-pronounce names for fictitious lands and fantastical figures. Like the four readers before them, they voiced not a single reference to anything resembling absurd realities of present day.

A perfectly innocuous looking middle-aged man read, "Gorzynstawlx-li said, 'And one day you will have the powers your father had, young warrior Jonqenzug-ahn,' as they walked amongst enormous blue flowers stained red by battle-slain bodies strewn across the frozen landscape, four moons spanning the sky."

It's not that I was relaxed—more like mind-numbingly comatose—but the next voice I heard was not the current writer reading a dystopian anthology.

"She's going to need protection if you keep using her to rile the HUMANS FIRST! subhuman contingent, not to mention evangelical terrorists. Rowan's in Vegas now. Someone already painted 'alien lover' on the senator's car along with a big red A on her front door."

It was a male voice not entirely unfamiliar, but I wasn't sure where I'd heard it before.

Part of me wished I'd continue to hear Red Orbiter conversations, odd as this one seemed, when the sixth and final reader of the evening read aloud: "The waitress was a member of the weaker sex, but at least she was hot, with long tanned legs in a skirt so short, you could almost see her twat and huge tits, and she was blonde. Not some nasty—"

The racial slur that followed ensured I was no longer relaxed, or comatose. But I did want to render the male reader unconscious. What would Luna Moth Woman do?

Should I be concerned that those present this evening might be Fox News aficionados or members of the ever-so-misogynistic Everlasting Evangelical Ministry? No one sported a HUMANS FIRST! ballcap, but you just never knew.

I made it outside, worried about getting lost while driving home.

Leaning against my car was Win, and the electricity that shot through me when I saw him was just wrong. Another tight black shirt, clinging in all the right places. Never believe it if someone tells you men over sixty can't have washboard stomachs.

I stopped abruptly. He crooked his finger at me. My mouth went dry.

I crept forward. "What are you—"

He reached out to snatch me with one arm, pulling me close and pointing to the sky. "That's Pleiades. It's easier to see if you look from the corner of your eye as opposed to directly at it."

I looked, and there it was, that tiny cluster like a mini–Milky Way.

Taking a few deep breaths to calm my racing heart at the heat of his body mixed with warm evening air, I was pleased with myself for refraining from accusing him of stalking me.

"I thought I might treat you to a late dinner at a place not far from here," he said.

"Oh good. I feel like I need to debrief after that meeting. Or rant for a few hours."

"Uh-oh," said Win. "Literary lamentations."

I peered at him. "Are you saying that because, along with everything else about me, you know alliteration's my thing?"

Chapter 22

"The restaurant is set up to be like a speakeasy," Win said as he led me through a back door from the parking lot of Capo's. We entered and passed a grand piano with retro hats displayed, plus a large photo of Frank Sinatra amongst various other Rat Pack pics on the walls.

It was so dark, they had mini lights attached to menus listing Italian fare. I was absolutely ordering cannoli for dessert, though I knew there'd be no message from Rauc in it.

After restorative sips of a divine Valpolicella and hunks of steamy garlic bread, I was ready to spill. "I don't know if this writers group thing will pan out for our purposes."

Win looked at me like I was a little kid trying to get out of eating my vegetables—not fair because I ordered a Caesar salad.

"It's not that I don't want to write fiction," I said, taking a bite of salad. "But most of those writers are drafting bizarre realms as if they're escaping from realities of their own lives and what's actually occurring in the world. Which, you've got to admit, is way stranger than fiction."

"Do you think they're grasping for originality?"

"Or they're in denial. Constant breaking news about aliens is overwhelming. It's too strange, too multifaceted. When things get really juicy, folks run for the hills, burying their heads and their minds, or they rebel and flatly insist it simply isn't so. But writers should embrace the challenge, should they not?" I waved my fork in the air. "Isn't our role to inform, even as we entertain?"

"I would think so. Maybe you should raise this at the next meeting."

"No time allotted for discussion about writing or current events. People nitpick each other's work, and then there's this vile dude who's like Archie Bunker meets Harvey Weinstein."

"So you're worried that when you read, no one will pay enough attention to catch on to concepts you're going to float?"

"That and I can't shake the thought that I just don't belong." I sighed and sipped wine. "It's starting to drag me down, this feeling of being alienated by life—pun intended—like I don't fit anywhere. Not in a small town, not at a writers group in the big city."

"We fit pretty well in bed. In fact we burn very brightly together," said Win who, as usual, was sitting too close to me in the half-moon booth. "Can I have a bite of your salad?" he asked.

"Okay. It's such a treat to have actual Caesar dressing and not some creamy white glop that more resembles ranch or—gross—blue cheese. You can taste the garlic and anchovies!" I babbled about salad dressing because I didn't know how to reply to his "burn very brightly" comment that made me burn, everywhere. Not to mention watching him eat from my fork as I held it out for him.

"Don't think I didn't catch that mention of a vile dude. Should I accompany you to the next meeting?" asked Win as I moved on to my seared scallops with shaved fresh parmesan over linguine.

I had a momentary visual of Win putting the Vulcan grip on the bigoted chauvinist. "Tempting, but no. It'll be agitating enough reading to this group—though funny you should mention that, because apparently there's a Red Orbiter who thinks I need protection. I heard him during the meeting. And I'm sure now it was the same voice I heard in my sleep at your place."

"Was he at the meeting? Who is it?" growled Win.

"No, I *heard* him. And I don't know who it is."

"What was said?" Win leaned in, and I pulled back. The man could engage in an entirely unnerving manner.

I told him what I'd heard, watching as he leaned back and took a sip of wine, somehow doing so without snapping the stem of his glass.

"The Omni Party National Convention is in Las Vegas next month," he said. "They're going to ask you to be involved, because of your newspaper columns supporting the otherworldly and this book you're to write about Red Orbiters."

"What does that have to do with me needing protection? Why would a political convention be dangerous? Won't there be security?"

With so much happening, I'd almost forgotten the OW Coalition had started a new political party.

"Putting you in the public eye is dangerous. The threats against the senator and other women in Congress and the media have become downright obscene in their frequency and intensity, all fueled by the president and lackwits at Fox stirring rage and retaliation against any potential threat to their tiny little—"

"Egos? No, that's not right," I took a sip of wine. "Their egos are huge, it's their self-esteem that's minuscule. Not to mention their brains. Inferiority complexes are easily triggered by aliens, aren't they? But doesn't Senator Rojas-Ortiz have Secret Service protection? I saw two of them when I met with her at Planet Wynne."

"Those weren't Secret Service. They're her own bodyguards. And they're Red Orbiters."

"Really? It's gotten that bad for her, even when folks don't know she's an alien?"

"Yes, and Olivia Warnock has guards too, especially since she's running for the Senate and married to a Red Orbiter," said Win. "But this guy—the one you heard—he protects Cassandra. And it's high time I have a talk with the peckerwood about what his job is, and what it isn't, namely protecting you." His eyes narrowed, his gaze granite.

"Wow, you're on a first-name basis with Senator Rojas-Ortiz? What's that about?" I said as the server brought dessert. "And did you know Olivia's dad, Oliver, was my law professor?"

"Yes, I knew, and stop diverting the conversation. If you're going to be at that convention, I'll be the one guarding your body."

"And did you also attend to the senator's body at some point? Intimately?"

"Yes, but a long time ago. You better eat that cannoli or I'm going to."

"Oh, how the plot thickens," I said, picking up my pastry, slowly licking the sweetened ricotta oozing from one end.

Win's eyes locked onto my tongue and smiled.

So much for me having the upper hand.

"So, this bodyguard of the senator somehow aims to watch over my body? Interesting. And handsome if it's who I think it is. I saw him when I met with Rojas-Ortiz. He told me how nice I looked."

"You're pushing it, sweet pea."

"Oh, come on. He's way too young for me. Can't be much older than thirty."

"Old enough to know better. And over my dead body he's guarding you."

"I'm thirty-three," drawled a potently masculine voice in my ear. "Old enough to take care of you, beautiful. And tell Oswald his dead body can be arranged."

I jumped, so good thing I wasn't holding my wine glass. And I could not pull off a poker face, though Win wouldn't fall for it even if I did.

"What did you just hear, Rowan? Is that mutt talking to you again? Tell him I'll be there if he gets too close."

"Not if I get to you first," the voice purred in my ear.

"What is it with you guys and being first?" I blurted. "Enough already with the testosterone. Both of you get out of my head and let me finish my cannoli!"

"Okay, beautiful. But I'll see you soon."

I made sure I didn't tilt my head and tried not to reveal any other tells to Win.

"Am I going to have to make you reveal what he just said?"

"You might shoot the messenger! It's not my fault he—oh no, you don't!"

Win was reaching for my shoulder, and I scrambled to exit the booth from the opposite side.

I wasn't fast enough.

Chapter 23

The next morning I walked Bodie at zero dark thirty to beat the oppressive heat before fixing my hazelnut coffee, wishing they'd make a pistachio-almond flavor like ice cream, and then checking the day's breaking news.

"PRESIDENT CONVINCED MOON IS SPYING ON HIM"

"MOON ATTACKING US SATELLITES, SAYS PRESIDENT"

Along with his predictable projection tactics, his attorney general waded into the muck:

"AG KAHN SAYS JUSTICE DEPT INVESTIGATING ALIEN ACTIVITY"

"JUSTICE DEPT WILL PROSECUTE ALL ALIEN CRIMES, SAYS AG KAHN"

I looked down at my coffee cup, made in England. It said, "The first thing we do, let's kill all the lawyers," from Shakespeare's *Second Part of King Henry VI*. It may have been about anarchy, but you had to love it in terms of on-the-money snark that applied to modern day.

Checking Twitter, I saw favorite and famed lawyer Terrance Scribe weigh in: "The AG might want to look into jurisdictional issues of prosecuting those he and this president claim either don't exist or lack citizenship status, because that makes them not subject to American jurisprudence, which does not have authority over the entire bleeping universe."

While I waited for my second cup of coffee to drip, I had the audacity to sneeze, causing disgruntled Morris to protest loudly. Yet I was still able to hear the ping of a Mom text.

"Did you see what the president said??? That jackass!!! He's the one who attacked the moon first!!! And on your birthday!!! (angry face, flipped bird, pile of poop emoji)"

Can I just say how disturbing it is that the poop emoji has googly eyes? I was feeling watched enough from so many angles, I didn't need it from poop too. And in texts from my mother? Plus, how'd she find that middle-finger emoji? Why couldn't she stick to the dog and cat she favored lately, emoji that resembled Bodie and Morris, her precious grandanimals?

What if Homeland Security still monitored her texts to me?

I responded to Mom, "Yes, he's a total nut-wing psychopath. (crazed face emoji)"

She answered, "Doodles, forgot to tell you your horoscope says you have a surprising new secret admirer!!! And new opportunities on the horizon!!! Cloudy here, due for rain. Ugh. (kissy face, shooting star, face with stars for eyes, dog, cat, cloud, umbrella emoji)"

Not-so-secret admirer, after last night. Surprising was accurate, however, as the senator's bodyguard was so much younger than me. I'd already attempted a hopelessly awful relationship with a crazy man thirteen years younger, which was traumatizing enough.

I checked Twitter again. I had three new followers, two of which were alien enthusiasts, but the third had the handle WillGuardYourBody. I checked for posts.

Sure enough, WillGuardYourBody reposted a presidential tweet, with reply.

The president tweeted, "Wimen who have sex with aliens are so nasty they can't get a humen man to look there way. Like that OW womin who thinks she can be senitor. And unruley Rowen Lain needs to be nicer if its men she wants. To agressieve needs to smile!"

The reply?

"Beautiful & brainy women so easily threaten lacking libidos of a diseased degenerate mind. What else is diseased? And tiny? Chalking up those harassment lawsuits!"

The cadence of writing, not to mention alliteration, were almost as if he knew me. Too well.

I dug out my burner phone and called Win.

"How come the president is still obsessed with the moonship and women having sex with aliens but isn't tweeting about the sparkly evil alien craft we've got blitzing the nation's skies? Is your grand scheme not working, Mr. Slick Spy?"

"Good morning to you too, Rowan. How are you feeling today? Why aren't you writing about Luna Moth Woman instead of scrolling social media?"

"Enough with Luna Moth Woman! You are not the boss of me and my writing! When are *you* going to teach me how to interpret Greens? And why aren't you stopping the ignoramus anus of a president from harassing me on Twitter!"

Bodie jumped off the couch and ran down the hall.

"Damn you, Win. You made me scare my poor dog. Why can't you leave me alone?"

"Maybe you shouldn't scream. And you called me. Why is that? Some subliminal need?"

I disconnected the call, walked into the backyard with the phone, and stomped the little black thing into oblivion. It was almost out of minutes anyway.

Twenty minutes later, Bodie starting leaping and yipping with joy, followed by the chime of my doorbell.

I looked through the peephole even though I knew who it must be. I thought about not opening the door, but I didn't want to learn how easily Win could gain entry.

"Open up, Rowan. I've got donuts."

I let him in, sniffling and clearing my throat.

"Have you been crying?" he asked.

"Out of utter and total frustration," I admitted, eyeing the pink bakery box.

"Get us some coffee. Then we can talk. And I brought you a new burner phone."

"You're so bossy," I muttered, headed for the kitchen.

Win greeted Bodie, who was clamoring for attention.

I handed him coffee in a CIA HUMINT (for *human intelligence*, as in spies) mug. He smirked, saying, "Jason Braxton," but chuckled when he read my "Kill all the lawyers" mug.

"You've got to ignore what the president tweets right now and trust the situation will be dealt with. As for our plan, he definitely knows about the new alien threat. But he'll wait to see what Cassidy spews on Fox before he weighs in with his own juvenile nickname for extraterrestrial insects."

"Heaven forbid he should have an original thought that doesn't involve sexualizing and degrading women. Thank goodness Mom isn't on Twitter. But wait, does this mean Calamity—that's what I call Ian Cassidy—mentioned me on his show?" I could feel my whole body clenching up for one massive cringe.

"Calamity? How appropriate. Are you going to start yelling again if I tell you that yes, he has? He uses your newspaper column photo and a clip of the announcement that you'll write a book about Red Orbiters. Otherwise the president would have no clue who you are because, for starters, he doesn't read." Win took a sip of coffee.

"So because Rauc spoke to the media about it, these demented thugs assume I had sex with him to get a book deal?"

"That and they deem you an alien lover regardless, because you don't embrace their humans-first mentality or perceived Second Amendment right to shoot anything they want."

"And here we thought disgruntled Greens were all we had to be worried about with me writing a book," I bit into a lemon-filled donut, my favorite.

"As far as the Everlasting Evangelical leader is concerned, you're going straight to hell, sweet pea," Win grinned. "I like watching you lick lemon filling off your lips."

I swallowed and hopped up for a glass of water, lest I scald my clogged throat with coffee. And I was definitely having a second donut, the cinnamon twist.

Why had I ever wasted time on a man who berated me for eating sweets?

"You know, the president tweeted about me meeting with Senator Rojas-Ortiz. Who spilled the beans on that?"

"I'd be tempted to accuse Octavius Wynne, shameless promoter of his hotel casino that he is, but he'd never cross Rojas-Ortiz, who's his niece. It could've been Homeland, but my guess is a SlayNews derelict gathered dirt to manipulate into conspiracy for Jax Smith."

"Well, isn't this flipping great!" I licked my fingers. "What am I, a walking cliché? Alien lover conspiring with the otherworldly to take over minds of people who, quite frankly, don't use what little brains they have to think cognitively? Will that slimeball soon offer an anti–Rowan Layne mind control pill for sale? Will he spell my name correctly?" I eyed the pink box.

"Have another donut. Third time's a charm. There's an old-fashioned buttermilk with your name on it."

"Okay, but I'm going to have to walk Bodie again, or find a way to work off all this sugar."

"My excellent cognitive brain already has a plan for that." Win grinned and my blood sugar spiked, making me woozy.

Chapter 24

I decided to do a search on Pleiades, thinking wherever it led could be an inspiring prompt for putting pen to paper for my Luna Moth Woman battle of the bugs. Whatever I wrote would be heavily laced with anxiety-inducing truths, so I might as well include factual data.

My mistake was in thinking it might also take my mind off yesterday's tryst with a certain talented ex-spy, given Win possessed Pleiades DNA and hailed from New Mexico. But what was niggling me was the memory of him on TV at the Monterey briefing after the spaceship landing that shocked the world last November.

I did an online search for excerpts, and there he was explaining how the Roswell crash was not a Red Orbiter mishap but an accident involving another alien entity whose intended destination was the Sandia Mountains, also in New Mexico. It had to be Greens.

Was one or more of them recovered from the crash? Alive? How would that have worked, what with their mind-manipulation capabilities? Area 51 did not exist in 1947, so where would they have been taken for observation or study? Theories abounded, including speculation that crash remnants were trucked to Wright-Patterson Air Force Base in Ohio.

I'd been to that base to teach a seminar on environmental law. At the time, its security was more paranoid than the Pentagon's, and that was after 9/11. I wondered why. What was there?

In any event, I couldn't write about Greens and I could just hear Win asking, "Why are you wasting your time with this, sweet pea?"

I googled Sandia Mountains and learned the range's highest point, Sandia Crest, was 10,678 feet. The Pueblo people called it Bien Mur, for big mountain, and consider it sacred. Interestingly, the Southern Tewa, Navajo, and Zuni all had names for these mountains. But *sandia* in Spanish means "watermelon." And popular belief said it was a reference to the reddish color of the mountains at sunset.

The thing was, when viewed from the west, the profile of the Sandia Mountains was a long ridge with a thin green zone of conifers near the top, making it look like the rind of a watermelon. I loved it when things were logical. And I loved watermelon. Maybe it was from Pleiades.

My phone rang, my sister G.

"You'll never guess what just happened!" she said. "I got a call about being on Rose Bergin's cooking show! I get to be a member from the audience who participates as her sous chef! Is that just the best ever?"

"Wow! You really are getting a reward for helping me find a house in Vegas."

"Yes, and she's doing OW dishes and ingredients so I'll learn a bunch of new things!"

"Good thing it's not French cuisine, or you'll be insisting we call you Gigi again. When and where are they taping the show?"

"Las Vegas, next month! I will see you soon, little sister!"

I got off that call and was poised to research Pleiades when my phone rang again, a Maryland number I now knew was not the NSA harassing me.

"Rowan, this is Olivia Warnock. I'm so sorry we weren't able to meet here in Baltimore in May, but I have an offer for you. As you know, the Omnipresent Party convention is in Las Vegas in mid-August. The OW Coalition would like you to be part of it. Right now we're thinking you could write speeches for candidates, but there may be more."

After I expressed interest and she said she'd be in touch soon with more details, I was typing "Pleia"—easy to misspell—into Google when my phone pinged.

"Your sister is coming to Vegas in August," Mom texted. "But it's too dadgummed hot for me to come too!!! I want to see my sweet grand dog and cat!!! Your dad just made popcorn. But it doesn't make up for him eating all the coffee cake this morning before I'd finished my first cup of coffee!!! Weather cloudy, may rain. Ugh. How is your weather??? (frowny face, dog, cat, coffee cup, cloud, heart, kissy face emoji)"

Was the universe trying to keep me from research on Pleiades? Or perhaps from writing my novel about Luna Moth Woman? Did it not want me to return to the writers meeting?

I answered Mom, "Maybe everyone could come at Christmas? Bodie and Morris send love and hugs to their grandmommy! It's July so very hot and sunny in Vegas. (sun, flame, thermometer, dog, cat, kissy face emoji)"

Bodie yelped in distress and came running for me on the couch, so I let him outside and told Morris the menace to stop chasing him and bopping him on the head—the popping sound was quite disconcerting. Was is a full moon?

Mom texted again, "I went out on the balcony to get popcorn your father is hoarding and we saw something flashy in the sky!!! Shiny and pinkish green. Your dad said he'd never seen one. I think it's tacky, whatever it is. (frowny face, flipped bird, kissy face emoji)"

I grabbed the burner phone and called Win.

"My mom just saw our iridescent UFO in the skies over Portland and was not impressed, or intimidated. I can't tell her the truth because she can't keep a secret." I paused for Win to stop laughing. "How do I convince her this is an evil bug craft invading Earth? And why would we want to cause distress in the elderly?"

When Win stopped choking on his own mirth, he said, "You're missing the point, sweet pea. Folks like your mom are not our target audience. She thinks the president is a first-class jackass, and she's right. It's the cockwomble and his cult members we're after. And tools like Cassidy and Jax Smith claiming everything's a hoax or fake news."

"Cockwomble? Isn't that a Scottish expression?"

"You bet your sweet ass it is."

"So you speak Gaelic? What are the other languages you know?"

"I'm in a meeting. Gotta run."

Was he getting me back for hanging up on him the other day?

Where was I? Trying to learn about Pleiades. But first I looked up *cockwomble*. "A foolish or obnoxious person."

Next I typed "Pl" and my phone rang again. It was an unknown number with a Las Vegas area code. I answered out of curiosity.

"Hi, Rowan. How are you today, beautiful?"

I recognized the voice, oozing charm. "Well, if it isn't the senator's bodyguard."

"At your service. And at your curb. Want to come out and play?"

Chapter 25

I marched outside to the street where he leaned, nonchalant, against what had to be a half-million-dollar sports car. Bright red, of course.

As I approached, he removed his sunglasses.

Hands on hips, I stared up at him. "A Red Orbiter observer without green eyes or red hair? What's up with that?"

"My hair is red. It bleaches white blond in the Vegas sun. As for eyes"—he leaned down, way down, to my level—"take a look."

His gold-amber peepers, kind of like Morris's, were flecked with green. As I tried not to pant in his perfectly sculpted face, the irises turned olive green, glowing brighter, almost unnaturally neon. At least his pupils were round, not shaped like a cat's—or a snake's.

"Yikes," I said. "Does that hurt?"

He smiled. "It happens when I'm looking at something I find appealing."

"Oh please. I'm almost twice your age." Not to mention I had on not one speck of makeup and hadn't detangled my hair today.

"Not really," he responded.

"So what brings you to my home? Were you spying on me? Listening to my conversations?" I peered up at him.

"Are you going to invite me into your home?"

"Is this like a vampire thing? Do you require a verbal invitation to come inside?"

He bent down to me again, which I had to admit was considerate as my neck could get a seriously painful crick looking up at him.

"An invitation is required if I want to be a gentleman. Do I? Haven't decided yet. How about we go downtown and get married? Then I can carry you over the threshold."

"But I don't even know your name," I drawled, all Southern belle and sultry moonlight.

"Roger Rogers, at your service."

"Seriously?"

"My middle name is William. My folks wanted me to go by Will, but Will Rogers was from Oklahoma, and you know we Longhorns would *sooner* be dead."

"You went to UT?"

"See, beautiful? We have much in common. Why fight it? It's inevitable."

"Are you a Texan?" I narrowed my eyes and pursed my lips.

"I'm a Red Orbiter. But I grew up in El Paso and met my best friend, Oggie West, at UT."

"Dr. Ogden West? Olivia's husband?"

"Yep, we had the same undergrad major."

"No way. You're not a physicist. You're a bodyguard!"

In a barely detectable blur, I was lifted and found myself on my doorstep. All in a hairsbreadth moment.

"You sure about that?" he drawled.

"What the hell did you just do?"

I was positive he'd had his hands on me and that's how I'd moved. But he stood there as if he never touched me—even if the tingling in my body said otherwise.

"Physics," he answered. Smug smile emanating from a square jaw, teeth unnaturally bright, like those eyes staring back at me.

Bodie was having a fit on the other side of the door, so I could invite Roger Rogers in or slam the door in his face. I debated.

But the man was a walking poster child for Dudley Do-Right. With emphasis on *child*, of course. And hell, I was only human, even if 83 percent OW.

Bodie pawed all over him as he sat on my couch. We scooched my coffee table out a foot to accommodate his legs, which Morris promptly leaped upon and kneaded with his claws.

"Doesn't that hurt? And would you like something to drink?"

"Barely tickles. I don't dare hope you have sweet tea. Do you, sweet pea?"

"What the hell? You *have* been listening in on me." I glared at him.

"Just those few minutes once I drove up to your house. Scout's honor."

"No way you were a Boy Scout. You're too lecherous. And no, I don't have sweet tea." I frowned. "This is not my mammaw's house."

"My goodness, you're prickly. I don't need anything to drink. I just want to talk to you. I've waited a long while to do so."

"Really? How long? Have you been observing me since you were five?" I sat at the opposite end of the couch, which was the dog's spot, making Bodie pace on the tile.

I patted the sofa, and Bodie jumped up to crowd in between us. Good, buffering.

"So why aren't you an observer instead of a bodyguard if you have the hearing skills?"

"Look at me." He gestured to his long legs. "I don't enjoy being cooped up in an orb. And I can use my skills for protecting others, which suits me."

I eyed him. He had to be more than six-foot-five, the tallest height I'd ever messed with, and the utter physicality of him emanated like a swoon-inducing force.

"And just what are those skills?" I asked, and almost clapped my hand over my damned mouth.

He stared at me, unsmiling, and his eyes grew bright green again.

I really wished he'd speak because the backs of my knees were starting to sweat.

"Okay so, you somehow transported me from your car to my door," I babbled. "Was it magnetic force? I know orbs do that, but you're not traveling in an orb, and I don't think that car qualifies. And how is it you can't be cooped up in an orb, but you're fine in a sports car?"

"The Ferrari's different. I don't have to be in it twenty-four seven. And yes, it's a magnetic force, but mine doesn't come from an orb. It's within me. I simply have a great deal more of it than most Red Orbiters. Along with stamina."

His eyes grew greener as he let that word hang in the air, and I gulped water.

"The first time I saw you," he said, "was that mine fiasco in Yearntown. I was the guy you approached. You thought I was a state trooper. So did the local-yokel police." He smirked.

"No way," I said. But I remembered a blond crew cut with mirrored sunglasses, so I hadn't seen his eyes.

"And I thought, who is this chick who uses words like *catawampus*?"

"Says a dude who uses words like *chick*."

"So I followed you home to see where you lived," he said.

Chapter 26

"You are seriously creepy," I said to Roger who, despite it being a total cliché, uncannily resembled a Greek god. "Is that when you started listening in on me too? You Red Orbiters are worse than the government." I stopped myself from gnawing my fingernails and clenched my fists to my sides.

"Says the woman who can listen to Red Orbiters."

"Yes but I don't *spy* on them."

"Some might not see it that way, and I'm all about their protection. That's why I'm a bodyguard. As I've already told you. Maybe you're not really into listening?"

I shifted toward him on the couch so abruptly, Bodie and Morris flew off.

"See now, I don't have to spy on you to know you look like you're fixing to yell and you might be thinking about taking a swing."

"I am not a violent person!" I hissed.

"Didn't you want to pulverize that jerk at your writers meeting?"

"Well, yes, and—damn it! You spied on me then too?"

"Beautiful, I've been looking out for you ever since I returned to your house that first night and heard you muttering about Space

Force. Before I listened to a fight between you and that seriously bad-news dude you lived with." His eyes grew somber, less bright.

"There was something else, though, wasn't there?" I said, looking away from those eyes. "You figured it out."

"You mean when you made a crack about your spidey sense, your potential superpowers? Yeah, that's when my ears really perked up."

"Well, butter my biscuits and call me breakfast." I slumped into the couch.

"I'd be happy to do more than that to your biscuits," he said.

I sat up like I'd been zapped. "My biscuits are too old and stale for you!"

Roger smiled, shaking his head. "Remember when you said you heard whomever it was talking about the stupid anti-alien sign, the one defaced by Rowdy Wilde?"

I nodded, feeling numb and yet tingling in places I shouldn't have.

"That was me you heard. Talking with Rauc and Rowdy. But it was during that fight, when I heard anguish in your voice, that I knew I was going to look out for you. You needed protection, Rowan."

"You weren't responsible for Lucas's disappearance, were you?" I cut my eyes at him.

"No, he did that all on his own. But I did make sure his application to go to Mars with that start-up outfit wasn't rejected. Even though it should have been."

"He wasn't right for me." I sighed.

"He wasn't right in the head."

"Can we talk about something else?" I fidgeted, wanting to bite my nails.

"Sure, I have some ideas. What's on your mind?" he leaned toward me, and I swear I held my breath.

"I recognize your voice now!" I said in a rush. "I heard you before you heard me. In Monterey in November. It was you who said, 'Word is out,' when the news about the moonship broke! In fact, it was your friend Oggie West who announced it."

"I was in Monterey covering security for the spaceship arrival."

"When I heard you, I thought it was the moon talking to me."

"You're adorable," he said.

"No, I'm not." I scowled.

"Why? Because you're over fifty?"

"No, because I'm pissed off at how men seem to think I'm the little woman they have to take care of—or worse, control."

"I don't want to control you. There's a great many things I'd like to do with you, but control is not one of them."

I glared at him.

"Aw, come on. Cut me some slack. Don't you have anyone like me on your bucket list? Secret Service agent, perhaps? I used to be, and will be again if Rojas-Ortiz becomes president."

"Your confidence is astounding. But you wouldn't be my first Secret Service agent."

"Who was that?"

"The service's top marksman. Won lots of shooting competitions."

"Damn. Well, what's left—if anything—on your list?"

I frowned, wondering if that was a *slut* dig like Lucas would have made, just for vicious grins. But I knew better.

"Firefighter," I said, biting my bottom lip.

Roger roared in triumph. Real king-of-the-forest stuff.

"There you go. Did it in Austin during college as a volunteer, and I'm still on call for big disasters. I worked up in California and in Colorado a few years back. You really need to stop fighting this."

"You need to stop telling me what I need!" I huffed.

Roger's eyes turned hazel gold, and his smile faded.

"And another thing! You followed me to Napa, and to Oregon! It's been your snarky comments I've heard! You made that crack about Columbusing while I was at the farmers market with my sister."

My mind ran rampant with all the times I'd heard a mysterious male voice in the past nine months. When it wasn't Rauc or Rowdy.

"Just checking in on you, beautiful. Making sure you were okay."

My burner phone rang, vibrating on the coffee table. I answered while staring into Roger's enigmatic eyes.

"You rang, master?" I said. Roger's facial expression did not change. But those eyes did.

"Watch it, woman," said Win. "This is a courtesy call. I'm outside your house looking at that pisser's Ferrari. I'm coming in. I suggest you not be in flagrante delicto when I get there."

The line went dead, and Win strolled through my front door to the happy yips of Bodie.

"You too with the Latin?" was all I could think to say as I rushed to head off a nasty confrontation.

Win looked into my eyes, and his entire demeanor changed. "Rowan, it's okay. I'm not angry, just a little ticked off. I'm not going to smash my fists into walls or break things. It's okay."

I felt the blood drain from my face. "I need to sit down," I said, somehow making it back to my couch.

Roger was there, and he reached out to me with long, strong arms. And just like that, a flashback hit me—of Lucas and not-so-great times. It was happening a lot lately.

"Please don't touch me." I shrank away.

Bodie was at my feet, whining and licking my hand. Morris appeared, rubbing against my shoulder. I stroked my cat's soft fur before leaning down to hug my dog, and I burst into tears. With two men in my living room. Mortifying. At least I had no mascara to run down my face in ugly black streaks.

"I should have killed that motherfucker," said Roger.

I shook my head. "I'm just glad I didn't."

Chapter 27

After saying he had more to discuss and he'd be in touch soon, Roger left, and I could tell he wanted to hug me but considerately refrained.

Win made a call for pizza delivery and opened one of my bottles of red wine.

I sat, drained, on my sofa with my critters.

"Did you know Roger's middle name is William and he was supposed to be called Will Rogers?"

"No, but funny," said Win. "I don't have a middle name."

I looked up in astonishment. "Neither do I!"

Win's smile made me feel a bit like my old self again.

Speaking of that…

"Do you know much about Red Orbiters? Because there's something odd about their age, I think, or how they age."

"That's what you find odd about them?" Win teased. "Dudes that fly around in pairs snooping on everybody?"

"Look who's talking about snooping. And it isn't always dudes. I know there's at least one married couple Rauc mentioned that fly together. What I'm wondering is how is it someone in his early thirties has managed to have so many careers?" I waved my wine glass around. "A Secret Service agent, a firefighter, a bodyguard, and who knows what else? I guess it's possible—but it seems like a lot of ground to cover. Not to mention the physics degree and observer capabilities."

"What I do know about Red Orbiters is that they're some of the finest folk I've ever worked with. Bruce and Ophelia, for instance. And Oz, crazy as he is. I think Roger rankles me because we're too much alike."

"You're in a similar profession, as far as I can tell. A gal can't have any mystery around you two." I frowned.

"Sure you can, sweet pea. But mysteriousness is not all that fascinating. Knowing what makes you tick is much more fun."

"Knowing what makes me tick, or ticked off?"

"Both, and speaking of that, I'm going to address the elephant in the room, say my piece, and then I'll butt out, okay? But let me get this out."

I nodded, feeling my throat constrict.

"I know you must have been with that guy in Yearntown because he was a Marine combat veteran and due to your past and your wonderful heart. But Rowan, abuse is abuse. And there's no excuse for it. You are not to blame. You're a kind, loving, giving woman."

"Thank you," I whispered. "It's just going to take time."

"I know. Makes it hard for us guys who want to fix it when we can't. But we mean well. Even Roger. Now, will you drink some of this wine so I don't have to work so hard to seduce you after pizza?" Win teased.

***

We were lazing in my bed, finishing off the wine and vying for space with Bodie and Morris.

"Will you tell me more about Pleiades? I started to research it this morning and got bombarded with phone calls."

"What calls?"

"Why do you always do that? Let's talk Pleiades, please?"

"Tell me about the calls."

I sighed. "Before Roger and you, it was my sister, Mom, and Olivia Warnock asking me to participate in the Omni convention, writing speeches—just like you predicted. Although I don't know if Senator Rojas-Ortiz will be there. Has she switched parties?"

"Not yet, but likely. Did Roger tell you who it was that tipped off the OW Coalition and the senator about your pro-alien newspaper columns?"

"What do you mean?" I sat up and pushed my hair from my face, reaching for my wine.

"Someone had to tell them about your local gig. You were living in relative obscurity despite writing about national and extraterrestrial issues."

"I guess I wanted to believe my writing was so amazing, it somehow reached important people." I moped. "But I knew it couldn't only be because Rauc and Rowdy put Yearntown on the media map by defacing that sign and leaving a 'Don't be stupid' message."

"Don't be a putz. Your writing is brilliant—it just needed a push in the right direction. I for one was happy you got some well-deserved recognition, though I worried it might pose risks. Roger was concerned for your welfare too, after the fact."

"Roger? Roger was the one who spilled the beans?" I nearly sloshed my wine.

"He told his pal Oggie West, who told his wife, who told her dad. And of course he also told Senator Rojas-Ortiz."

"Roger's had his hands in a lot of pies lately."

Win almost spit red wine on my blue cotton sheets. "Please tell me not literally?"

"Was I not fully clothed when you barged into my house at a mere moment's notice?" I swatted his thigh. "Now will you please tell me about Pleiades?"

"Okay, but that wasn't really an answer," said Win.

"I'm learning from the best." I smirked.

"I'll tell you, as long as you'll use it to write about Luna Moth Woman."

"And you call me stubborn?"

"Pleiades is a star cluster also called the Seven Sisters, but with thousands more stars than that, plus what we now know are planets like the ones my DNA derives from. What you might find interesting," Win tucked a curl behind my ear, "is that on Earth there are multiple structures, on multiple continents, built by multiple cultures, with one thing in common. They were all placed in alignment with Pleiades, which they revered."

"Do we have such a structure in the US?" I knew the answer almost as soon as I asked.

"In New Mexico. Chaco Canyon."

Morris grunt-meowed his displeasure when I shifted abruptly. "I love that place! Went there years ago, and boy, was I furious!"

"That's an unusual reaction to ancient Puebloan architecture."

"That's just it! Here I'd traveled to Great Britain to see, touch, and experience thirteenth-century castle ruins, all to later discover ninth-century dwellings right here at home that were conveniently never mentioned in American history textbooks. First in time, my patootie!"

Chapter 28

The next morning I dug through a box of books I hoped might also have a pamphlet on Chaco Culture National Historical Park (try saying that quickly), situated between Albuquerque and Farmington in northwestern New Mexico. As luck would have it, I'd kept one.

I sat down with blueberry-vanilla coffee (who knew it would taste good?) in a favorite mug with a picture of Bodie and Morris cuddling on the couch. It said, "Can you tell me the story of how you rescued me again?"

Scanning the pamphlet that said, "Massive buildings of Ancestral Puebloan people are testament to engineering and organizational abilities not seen anywhere else in the US...central to thousands of people between 850 and 1250 AD," I realized I wanted more tantalizing tidbits than federal-government-approved text.

On the internet, Chaco Canyon was described as, "Architecture without precedent in prehistoric North America, precisely aligned sandstone buildings with cyclical positions of the sun and moon during pivotal times such as solstices, equinoxes, and lunar standstills" with "masonry techniques unique for their time" and "an enduring enigma for researchers."

Pueblo descendants described it as a special gathering place to share ceremonies, traditions, and knowledge. Archaeologists speculated Chaco Canyon to have been a trading hub because of turquoise, copper, and seashells from distant lands they found in dwelling spaces.

Many questions remained about the mystique surrounding this ancient marvel, due to a lack of written record. A location in high-altitude, semi-arid desert where mere survival was an accomplishment.

But the ultimate mind-boggling questions were: Why did these people vanish without a trace in the late 1200s? If they left for a better life elsewhere, where did they go?

Despite a most enthralling subject, I couldn't shake questions and mysteries of my own swirling through my head. Plus, Morris was now sitting on the paper I'd had at the ready for taking notes. Another sign from the universe that I was not to write about this for my Luna Moth Woman's adventure series?

The next writers meeting was days away, and I'd not written a single sentence.

I couldn't stand not knowing anymore, so I redialed an incoming number from yesterday. I knew I could probably summon him by speaking aloud, but I wasn't ready to accept he might already be listening, waiting.

"Howdy, beautiful! To what do I owe the pleasure?"

Now that I had him on the phone, I didn't know what to ask or where to start.

"You there? Everything okay?" said Roger.

"I'm fine. Just trying to wrap my head around too many things. Win said you were the one who had folks reading my columns. I figured you were planning on telling me. But why did you know about me in the first place? Plus, how did you get to the Yearntown mine so quickly—and dressed as a state cop?"

"Undercover work in that town and county."

"Why? I thought you were a bodyguard for the senator."

"I guard her when she's in Las Vegas. Otherwise I work security issues for the Red Orbiter organization."

"What does that mean, exactly? What are you?"

"Someone who could make you very safe and very satisfied, beautiful. But right now, I'm not in Vegas and I don't have the time I'd need to answer your questions. Why don't I meet you after your writers gig Tuesday night?"

I squeaked out an okay as I could tell he was in a hurry.

"That alien is seriously, disturbingly hot," I said to Bodie while stopping Morris from chewing on my still-empty pad of paper.

I got a second cup of coffee and willed myself to focus.

It turned out there were petroglyphs in Chaco Culture National Historical Park at a spot called Fajada Butte. One in particular I had not known the story behind was dubbed Sun Dagger. What sparked my attention were its two spiral petroglyphs, reminding me of the inner portion of the ear called the cochlea, of which mine are freakishly hairless.

Anyway, these two spirals were bisected by shafts of sunlight, interpreted as daggers, passing between three slabs of rock in front of the spirals on the day of each solstice or equinox.

Was it possible there was a different way to look at this? Could the two spirals be a set of ears, with shafts of sunlight representing incoming auditory communication at specified times?

There were also pictographs—painted images on rock as opposed to the carved petroglyphs. One pictograph was thought to represent a supernova occurring in 1054, and another was a crescent moon.

That led me to wonder, was Earth's moon always a moonship? Or did something happen to the real moon and then it was replaced by a spaceship so as to not discombobulate human populations on Earth? Why had I not thought to raise this with Rauc?

Chapter 29

Thinking of Rauc led to me to think of Win, and then Roger, so guilt flooded my senses, making rational thought impossible.

I gave Bodie a rawhide chew to keep him occupied so he wouldn't pester me while I called my big sister. "New development," I said.

"Another man?"

"Why do you assume that?"

"Am I right?"

"Yes, but it peeves me to be predictable."

"Some women collect spoons—you collect men."

"Not funny."

"Yes, it is," said G, giggling.

"This is not helping."

"Okay. I'm sorry," she said, but I could still hear mirth in her tone. "So who's the newest caped crusader?"

"Funny you should say that because he reminds me of this cartoon when we were kids, but I was really little and barely remember so I don't know why it comes to mind when I see Roger, but—"

"Roger? That's his name? Same as my favorite tennis pro!"

"And my fav legendary quarterback, but that's not the point. He reminds me of Roger Ramjet."

My sister laughed so hard, she held the phone away from her ear and it sounded like she fell down a well.

"Okay, sorry. I swear I'm listening. And Phil is googling Roger Ramjet because I barely remember it too," she said, still giggling.

I could hear Phil in the background saying, "Comedy cartoon series from 1965 to 1970. Big muscle-bound redheaded dude in a white flight suit with blue wings. Tagline, 'Hero of Our Nation' fighting against forces of evil, including N.A.S.T.Y. He's a 'Man of Adventure!'"

Uncanny, given *nasty* was the president's word of choice when speaking of women, or aliens.

"Is this guy a pilot like Rauc?" asked G.

"No, but he's a Red Orbiter, with observer capabilities."

"What does he do?"

I hesitated, for good reason. "He's a bodyguard for—"

The burst of laughter had me pulling my phone away from my ear. "I do not see what's so funny!" I yelled.

Bodie stopped chewing and cut his eyes at me as Morris meow-screeched his displeasure at being awakened from slumber.

I could hear G come back on the phone, so I said, quietly, "And he's apparently some sort of spy too, so have at it. Laugh yourself silly."

She was howling again as soon as I said the word *spy*.

When she calmed down, G said, "Wasn't that Navy SEAL of yours a redhead? And the government agent on some super-secret paramilitary team? Was he redheaded?"

"Only the SEAL! And Roger's hair is not that red. It bleaches white blond in the sun! And he's about six-foot-seven and built like a linebacker, but now I'm afraid to tell you anything else."

"Okay, so he's Tarzan," she chuckled. "I promise I won't laugh anymore. What's his last name?"

My burner phone from Win buzzed before she could also ask me about Roger's age.

"Gotta go! Win's calling on the phone he gave me."

"Great. Another bat phone. Love ya, sis! Not sure I'd want to be ya, but it might be fun!"

I answered my burner bat phone, "Why are you calling and distracting me from writing?"

"Because apparently, when we were having all kinds of fun last night, Calamity was a busy bag of wind and dubbed our latest UFO a *flaming flying fairy* on his show masquerading as news, so today the president is tweeting about the, quote, 'Flaming fairy UFOs that look like rainbow balls and that's a gay thing.'"

"Can bugs be gay?"

"Ha ha. Now we've got the Everlasting Evangelical leader frothing at the mouth about toxic chemicals spewing from 'fruity aliens' that will make you gay if you have sex with them. Turn on your TV—the decrepit geezer's going at it right now."

I grabbed the remote and selected the channel Win told me, but I had to turn down the volume because the demented deacon of damnation was painful to listen to.

"It's unnatural, unnatural I say! Against all decency! These flaming fruity aliens do unnatural things. Things no one in my day ever did! Their body part chemicals will contaminate Earth and cause a pox on us all if feminazis don't stop fornicating and doing unnatural acts with aliens! We must smite them down before they bring a homoalien plague!"

"Homoalien plague? Who's that prune-faced fossil kidding? And I guess he didn't get the fairy memo, or maybe he misread it as fruity? He reminds me of the geriatric Supreme Court justice who said he'd never heard of anyone *he knew* engaging in oral sex." I huffed. "But how are we supposed to propagate our bug scheme now?"

"We've got Red Orbiters taking to the skies as we speak, wearing masks created on the fly exclusively for our caper, with bugged-out eyes and antennae plus iridescent wings."

"So how is that going to work, exactly, if they're up in the air in pistachio crafts?"

"They'll land in various hot spots, pop out, and spray bug juice at civilians who attempt to attack them. It'll be known as the Double-I War, for Iridescent Insect. I promise you Calamity will use that term this very evening. And you know why?"

"Because the president will never be able to spell or say *Iridescent*. What is this bug juice?"

"A Red Orbiter chemist at OUTWARD concocted something that's apparently a cross between nitrous oxide, helium, and sodium pentothal. Harmless, but it'll relax them while they babble inner truths in a voice like Porky Pig."

Once I stopped laughing, another thought dawned. "Aren't we worried about Red Orbiters getting shot by the lunatic fringe?"

"Rauc never told you? Or Roger?"

"Told me what?"

"Red Orbiters have a magnetic shield that protects them from the impact of projectiles."

Chapter 30

This morning my coffee was mere French roast, but should have been the Highland Grog roast because I used a mug I'd gotten in Scotland that said, "Highland Tryst" with adorable long-haired, burnt-orange cattle resembling longhorns. Were they alien?

I needed to grocery shop, dye my hair, and print copies of my excerpt from the Luna Moth Woman series for reading at tonight's meeting. Problem was, my printer was giving me fits. Maybe if our government wasn't so busy secretly reverse-engineering extraterrestrial aeronautical technology without considering alternative forms of energy and fuel, we'd have simpler things like printers working properly for more than a year. With ink that didn't require a personal loan to replace.

That wasn't all that was consuming me with consternation. Maybe I should move to Scotland. Maybe Red Orbiters there would not feel such a need to keep secrets, because this passive-aggressive method of treating me like I was the greatest thing since sliced bread for writing about their world, yet not worthy to be privy to some pretty freaking crucial details about them, was wearing on my last nerve.

I spent all day yesterday—when I wasn't writing so Win would get out of my hair—racking my brain for reasons why Rauc would not have confided in me during our April trip to Monterey and Valley of Fire. It was our only real alone time to date.

Was I partially to blame for talking about myself too much? Or did I not ask the right questions? Was it possible Rauc didn't realize what I might find of interest about Red Orbiters? About him in particular?

Would Rauc ever speak to me again, given my recent exploits?

What would Roger tell me if I asked? Or better yet, what could he divulge without me asking? What would I have to do to get him to do so?

And would I mind it?

I checked news headlines to stop thinking about Roger, which backfired.

"ANNUAL NRA FUNDRAISER INVADED BY GIANT ALIEN INSECT"

"TOWERING DAY-GLOW BUG SPEWS TOXINS ON GUN-TOTING TOWNSFOLK"

Those headlines came from our Las Vegas newspapers but were about Yearntown, which prided itself on an annual NRA fundraiser held at the local Boys & Girls Club facility where they auctioned off a semiautomatic rifle to the highest bidder. I personally was shocked it wasn't held at the evangelical church with the district attorney as auctioneer.

I said, out loud and from my living room, "Way to go, Roger Ramjet!"

Moments later I was rattled by a response in my ear, which felt a bit like a caress, followed by a threat. "Thanks, beautiful. I think. What did you just call me?"

"Um, Roger Ramjet. It's a cartoon from the sixties, which you wouldn't know because of your age, but you sort of remind me of it."

The pause was excruciatingly long.

"I know what Roger Ramjet is. We'll talk about this tonight."

I waited a bit to see if he'd say anything else, perhaps not in a tone so domineeringly enervating.

Silence, so I scrolled national headlines:

"IRIDESCENT UFO PILOTED BY BELLICOSE BUGLIKE ALIENS"

Excellent for our purposes, and not one mention of a fruity fairy, but how many HUMANS FIRST! cult members would know *bellicose* means "demonstrating aggression and willingness to fight"? I knew the president wouldn't.

My burner phone rang.

"Did you see headlines?" I answered. "Looks like Roger and others are busy being bugs."

"I did," said Win. "That's partly why I called. We'd like a meeting with you today."

"Why? To avoid imparting pertinent information while using me for your own ends?"

"What the hell, Rowan?"

"I have to grocery shop and find something called red yeast rice supplements for cholesterol, and I've got a writers meeting tonight, and I don't need to drag my butt all the way out there today. With no advance warning. Or consideration of my time."

"Explain, please."

For once I paused before speaking, but only because he said please, though it sounded way too much like an order.

"I already explained. Red Orbiters want me to write speeches for them, and books about them, but I'm not entitled to know the most basic and pertinent facts about what they are, or to stick my pinky toe in their headquarters area, or to get more than messages in my food from one who told me I captured his Red Orbiter heart! If he even has one!"

"You need to breathe, sweet pea."

"You need to back off. Because no one's going to control what I write, or how I write it, nor will there be meetings for autocratic review of what I write beforehand."

I thought my head might explode, so I hung up on him. Again. At least this time I didn't stomp the phone into oblivion.

And I deserved points for not smashing my printer to smithereens either, when it decided to attempt to reject my generic, much cheaper ink by claiming it didn't recognize it. Who the hell programmed printers to be elitist about ink brands? And where do machines get off asserting it's their job to have cognitive thought about anything, much less expensive, extortionist ink?

After hanging up on Win, I realized my ears were bleeping in that crazy electronic pattern others find similar to Morse code, like Dad. It had to be Greens. Had they heard me yelling? Were they worried about what I might write? They could be such touchy creatures.

And good grief, the government was bad enough, but how many different types of alien species did I now have to worry about analyzing my every utterance?

I leashed Bodie for an exploratory walk, but there were no menacing telltale clouds in the sky to camouflage a potential UFO. Bodie didn't detect anything suspicious nearby and only peed and sniffed and hopped erratically on the sidewalk, which meant it was too blistering hot for either of us to be out there. Back in we went, and Bodie drained his water dish.

Shopping took little more than an hour, as I no longer traveled fifty miles for a Trader Joe's. After making my hair roots copper red versus silver, I still I had hours before my writers meeting—and my post meeting with Roger. I didn't know which I was more nervous about.

Crafting might help calm my spirits, but that room was a disorganized mess. Yet I might as well unpack a box or two.

I got as far as a container with miscellaneous rubber stamps. Catching my eye was one that said, "It ain't easy being green."

I'd gotten it years ago at the best-ever rubber stamp store, Viva Las Vegastamps right here in Sin City, which I'd been too busy to visit since I moved. Did they know about Greens? This gave me a stellar idea for easing alien concerns.

Before I left for my meeting, I took a printed copy of what I planned to read for critique and placed it in the garage with the unearthed rubber stamp.

I said aloud, "I'm leaving this copy of what I wrote here for you, so you can come get it without worrying about my dog or cat. The side door from the yard will be unlocked. And, just so you know, we writers can be kind of touchy about our work, but I do hope you approve."

Chapter 31

I sat uneasily at the meeting, up next to read, unfortunately with the same bigoted chauvinist from last time seated opposite me and reading his own inane text.

Taking a deep breath, I began:

> She started life in the nation's capital, destined to champion truth and justice, but she didn't know she was born alien. And the truth would not be revealed for another fifty years. She had DNA from Jupiter's moon Elara, actually called Actius, named for the insect persona she donned, Actius Luna.
>
> Luna Moth Woman. It was her calling, and her greatest challenge. It wasn't easy being a post-middle-aged, menopausal, Earthbound female, much less a recovering government lawyer sporting alien-green combat boots to battle the latest threat to life as we now knew it.
>
> Her task? Keeping Earth dwellers safe from a deceptively sparkly but sinister species determined to wreak revenge on humans for their foibles and

fallacies and fantastical imaginings that all alien species were out to get them.

I could hear the aforementioned Neanderthal thrash in his chair, mouth-breathing his impatience. Or maybe he needed to "take a piss," like his protagonist he'd read about, who yet again blathered racial slurs and feminist slights.

"Sometimes she wondered if it was worth it," I continued reading, "if, perhaps, human hybrids were ultimately deserving of alien ire for their callous disregard of the world around them and of those in it who did not look and think and feel the way they did. Earthlings who needlessly squashed legions of harmless bugs out of revulsion, fear, or meanness. Was it time to surrender them to a similar fate, or were they worth protecting in this Iridescent Insect War?"

So yes, Luna Moth Woman was me, Rowan Layne. But was there ever any doubt how this would play out? I finished up with a paragraph that succinctly described a dramatic, action-packed attack by a rainbow-bright craft, overtaking Las Vegas skies, seeking out its prey for a fate to be determined...in subsequent chapters.

The bigoted bonehead audibly exhaled his disdain and launched into commentary without following meeting protocol. "What's the point?" His toxic energy leapt across the table to pummel my aura. "There's not enough action! Is something going to eventually happen?"

His statement was a repeat of commentary he'd received, and not for the first time, about his own written offering. I knew this when someone began a critique by noting, "As I and others have said before," followed by the part about an actual plot needing to take place.

I stared at him with utter contempt, learning for the first time in my post-middle-aged life how powerful my silence was. His eyes went squirrely and he fidgeted, shuffling papers underneath his hands. My written words. He was touching them yet would never comprehend their import.

But I would remember that sweltering silence when it came to Luna Moth Woman and her superpowers. It might not be bugs she ultimately made squirm and run for cover as if they were cockroaches scattering from sudden light.

I endured various additional commentary. One guy "corrected" my reference to the Pentagon for whom Luna Moth Woman once worked, arrogantly informing me it was in Washington, DC, not Arlington, Virginia. I responded by asking where he was from and had he worked for the military? California, and no, he had not. But the meeting proctor chided me for being defensive about receiving feedback.

One woman named Alice seemed like she might actually get it but probably not in the way the bug-scheme team wanted. Plus, she was the writer I'd enjoyed at the last meeting because she wrote about her career as a private investigator.

"I like where you're going with this. Luna Moth Woman has spirit and spunk," Alice said.

She approached me after the meeting, and we chatted as we left the building.

"I've seen them, UFOs. Many times on night stakeouts here in the city," said the soft-spoken private eye with well-honed wisdom in her blue eyes.

"I'd love to hear more about that. Have you seen the latest craft, this iridescent one?"

"It looks like a piece of jewelry in the sky, or a Fabergé egg, despite some saying it's dangerous, piloted by evil beings." Alice smiled. "But I've never had a problem with an alien or a UFO while on the job, though I sure can't say that about humans."

With her light-red hair, she could've passed as Win's sister, including the deceptive strength lurking below the surface.

"I'm with you on that," I said. "I tend not to automatically see aliens as the bad guys, though the jury's still out on this latest UFO, which gives me creative license to imagine! But I'm going to wait and see before I demonize them. There's enough of that already."

We'd reached the parking lot as Alice said, "I hear you, and I look forward to seeing what you come up with for Luna Moth Woman!"

Roger was leaning against his red Ferrari, lit up in all his glory underneath a lamppost. His hair looked positively white, angelic. I knew better, but Alice didn't.

"Good evening, ladies," he drawled, standing to his full height. "How'd your reading go, Rowan?"

"My goodness, you always have such interesting men waiting for you after these meetings," said Alice.

Chapter 32

I slipped into the passenger's seat of Roger's Ferrari, which I had to admit was a bit of a thrill.

He leaned toward me as I clicked my seat belt, so I drew back. "What, Roger?"

"Don't you mean Roger Ramjet?" his currently bright-green eyes seared into mine.

"It wasn't intended as an insult. How'd you know who he is anyway?"

"I know many things." He started the engine, which seemed to vibrate through me. "I'm taking you to my place so we can talk privately. You okay with that?"

"I suppose so. Where's your place?"

"Planet Wynne. I have a suite there, more convenient than Red Orbiter headquarters."

"You don't like Valley of Fire?"

"I like it just fine, but living on the Strip is better for my work."

"About that, I kind of get terrible motion sickness, and I'm not sure I can handle those elevators moving in a circular motion at Planet Wynne."

"Not to worry, beautiful. I'll take care of you."

"That's what I'm afraid of," I muttered, seeing Roger smile when I cut my eyes at him.

Driving into the hotel parking lot, we somehow ended up in an elevator while still riding in the Ferrari. Large doors slid open at the end of a row of parking, and there we were.

Roger applied pressure to my left wrist and said, "Here we go."

We moved on what I presumed were the rings of a planet, which the ground level was designed to look like, but it didn't make me queasy.

Another set of doors slid open in front of us, and Roger drove the Ferrari out to the open glare of night-bright Las Vegas on the second level of Planet Wynne, shaped like a flying saucer.

We parked on the outer edge of the saucer, perhaps fifteen stories above ground.

"Holy cow, we're sky-high in open air like a bridge! My knees will cave on me!"

Roger opened my door and lifted me from the car. I was cradled in his arms feeling like I'd slammed a shot of tequila.

"Whoa!" I said, looking around at what appeared to be a flight deck not unlike a naval aircraft carrier but with orbs and pistachio craft parked along the flat surface. "I bet they don't charge for parking up here. But can't people see everything? What about drones?"

"A magnetic force acts as a canopy. Can you stand now? Would you like to see our new spaceship up close?"

"Okay, but please don't let go of me," I said as he lowered my legs to the ground, which was also sparkly and florescent.

We walked toward the shimmering surface of a large spacecraft with a dark band around the center, placed where the split in a pistachio shell would be. Keeping one hand glued to Roger's arm, I reached out to touch its smooth exterior, surprised to find it cool to the touch.

"Can we go in it?"

"Not tonight, beautiful. I'm not the pilot, who's likely sleeping inside. We've been busy these past couple days."

"Don't you need to rest too?"

"I've got more important matters to attend to."

"I'm a matter to be attended to?" I said as Roger led me to another set of large doors, sliding open to an enormous circular hallway that made me think of the Pentagon. But it definitely wasn't government-issue décor, boasting a color scheme remarkably like the glittering pistachio craft with the addition of a galactic theme, a fluorescent Milky Way.

A smaller set of double doors led to Roger's suite and a disorienting contrast. Entirely masculine and sharper edges with red, black, and silver accents. Plus, I felt woozy. Indoors and up close, Roger's towering height and muscle might were wholly intimidating.

"Are we alone?" I asked, wishing my voice wasn't quavering.

"Yes," he said, looking down with those startlingly bright eyes. "But that's a good thing, beautiful. You can ask questions, and I'll answer what I can. I don't want you frustrated with me like you are the others."

"For crap's sake, Roger! I'd have thought you were too busy to spy on me this morning!"

"I was," he said, taking me by my wrists, his thumbs stroking pulse points, which immediately instilled a sense of calm. "I heard you were upset from Oggie, who heard it from Bruce and Ophelia, who were told by Oz that you were none too pleased with Red Orbiters."

"You guys have quite the gossip chain." I scowled.

"Not gossip. Concern. About our favorite human hybrid with Red Orbiter DNA and capabilities. Can I get you anything before I let you interrogate me?"

"No! I already feel like I've had several shots of tequila."

"It's the magnetic force."

"It's you," I said, wanting to smack myself for saying it.

Roger stared at me so intently, I thought twice about being alone with him.

Chapter 33

"You asked before, what I am and what I do?" said Roger, folding his long frame into the opposite end of a red leather couch where I was seated. "Security is the umbrella that describes my role, which includes personal protection but also intelligence gathering. Which means I infiltrate, undercover. Disguised as a state trooper, for example."

"So you're the Red Orbiter equivalent to Oswald Winslow's former profession."

"Except I provide individual protective services, not the forte of the CIA, which Win may be retired from, but you'd do well to realize there's nothing former about what he does."

"Was that a warning? Is that why you're determined to protect me? Or is this a who's-got-the-bigger-wanker contest?"

"When you're ready to learn the answer to that question, let me know."

"Not an answer!"

"Sure it was."

"Do you have some sort of enhanced sexual powers you're alluding to?" I peered at him, frowning. "I thought you weren't going to keep Red Orbiter secrets from me anymore!"

"All in good time, beautiful. You haven't learned how to fully apply your skills. There are unknowns involved."

"I am not a risk to Red Orbiters!"

"Maybe not. But you're still at risk personally, because of what you know, what you can find out, and what you don't understand about your abilities."

"You make me feel like I'm the one who's twenty-four years younger here." I shifted on the couch, crossing my leg away from him. Which those green-glowing eyes tracked, damn him.

"All right, to show good faith, I'll answer a question you haven't asked."

I flipped my leg back and crossed the other in his direction. He smiled.

"Red Orbiters do not fly in combinations of pilot and copilot," Roger began. "There's a pilot, but there's someone like me on every orb, trained to gather intel for security purposes. As opposed to observers like Raucous Wilde, who learn about species to study and document them."

"What are you saying?"

"Rowdy Wilde is not a mere copilot. He's a spy, gathering information about groups or individuals who pose a danger. Rowdy identifies risk for Red Orbiters."

"Son of a bitch," I slapped my leg and winced. Damn if Roger Ramjet's eyes didn't track that too, his smile loaded with import.

"That looked like it smarted," he said. "But before you get all twisted—"

"You're the one who's twisted!" I huffed.

Roger's face swooped at warp speed to within an inch of my face. I stopped breathing.

"I'll rephrase that. Before you get your panties in a wad thinking Rowdy identified you as a risk, he did not. You were an enigma, but not dangerous. And you need to breathe before you pass out," he said, pulling back, but not far enough for me to relax.

"I don't know how I'm supposed to feel." I frowned. "I've got Win telling me I'm not mysterious, and you Red Orbiters treat me like I'm some sort of puppy-dog fascination."

Those eyes again—so close, my vision blurred. "Don't you have more questions for me? Your middle name should be Question."

"I don't have a middle name," I whispered, his lips an inch from mine.

Roger slid away from me on the couch.

"What was that? Were you trying to mind meld with me, or is it all about intimidation?"

Roger's eyes returned to amber gold, and I felt like a deflated balloon.

"Not intimidation. Perhaps a chance to recognize the difference between a man who gets in your face to shout you down versus one who likes the feel of you up close. Quivering, but not trembling in fear or rage. You're a strong woman. And I like what I see, Rowan. I'm not one to want to vanquish that fire in you."

"I realize that," I said—and meant it.

"There's more you need to know. Yearntown, and the entire county where you lived, is a hotspot for anti-alien activity. They're organized because this is a group that's stockpiled guns for a while now, promoting anti-government conspiracies."

"And racial supremacy." I sneered.

"Yes, despite not being what you might call intellectually supreme. Although some have enough education and experience to know better."

"Let me guess. County commissioners are involved, along with sheriffs and perhaps the district attorney?"

"The county sheriff, deputies, a police chief, teachers, preachers, lawyers, even firefighters and medical personnel. It's pervasive, and it's festering. They all have a fresh new target for their hatred and rage and paranoia: aliens."

"Which I championed in my columns."

"That you did, and did well. Perhaps too well for these vigilantes."

"No wonder Dad worried about me." I sighed. "I thought I was relatively safe because most of them didn't read anything, much less my column. I'm lucky I got out of there unscathed."

"There's more," said Roger.

"What?" My stomach roiled.

"Your guy Lucas, the veteran you thought to help? He was one of them. He spent too much time in a bar owned by one of the ring leaders, and he was easily pulled in. I'm sorry."

"I somehow knew that. Or had daunting suspicions. Especially about the police." I wrapped my arms around my middle. "Lucas taunted me to call them when he got in my face."

"You were concerned about calling police? You thought they'd take his side?"

"He told me they would. And that they'd shoot our dog." I murmured, "He said they liked to do that."

"That's wrong, Rowan. Crazy, sick talk. You know that, right? Not all cops are bad."

"True." I shrugged. "Neither are all combat veterans. But too many people assume they're all good. Which is kind of unfair to their victims." I looked up. "This isn't such a fun conversation, is it? Here I am with a dashing alien and I'm talking horror stories when I should be asking questions."

Roger smiled, so I smiled.

"Always with the questions. I'm ready when you are, beautiful," he said.

My mind was mushy, so I said the first thing that surfaced. "Are there bad aliens?"

"Depends on how you see bad. Lots of humans would probably think Greens are bad, with their tendency to abduct and indulge in memory manipulation. But Greens might claim they're simply defending themselves against a bullying species."

"Makes sense to me." My mind jumped to what I'd learned about Rowdy and I chuckled.

"Whatever caused that amusement, it's gratifying to hear," said Roger.

"Does this mean Rowdy isn't a goofball?" I shifted towards him. "It was all an act?"

"He's goofy, all right, deceptively so when it's useful. He can be very effective when he poses as a harmless clown looking for a party. I helped him infiltrate Yearntown. He agitated locals by defacing that sign because he knew who made it and how they'd react."

"So why'd Rauc and Rowdy end up in hot water over it?"

"It wasn't pushback from Red Orbiter headquarters because it worked. The problem was he got Greens riled up about using their image, making it look like they were involved. Although it's not like he could use a Red Orbiter likeness."

"So Greens really do look like the stereotypical caricature?"

"Yes, except they don't have mouths. Rowdy improvised the mocking laugh."

I sat there, pondering. "Was Rauc's behavior toward me all an act too?"

"I can't speak for him, except to say he's not a spy like his brother. It's not his role to pretend to be something he's not." Roger's eyes locked with mine. "As much as I wish otherwise, his interest in you is likely genuine. Although his job requires prudence in ensuring you don't compromise Red Orbiters."

"Are you talking about Rauc's job or yours?" I asked.

"You're very astute."

"That wasn't an answer."

"You already know the answer, beautiful."

Chapter 34

When I got home—which I did without going the wrong way on the freeway, so there's that—a text from Mom pinged as I pulled into my driveway.

"Your father wants you to know he sent you an email. I don't know what it's about but he was in the kitchen sneaking cookies and it is too late at night for him to be eating. How was your writers meeting? Give my grand dog and cat a kiss. Love you oodles Doodles! (kissy face, dog, cat, heart, moon emoji)"

I assumed the moon emoji was because it was nighttime.

Getting out of my car, I noted the pages and rubber stamp I'd left in the garage were gone, the door to the side yard now locked. All safe and secure, so Greens could be considerate.

The critters didn't seem agitated. I sat them down and said, "Okay, family meeting. I know you didn't get a vote in moving here, but we're much better off, and I promise I will keep you safe. We've made some new friends, and that's a good thing, I think."

I hugged Bodie and stroked Morris, and we all climbed into bed, where I checked my phone for emails. Sure enough, one from Dad a half hour ago:

Doodles, I am getting old so this may seem strange, but I heard something tonight I wanted to share with you. There were messages I could tell were about you, and someone out there really likes you and is happy you're living in a safer place. They like how you write, and think you are a very nice person. Do you know who these people are? I am happy you are enjoying Las Vegas. Pet those critters for me, and send more pictures!

Love you, Daddy

I smiled through tears at how amazing life can be, writing back:

Hi Daddy, thanks for emailing me. Remember when you met Rauc, my Red Orbiter pilot friend in Portland, and he said there are alien species who have a language like Morse code? I think that's who you heard talking about me. They're careful about their identities but mean no harm to those who don't try to harm them. I'm attaching a picture of Morris and Bodie snuggling on the couch. We're settling in to life here, and it's good.

Love you, Doodles, Bodie and Morris

I had another email from my pal George and felt a pang of guilt even before I opened it.

Rowan, I want to say I'm sorry in whatever part I might have played to make you feel like we were keeping things from you here at OUTWARD. I wish I could say more, but just know we all love you and appreciate your help and support. You are a valued member of the team. I hope we're able to talk soon, and you and your pets are doing well.

Boy did I feel like a doofus for overreacting.

George, please know I am very sorry for causing you to think I was mad at you or anyone else at OUTWARD. I've been anxious adjusting to my new life, but I am grateful to be here and to know I have friends like you on my side. And you will be happy to learn I read for the first time at a writers meeting tonight, and it went better than I thought it might. I'll give it another shot next week, and we'll see how it goes. Luna Moth Woman is on the job! :)

Next I texted Mom back, "Writers meeting went okay. Wish you could be there to respond to various commentary, as some people are really out of it (smiley face emoji). Morris and Bodie and I are ready for bed. Sleep tight, sweet dreams (dog, cat, heart, moon emoji)"

And because I was bursting at the seams about the later portion of my evening, I texted my sister. I didn't dare gush it aloud. "You'll never guess where I ended up tonight. And I got to ride in a red Ferrari. (spaceship emoji)"

"Were you with Roger Ramjet?"

"Yes, and still have much to tell you about him, but he resides at Planet Wynne and he's been looking out for me for a while now. So yes, I finally seem to have my very own bodyguard. And we were outside on the second level of the hotel, the part that looks like a flying saucer!"

"You didn't get vertigo being up that high? (shocked face emoji)"

"Not with him holding on to me!"

"Next thing you know, you'll be flying around in his arms like he's Superman."

"Ha! Maybe you'll meet him when you're here next month for your cooking gig. And speaking of cooking, I don't think I've been eating right despite not eating meat because I have cholesterol issues and I'm taking red yeast rice pills."

"It's hereditary," said G. "I have high levels of both good and bad cholesterol. So do Mom and Dad."

"What's with that? How is it one can have good and bad cholesterol? It reminds me of the ozone layer in the atmosphere. There's the good protective ozone up high, and bad ozone from air pollution down low. Do you suppose some aliens are like that? Good when they're up far away and bad when they're down here?"

"Did you make it home safely, beautiful?" said a throaty caress in my ear.

"Yes, just a sec," I answered Roger. "I was texting my sister."

I texted G, "Gotta go! Roger's checking to make sure I got home okay."

"You go, sister! XO"

"Okay, Roger, I'm here!" I said, feeling out of breath.

"You all cozy in bed?" he asked. My toes curled and Morris grunt-meowed when my foot nudged him.

"Yes. But I'm not alone."

Silence.

"Morris and Bodie are hogging the bed!"

Roger laughed, low and sexy, supremely self-satisfied. "Lucky critters. I'll let you get some sleep. But I just want to say…whatever you do, don't dare think about me in that moment when you drift off to dreamland."

Chapter 35

When I was little, Mom used to tuck me into bed saying, "Whatever you do, don't think about lollipops!" It was her way of staving off my nightmares, likely from hearing aliens I thought were ghosts.

Thanks to Roger, I had a few waking thoughts through the night that were not about lollipops.

I stumbled about on my walk with Bodie, pleased to discover hummingbirds frequented the desert when one flitted then hovered in front of us. Did Win speak their language? It could be interesting to learn what they'd been chirping at me all these years.

Bodie strained against his leash as we rounded the corner for home, making me tense until I saw Win's Jeep parked out front. I relaxed but was wary, recalling our last conversation.

He was in his car on the phone. Bodie jumped up to his window with a happy yip, so Win emerged from the Jeep holding a small cardboard box above his head.

"I guess that probably isn't donuts," I said, trying for breezy humor but sounding like wistful disappointment.

"No, but I'll take you out for breakfast if you like. Let's go inside and talk first."

"Okay, but can you make your voice a little less foreboding?"

"Sweet pea, you may be able to hear better than a moth does, but your ability to detect accurate emotion sucks. I came to apologize."

We entered my house, and he handed me the box and bent down to stroke Morris. I unlatched Bodie's leash and went to my kitchen for a boxcutter.

"Be careful with that thing," said Win, eyeing me opening the package.

"With the box?"

"With the blade. We don't need a visit to the emergency room if you slice open a finger."

"How did you—? Damn. You even know about my kitchen clumsiness."

I pulled a mug in bubble wrap out of the box. As I unwrapped it, a big red question mark came into view, the mug handle. Printed on the mug itself were questions.

I read aloud, "If a word is misspelled in the dictionary, how would we know it? You can be overwhelmed and underwhelmed, so why can't you simply be whelmed? Why do we say something is out of whack? What's a whack?"

Win snorted and said, "Ha!" so I moved on to more questions depicted on my new mug.

"Why do *fat chance* and *slim chance* mean the same thing? How do people get discombobulated? Is someone ever combobulated?"

I put down the mug and sighed. "Yes, me. I was discombobulated, combobulated, and altogether agitated about getting something written and then reading it at that meeting. But I shouldn't have taken it out on you, or Oz. And thank you for this mug. I love it."

"It's okay. Honestly, I thought you loved Valley of Fire and wouldn't mind coming for another meeting. It wasn't about what you wrote, more for discussing events currently going down, and when's the right time to reach out to Homeland."

"Do you think I should call Tim Rider this week?"

"Not yet. He'll want to meet immediately when you make contact. Give it another week. You can concentrate on more writing, only if you want to." He shot me a steely eye. "Or sightseeing. You could probably go to Mount Charleston because apparently Greens are your new best friends."

I looked askance at him, trying to gauge his reaction. Waste of time. "My dad sent me an email that he heard them singing my praises."

"Whatever you did was good. Care to tell me what it was?" Win's tone was casual, but not really.

"Let me get coffee in my new mug, and I'll tell you all about it. Would you like some?"

***

Why did I always end up tangled in sheets with this man? At my age it was bad enough, but in broad daylight? And thank goodness for air-conditioning!

At least the critters didn't mind. Morris was now perched on Win's chest. As I watched his hand stroke along my kitty's back, making his furry butt rise in the air, I flushed.

"Are you hungry?" said Win. "We can go for a late lunch. First, I have news Oz wanted me to impart."

Was I hungry? Maybe so, though I felt like a limp noodle. "Okay, fire away, and then I'm going to shower."

"Oz says Rauc and Rowdy and recruits training in the moonship will return in time for the Omni convention next month. We're stepping up our game on this Iridescent Insect War."

"I see why you waited to tell me until *after* we had sex."

"Oh, I'm happy to go another round, sweet pea."

"That's not what I meant!" I whacked his arm.

"You're getting defensive again."

"Do you blame me? I'm lying in bed with you while you tell me Rauc is returning."

"Something to consider the next time you meet up with Roger. Because I have to go out of town and don't like the idea of leaving you at his mercy."

"Please! I'm no cougar, and I can barely make it through a round with you."

"You made it just fine, sweet pea."

"I didn't want to miss anything," I said, suddenly feeling sad. "Where are you going? Will you be gone long?" I didn't like sounding needy, but no point in trying to hide it.

"A week or so. I'm headed to the East Coast for Origins board meetings, then to the convention in Seattle, and I'll stop in at OUTWARD while I'm in Washington State."

"Why in hell are you going to the Republican National Convention?" I sat up.

Win smiled. "Just doing my thing."

"Intel? I guess you really aren't retired."

"Sure I am. From the government."

"Never mind." I rolled my eyes. "Can you believe they switched the Republican convention to right before the Democratic convention thinking to steal their thunder?"

"Narcissism is as sociopath does. My hunch says it'll backfire on the president."

"Hunch or intel? What do you know?"

"Nothing definitive or otherwise shareable."

"Oh, fine." I huffed. "Tell me about Origins. Where is it?"

"In Virginia, not far from Langley and near my townhouse. I need to check on things at home, do laundry. Long-term living in an RV is not the greatest."

"I can imagine. You're welcome to do laundry here in the future. I could live without some things, but not a washer and dryer. And a full-sized bathroom. Speaking of which, will you head into the living room so I can shower?"

"I think I'd rather shower with you—put you through another round and prove you wrong." He smiled.

Chapter 36

I finally had a week in which I could write without distraction or otherwise do as I pleased, but a few days in, I felt stuck. And I didn't relish going anywhere on my own, especially in this heat.

Win was being a spy and Roger was off doing his bug thing, leading to headlines:

"FAIRY BUGS ABDUCTING, TORTURING CITIZENS, CLAIMS PRESIDENT"

"EVERLASTING EVANGELICALS WARN OF HOMOALIEN PLAGUE"

"PRESIDENT SAYS BUG ALIENS DENIED HIM ACCESS TO MOONSHIP"

"PRESIDENT ANNOUNCES MINING PLANS FOR MARS"

Some things were working in the great alien bug scheme, except the president was still fairy obsessed and steadfast in his determination to maraud and exploit other planets.

I read the article about Mars mining, and it had a quote from my law school professor, Oliver Warnock, founder of the OW Coalition: "The president persists in an egocentric misconception that the US is the center of the universe and somehow has a unilateral claim to activity on Mars, or anywhere else in the galaxy, including Earth's moonship, where he was denied access solely because his first and only instinct was to attack and destroy it."

There was also a quote from an unnamed source with ties to human-alien relations: "The president and others should cease with homophobic and other juvenile slurs against any and all extraterrestrial beings. Bigotry has no place in intergalactic relations. We need a leader who forges alliances with the otherworldly, as opposed to projecting a posture of dominance and destruction while throwing dangerous tantrums worthy of a chastised toddler."

Good job, Win. Couldn't have said it better myself.

Meanwhile Mom weighed in with a text, "People are out of it!!! Those aliens are not gay bugs!!! They wear the tackiest outfits I've ever seen!!! My gay friends have taste and would never dress like that!!! How is weather??? Not cloudy here. For once!!! (flipped bird, smiling sun, plain sun, pink shoe emoji)"

Again with the flipped bird. Maybe she didn't realize what it was?

Evidently Mom saw one of our insect marauders on the Portland news, as the media was providing excellent footage of various extremist nests getting sprayed with bug juice. Win told me Oz was in the Pacific Northwest flying in costume and having a blast reliving his Navy test pilot days, as was Dr. Bruce Robertson, former Marine pilot conscripted to temporarily fly a pistachio craft. It was all Red Orbiter hands on deck for our Operation Bug Attack.

I checked Twitter, where the president responded to media coverage: "I have toatal control over other planits. Warshingtun Post is all lies. Nasty reporters. OW groop fake to. Aliuns after your guns and my money!"

I guess that *Coalition* word was too much of a stretch for him.

Responses included:

"President grasps for absolute power to loot other planets, but can't accurately spell anything projected from within the demented kingly realm of his diseased mind."

"Concerned citizen here. Anyone think we have a problem when our own president can't spell Washington? Who voted for this?"

That first one sounded like Roger. And okay, I admit the second tweet was mine. It wasn't about our bug scheme, so I put my two cents in.

My favorite response came from constitutional law expert Terrance Scribe: "A president does not have absolute rule over this nation, much less the universe. He should try reading the Constitution. If he can."

Win might fuss at me, claiming I was wasting time surfing social media instead of writing, but this provided fabulous fodder for the exploits of Luna Moth Woman.

I'd been busy in my craft room too, because I had a rubber stamp that said, "PROCRAFTINATE: a verb meaning avoidance of adult responsibilities to partake in crafting." I also found a stamp with a quote perfect for responding to members of the Everlasting Evangelical Ministry's deluge of tweets spreading fear-mongering about fruity homoaliens: "I do not feel obliged to believe that the same God who has endowed us with sense, reason, and intellect has intended us to forego their use. Galileo Galilei."

Plus, the planet (not *planit*) we called Neptune was actually named Galilei for the esteemed physicist.

But my greatest inspiration came from the rubber stamps I unpacked with a fairy theme. I put together a bright, glittery greeting card to give to Roger the next time I saw him, because yesterday I heard him ranting from afar: "If I get my hands on who came up with the monumentally stupid idea of having us wear sparkly glitter wings, it's not going to be pretty," he said. "There are plenty of insects without wings! What were those engineering idiots thinking? Didn't it occur to them that someone as simple and demented as the president would see us as frigging fairies?"

Chapter 37

Star date: Third Tuesday-night writers meeting. Same bat time, same batty people, or at least a few of them. The bigoted blowhard actually sat his annoying ass down next to me. He came in late after the meeting started, providing no opportunity to switch seats without being obvious.

I absconded to the bathroom after he launched into reading and his protagonist referred to yet another female as a "bimbo with bursting boobs." The inevitable racial slur followed.

I was up last to read, and I didn't even want to because Alice wasn't there, and she was likely the only person who would give me uplifting feedback.

Taking a deep breath, I prepared to begin, but a voice in my ear made me pause.

"Howdy, beautiful. I'm right outside in case you have trouble with Archie Bunker in there. What the hell are *bursting boobs*, anyway? I hope you're not wearing a lowcut top. Might have to spray some bug juice on bigot boy."

Wasn't that a nice image to have in my head as I read? And no, I wore plenty of flowing, cottony gauze fabric in this infernal heat.

"Are you going to begin reading? I've started the timer," said the meeting proctor.

Taking another deep breath, this time with an exasperated exhale, I stated I would read chapter two and only part of chapter three due to time constraints. As I read, I wished Win would teach me his Vulcan grip for the spastic psycho bigot twitching mere inches from my elbow.

The president stood on a festooned podium, cowering behind Secret Service protection after launching a tirade at a journalist's inquiry. "What source are you citing when you claim to have absolute power over all planets and otherworldly beings?" she asked.

He answered with a pointed finger, shouting his condemnation, "That nasty woman and all like her should be silenced!"

Egged into a frenzy by their ignominious leader spewing spittle-flecked rage, the derisive, panting crowd turned their ire on the targeted female reporter—who happened to be Luna Moth Woman, though she wasn't equipped with protective luminous shielding on this day.

She'd not anticipated the need to battle emboldened forces of evil. Today she merely performed her day job's mission: to obtain truth where too many lies prevailed, to attempt to wrangle reason from insanely babbling chaos.

When a pair of towering aliens with glowing antennae attacked, she stepped out of their way. It was too late to intervene, and she knew to be wary of toxins spraying over the crowd.

By night Luna Moth Woman was tasked with taming these turbulent beetle beings from another world, tracking their rainbow-hued crafts as they marauded the skies waging a war of intimidation, and retaliation. But on this day, it was Lacey Mae Wordsworth who was instead lifted skyward by a supposed alien nemesis. Away from vicious vigilantes and a president intent on doing her harm.

I looked up as, unfortunately, a certain someone spoke.

"I don't get it, who is this Luna Moth Woman? Some kind of bug bimbo? But what does she do? Where's the action?"

This time I stared not at the misogynist mouth breather seated next to me, choosing to rest my gaze upon the unlucky individual presiding over this meeting. If I stared at her long enough, would she take control?

Before that could happen, another asked, "Are you sure the president doesn't have absolute control? I think the Constitution says he does."

I responded, "My legal background compels me to make sure I get these things accurate. What's your background?" and received yet another admonishment telling me I shouldn't be asking questions because it took time away from feedback on my book. If only.

To add insult to injury, the meeting presider also weighed in with how she didn't think a "media person" would actually ask that kind of question. I refrained from responding how my journalism background also led me to some sort of instinctual accuracy on such things, or from suggesting she watch the effing news.

Next and final feedback: "That last chapter kind of fell flat on the ending. I tend to expect more from a chapter."

"Comment noted," I said. "I'll look into that in the rest of the chapter I didn't read for you. As mentioned beforehand."

"You ready to go, Ms. Layne? Your chariot awaits!" said the towering towheaded alien swooping into the meeting and rescuing me. No bug juice though.

I half expected a red orb or pinkish pistachio hovering at the ready to fly me away, but it was the red Ferrari, which was still impressive.

I heard a guy from the meeting who walked out behind us say, "Damn, that is one big dude. How does he fit in that car?"

"I don't know," said another. "But killer wheels."

I was inside Roger's killer car before I remembered the card I'd made for him. "Be right back," I said.

I dashed to my car, grabbed the card, spun around, and ran smack dab into Roger Ramjet's massive and very hard chest. "I think I broke my nose," I stepped back, eyes watering.

Roger was laughing, damn his muscle-bound hide. But he pulled me into a hug and kissed the top of my head. "You okay, beautiful?"

"Yes, but why did you feel the need to stalk me to my car?"

"Because one of the people at that meeting shouldn't have been, and he's still inside," he whispered in my ear, and I felt my knees go weak as if I were back on the flight deck at Planet Wynne. "I'll tell you all about it at my place."

Chapter 38

"Tell me again why you drive this flashy car," I asked Roger, buckling my seat belt.

"Just another cover, beautiful. Most folks think my Vegas job is Planet Wynne promotion."

"So what'd you do for your Yearntown undercover infiltration?"

"Pickup truck and a military crewcut with ballcap, plus poser camouflage hunting garb when I was in civilian, as opposed to state trooper, mode. My hair's grown out since then."

Yes, it had. It was all spikey and sexy.

"Please tell me you didn't wear a HUMANS FIRST! hat."

"What? You don't think those are hot?" Roger started the engine and eyed the white envelope in my hand. "That's what was so important you had to dash to your car?"

"I did some paper crafting yesterday and thought of you. So I made you a card."

"Oh yeah? I'm not sure about the sound of that giggle," he said, his tone making me squirm in my seat.

"Maybe I should give it to you in a public place. Why don't we go to Galaxy Grog? Except no, I can't drink because I still have to drive home. I hate that route too, because I'm afraid I'll go the wrong way coming off the freeway and end up sitting at red lights an extra twenty minutes."

"I'll take you home tonight and arrange for your car to be returned to you without the tracker that is likely being placed on it."

"By the guy from the meeting? Who was it? Not the bigoted buffoon. He's too clueless."

"We'll talk about that later. Let me see the card."

"You're driving. It can wait." I looked out the window, away from those eyes.

"Open it."

"But I—"

"Now."

"You sound so domineering." I turned towards him. "It's only a funny card. Lighten up."

"Don't make me pull this car over."

"Now you sound like someone's mother."

"I'm fixing to feel like someone's daddy."

"Oh, good grief! I'll open it, okay?" I tore into the envelope.

For the front I'd used one of my rubber stamps of a short-haired fairy with huge wings. I decorated the wings with glitter pens, rhinestones, even some fluorescent embossing powder—in every glistening color of the rainbow. Underneath it I'd stamped the phrase, "Her wings were made of bold patterns and bright colors," except I'd crossed out "her" and inked in "his."

Roger glanced at it and somehow remained expressionless. "Looks like someone's got too much time on her hands."

I babbled as I cringed, "I also used a couple of my rubber stamps for a message inside."

"Read it aloud to me."

I was never, ever going to use another rubber stamp. It was too perilous.

"Can we just wait until later for that part?"

We pulled into the first elevator taking us to the second deck where red orbs and neon nuts docked.

"Read it."

I swallowed my parched throat and read, "Don't let anyone dull your sparkle!" and "Don't forget to spread your wings and fly."

As Roger parked and cut the engine, still showing no reaction to my card, I slumped my shoulders and said, "I heard you complaining about your wings. This seemed sort of funny when I made it. And I used a very long-legged fairy."

Roger came around to remove me from the car, like last time, except tonight I wasn't thinking about queasiness. I was already there.

"Can I get another look at the new spacecraft?" I dashed away to touch its cool iridescent surface again. "At least I got the color right, but I should have made the wings blue, like Roger Ramjet."

I heard him chuckle. "Come here, I want to show you something."

"I'm not falling for that," I said over my shoulder.

"I promise you'll like it."

"That either!" I nervous-laughed.

I felt a whoosh in my stomach like I was in a plane that had suddenly dropped in altitude. It left me up close and personal with Roger, backed up to the parked Ferrari.

His hands moved from my waist, upward.

"Please don't tell me you've got a Vulcan grip too?"

"Oh no, beautiful," Roger's voice purred, the deep timbre tweaking my—

"Whoa!" I shivered as his hand moved across the back of my neck, stroking the sensitive spot at my spine's apex.

And...I orgasmed. Just like that. Standing right there against his red Ferrari.

"I bet Roger Ramjet can't do that," he said. "Oh, and thanks for the card."

Chapter 39

I staggered to double doors leading to the circular Milky Way hallway, holding onto Roger's amazing hand.

"Still want to get that drink at Galaxy Grog?" he said, smiling down at me.

I shut my eyes so I wouldn't have to look at his smug green ones.

"No? Okay, we'll just have a little something at my place then."

I was back on the red leather couch, holding an icy tumbler with what tasted like Amaretto, or was it Frangelico? Except it was light green. I hope he hadn't given me absinthe. I rolled the sweet liqueur around on my tongue until I realized Roger was watching me intently.

"Pistachio laced with cherry. Kind of like spumoni ice cream."

"It's delicious," I said, sipping and smacking.

"You have very enticing lips."

Why did I feel as if his mind pictured a different set of lips? I crossed my legs. He smiled.

"So what do you want to ask me about tonight?" he said. "The origin of pistachios, or that little maneuver I treated you to outside?"

I stopped sipping, looking away. "Is that your special gift? Or is it a Red Orbiter thing?"

Roger moved from across the room to crouch down in front of me. "And here I thought for sure you already knew," he said, alien eyes penetrating mine.

It was a searing slap to the senses to realize his meaning. Why hadn't Rauc brought me such pleasure so swiftly and easily?

I looked away from Roger again. My orb-tryst time with Rauc had been immensely pleasing—don't get me wrong. Yet it was remarkably ordinary, given his Red Orbiter capabilities. He'd clearly held back, but why?

"Is there more?" I asked, sheepish. "How much do I still not know?"

"I can only speak for me, beautiful. When you're ready, I'd be most honored to show you. I probably shouldn't have sprung that on you tonight, but you were so adorable, all worried about that hilarious card." He chuckled. "I admit I lost my head."

"Can I please have more of this?" I held up my glass. "And then you should tell me about the plant at the writers meeting and why you think he'd put a tracker on my car."

Roger raised to his full breath-robbing height, and I watched him glide across the room, trying not to imagine what it must be like to entwine with the embodiment of, and perhaps magic within, a Greek god—gods who, I'd learned from Rauc, were actually extraterrestrial beings from another galaxy.

Would it not be daunting to lie with one who's physical beauty so outshined my own? Not to mention one so much more youthful?

Roger handed me a replenished glass and sat down in a chair across from the couch, keeping his distance. Did he feel guilty about what he'd done?

"It was the man who told you he thought the Constitution gave the president absolute power. And because of that, it likely won't be him at the next meeting. His instructions were to observe, not speak, and to definitely not mention the president in any capacity. He couldn't help himself. Not surprising, as these idiots are more like indoctrinated cult members."

"You have ears listening outside the White House?" I asked.

"We have ears inside the Executive Office Building too, where the president's baby brother pretends to be a spymaster." Roger snorted. "These are his flunkies, picked from the crowd at rallies to infiltrate gatherings of those who might speak with disfavor about the president. But they don't need HUMANS FIRST! ballcaps to stick out like neon signs."

I thought back to the guy sitting at the end of the table. I hadn't noticed much, other than bad skin and the croak of a heavy smoker. What stood out was how he'd introduced himself. "A real charmer," I told Roger. "He said he didn't really like to read books but thought he might write one so he could, quote, 'Rake in the Benjamins when they make a movie out of it,' and 'How hard can it be if that Stephen King guy does it?'"

"Oh yeah, he's public enemy number one with these pissants. But Rowan, you are too. So you might want to lay off Twitter for a while. I can't protect you every minute of the day right now, especially when I'm flying around flapping fairy wings."

I giggled.

"Write whatever you want for your book, and I or someone else will cover you at meetings. And the Omni convention. Are we clear on this? You good with me hovering when I deem it necessary?" Roger pinned me with glowing green eyes.

"Yes." I sighed, wishing my libido weren't so damned thrilled with it. "But after tonight I don't think I want to go back to that writers meeting. It wears me out."

"It's your brain, beautiful. It moves too quickly. The rest of us can't keep up."

"But you said you had superpower stamina!"

"You remembered," he drawled. "Been thinking about that a lot, have you?"

Chapter 40

The cat's on my shit list this morning. Last night he spent a good hour bouncing off walls and crashing into things, screeching and caterwauling like he was squeezed in a vice after Roger dropped me off. I didn't know if it was because Roger came in to make sure everything was okay or because he was mad I'd left the house to begin with. Something was up his furry butt.

Now, after walking Bodie, who for once acted like an angel and didn't tug on the leash or stop dead in front of me and almost cause me to break my neck, I found a cat toy in the litter box. Sitting right on top of clumps of poop was a little pink ball with a bell inside.

Could it be some sort of feline alien protest against plastic? Should I stick to cloth catnip toys? I recently bought him hilarious little "fish tacos," and Mom got a pink octopus at Christmas that I dubbed kitty calamari. He didn't leave *those* in the litter box.

I supposed I should have been glad it wasn't a dead mouse. But was that the problem? Was he peeved this house was not mouse-invasion central like our last residence?

I plopped myself down with a second shot of caffeine, seriously considering prodding at the sleeping orange monster on the back of the couch. A voice in my ear stopped me from such folly.

"Good morning beautiful. I'm outside with your car. Want to open the garage? I don't have an orb picking me up for another hour, so can I come inside and watch TV?"

"You sound like a little kid," I said as the garage door lifted to reveal Roger in all his towering titillation. "Did you want to watch cartoons?"

"Sure, I thought we might see a few episodes of Roger Ramjet. Do you have a rubber stamp of him too?"

I paused, thinking no, but that would be a good suggestion for Viva Las Vegastamps.

"Actually, I thought we might watch the news. Senator Rojas-Ortiz is making an important announcement in a few minutes," said Roger.

"Okay, but did you check for a tracker on my car and remove it?"

"There was none. Not that he didn't try."

"What happened?" I asked as we walked in the house and Bodie practically leapt into Roger's arms. "Do you want coffee?"

"Sure, with sugar if you have it."

"Aren't you sweet enough already?"

"Come here, and I'll show you just how sweet I can be," said Roger.

"No way, no how!" I said, scampering into my kitchen.

Roger followed with Bodie at his heels while Morris yowled from the counter.

"When our author wannabe infiltrator trotted out in the dark after everyone left the meeting, he was unsuccessful in his mission," said Roger. "He screamed this morning about how he was abducted and held captive by horrifying little gray creatures who tortured him for information about who he was and what he was up to."

"You have got to be kidding me. Did anyone believe him?"

"Hell no. They think he's making it up because they canned him from further assignments. And they warned him he better not tell his tall tale to the fake news media either."

I snickered.

"So what'd you do to get Greens all sweet on you, beautiful? Looks like I've got some competition protecting that lush body of yours."

I stood looking up at Roger, realizing I was wearing clinging yoga pants with no panties and a cotton jersey top over my sheerest, unpadded bra.

"I'll just go change—"

Roger snagged my wrist as I headed for the hallway. "I don't have the time it will take to properly show you the attention you deserve, so let's turn on the TV, and soon I'll be out of your gorgeous curly red hair."

"I didn't mean I was going to change into something more comfortable! Jeez. Is everything a double entendre with you?" We sat in front of my TV, Roger holding the clicker. "So what's the senator's big announcement? Surely she's not going to tell the world she's a Red Orbiter."

There's apparently some unspoken rule that men, including alien males, must be in command of the remote control at all times or they'll self-destruct.

Roger selected a channel in time for us to see Senator Rojas-Ortiz step up to a microphone, a row of American flags behind her and a tall black male at her side.

"That's my congressman," I said.

"I am Senator Cassandra Rojas-Ortiz of Las Vegas, Nevada, speaking to you today from our nation's capital with my fellow Nevadan, Congressman Warren O'Neill. We are here to share an exciting announcement. But first, I'd like to say a few words."

The congressman had light-green eyes, like Smokey Robinson.

Senator Rojas-Ortiz said, "Well before the alien revelation and formation of the Other Worldly Coalition, millions of Americans tested their DNA to learn where they came from. Not one single person received results identifying them as being from the United States. Why? Because DNA doesn't work that way. You're an American if you were born here, live here, hold citizenship status here. All of which entitle you to support the candidate of your choice, or choose to serve your country—irrespective of where you might hail from or how long you've called America home. The inalienable right to participate in our democracy as a human, an alien, or some combination of both."

"Those are my words! I wrote something similar for her about property rights! How cool is this? You sure she's not going to pop right out and say she's a Red Orbiter?"

"I'm sure," drawled Roger. "But nice words, beautiful."

The senator continued, "Facts matter. And the truth is, every single human in this nation and on this planet possesses extraterrestrial DNA. If the otherworldly can't serve our nation, no one should. Aliens are among us, and we are them. Now, as in the beginning."

"I wrote that too! And I think she did reveal she's an alien, though no one will realize it!"

Congressman O'Neill moved in front of the microphone as the senator stepped away.

"Thank you for those inspiring words, Senator. My fellow Americans, for the first time in our nation's history, we the people have a political party, the Omnipresent Party, which represents the otherworldly in all of us. The Omni Party seeks to ensure all Americans are instilled with a voice, an opportunity to be heard, and representation so that they may share in the blessings of liberty."

"Oh my gosh," I murmured.

"That is why," said Congressman O'Neill, "Senator Rojas-Ortiz and I announce today that we are joining the Omnipresent Party of the United States of America! But we do not entirely leave behind the Democratic Party that brought us to Congress. We will continue to work alongside our colleagues for the betterment of all Americans. And due to the timing of this announcement, both the senator and I will be participating in the upcoming Democratic and Omnipresent conventions."

"He's an alien too." I turned to Roger once the press conference ended. "Those eyes, light green with black around the iris. Just like my friend Oapule and my mom's personal Uber driver Karim. They're from Venus, less than one percent human."

"You figured that out, did you?" Roger grinned.

Chapter 41

I sat there on my couch after Roger left and wondered if he'd seen what I had.

When the senator and congressman left the podium, the camera followed them. There, leaning against a wall, was Win. Not at all noticeable—unless you knew him. I hadn't expected he'd be hanging out in the halls of Congress, visiting his ex-girlfriend.

As I put Roger's and my coffee cups in the dishwasher, I muttered, "It's not like I've been a nun myself. I should just get over it. Who knows why he didn't tell me he was going to be there?"

"Beautiful," said a silky voice in my ear. "Don't beat yourself up over this."

"Damn you, Roger Ramjet!" I screeched "Why are you spying on me? We have privacy rights under the penumbra of the Ninth Amendment to the Constitution, and you should damn well respect that!"

I was immediately sorry about yelling, but only because the critters ran from the kitchen where they'd been underfoot, as usual.

"I wasn't spying," said Roger, too calmly for my blood. "It's not like when we're deliberately focused on hearing someone. I was thinking about you, so I heard you."

"What the hell does that mean?"

"Why don't you sit and I'll explain."

"I don't want to sit. Tell me what's going on!"

"It's a Red Orbiter thing. We can often hear one another at the moment we think of someone."

My blood pressure rocketed. Yet another bombshell Raucous Wilde had neglected to reveal before disappearing.

"Before you lose it over Rauc not telling you this—"

"Oh, so now you can read my mind too?" I stomped around my living room.

"I don't think he realized it. You're not a Red Orbiter. But you have our DNA and our auditory abilities, so that's likely why I could hear you when I thought of you."

"Are you sure? What if Rauc can hear me and has been listening all this time?"

"He's on the moonship, and even he can't hear you from there."

"Oh good. Here I thought I'd been listened to since childhood, spied on by Labyrinthians."

"I don't have time to find out what that's supposed to mean. But will you let up on us Red Orbiters? We're still learning about you too."

"I'll try," I grumped.

"And as much as I dislike saying it, will you also give Win a break? He's just doing his job."

"I know." I sighed. "I don't really know why I'm so upset. It's not like we're in an exclusive relationship."

"Happy to hear you say so. But his thing with the senator was some time ago. They met at Oxford, long before she was in Congress."

"So we have Red Orbiter Rhodes Scholars?"

"Hey, we aren't all brawn—we've got superpower brains too. Catch you later, beautiful. Gotta go be a fairy bug."

I checked headlines on my phone after bugging out with Roger, and there it was:

"TWO NEVADA DEMS FIRST TO SWITCH TO OMNI PARTY"

Another headline made me chuckle:

"BUGS GET REVENGE, SPRAY HUMANS LIKE PESTS"

I read the accompanying news story, about a presidential rally in the Florida Panhandle gone awry. Ironically, big scary bug aliens fell from a jeweled brooch in the sky, wreaking unspeakable toxic terror on HUMANS FIRST! thugs threatening a reporter from a news channel they deemed fake news. At least that's what one bug juice victim claimed, because the article was written by the targeted reporter who, uncannily, was attacked by a mob right after the president bashed the cable news organization he worked for. Hence the headline.

Even I couldn't make this stuff up for a Luna Moth Woman tale.

My burner phone rang.

"Did you see the senator's press conference?" asked Win when I answered.

"Sure did. Exciting news."

"The congressman told me he's very impressed with you. And you're practically neighbors."

"Wow. So where are you now? It sounds noisy."

"I'm at National, waiting on my flight to Seattle."

"Good thing you called it National and not Reagan, or my mother would not approve."

Win laughed. "Whatever this airport's called, it's nuts here now. There was a HUMANS FIRST! rally out in Manassas last night that got a visit." Win's voice cracked on a chuckle. "Bunch of bug-juiced dudes wandering the airport, babbling. They don't sound like Porky Pig, but either the sodium pentothal didn't wear off or we made those bugs way too attractive. You'd be surprised how many of them have sexual fantasies about aliens."

I shuddered at the thought of those guys having sex with anyone.

"You still there?"

"Yes." I composed myself. "Hey, speaking of aliens, I had a thought."

"Uh-oh, not you too," said Win.

"Seriously, it's about the OW Coalition. When Oliver Warnock and his daughter Olivia founded it, it wasn't only about human hybrids, was it?"

"Not entirely, though it aimed to recruit like-minded individuals such as yourself. But aliens are and were involved. How do you think we have spaceships to travel to Mars and the moonship?"

"And you? You didn't just start Origins for DNA testing—you were part of forming the OW Coalition."

"That I was. My flight's boarding. I'll give you a shout from the convention. Stay away from presidential rallies." He chuckled.

A text arrived when I got off the phone with Win, and it wasn't Mom. It was a Las Vegas phone number.

"Ms. Layne, it's Tim Rider. Would it be okay if I gave you a call?"

DHS was extending every courtesy to me these days. Interesting.

I texted, "Sure. Now is fine. (smiley face, flying saucer emoji)"

I didn't use the green alien head emoji out of respect for my little friends. It wouldn't do for them to think I might somehow be outing them to Homeland.

My phone rang.

"Nice emoji," said Tim. Good for him.

"I figured Bart would enjoy them."

"I suppose he would, but he won't see them. I'm calling you from my personal phone."

"Seriously? What's going down?"

"Nothing good," he said. "That's why I want to meet with you tonight, but somewhere relatively private where we can talk after work, around seven? I'd be happy to take you out to dinner for a few hours of your time."

"Why don't I see about getting us in at Galaxy Table in Planet Wynne? Would that work?"

"Really? I've wanted to eat there but can never get a reservation. My mother loves Rose Bergin."

"I'll give them a call and text you back."

I dug up the business card Octavius Wynne handed me when I'd met him with my sister. It was quite a shocker to have the man himself answer my call.

"Rowan Layne, how lovely to hear from you."

"Hi, O.W., I need a favor. I have to meet with Homeland Security and wondered if you could squeeze us in at Galaxy Table tonight?"

"For you, absolutely. Rose has just such a private table reserved for these things."

I got off that call and realized the timing of this had Win on a plane to Seattle, with Oz and Roger off doing the bug thing, and no way for me to let any of them know my plans. But if O.W. knew, maybe the issue would resolve itself, at least for Red Orbiters. The Las Vegas mogul had the look of a total gossip queen.

Chapter 42

What to wear to meet with an agent of the Department of Homeland Security? This wasn't a social date, and the guy was the same age as my best college friend's son. But it was a swanky restaurant, which also meant no way could I let Tim pay on his government salary.

A flowing, azure-blue linen skirt with matching top would do, and the other issue resolved itself when the famous chef's voice slipped into my ear on my drive to the Strip.

"Hi, Rowan, it's Rose. Thrilled to have you returning! Wanted to give you a heads-up that your meal's been comped by O.W. and me, and your table is in a corner, screened off for privacy. Also, use valet parking. See you soon!"

I'd lived in Vegas a little over a month and already felt like a high roller without having gambled a dime.

From valet parking, I zipped up the escalator and over to the restaurant to find Tim Rider waiting. He'd changed out of his workday suit into khakis and a polo shirt, making him appear even younger with his short brown hair and clean-shaven face.

"Ms. Layne, thanks for meeting me."

"Please, call me Rowan, and my pleasure. Rose has a table ready for us, and it's all taken care of. Having Red Orbiter friends has its perks." I grinned.

"This is great," said Tim as we were led to a table behind a screen painted with a starry, cloudy sky. "Good thing I'm not married or someone might think I'm having an affair."

"Yeah, with your mother," I snarked.

"I've always been attracted to smart-mouthed older women." He winked.

"Greetings, dear friend," said Rose, appearing at our tableside. "I won't intrude on your time, but here's a special chef's taste treat to whet your appetite." Rose placed small plates on our table. "Please enjoy, and I'm happy to answer questions about the menu."

"Thank you," said Tim. "My mother adores you and has all of your cookbooks."

"You must bring her to dine with us!" said Rose, leaving us to our treat.

Tim looked down at the artfully presented little plates of marinated shrimp and glanced up at me with anguish on his face. "I so appreciate your willingness to meet with me. I know you aren't a fan of Homeland Security, and these days I can certainly understand why."

"These are difficult times, and I don't envy the position you're in," I said, taking a bite of shrimp. "This is delicious. Let's peruse the menu, and you can tell me what's on your mind."

I watched Tim's shoulders relax and decided to order wine. It might help flush out the intense electronic beeping in my ears. Were Greens in a flap about my meeting?

We'd barely had two bites of our entrée when Tim put down his fork and leaned across the table, speaking in a low tone.

"I want to be a whistleblower, but I'm barely thirty, and it would destroy my career. You know how they're treating anyone who raises any issue whatsoever about this administration, which is totally out of control." Tim threw up his hands, his shoulders hunching. "It's been bad for a while now, but this is the last straw for me. I took an oath to defend against all enemies foreign and domestic, and, like you, I no longer think the enemy is who they're claiming it is."

Whoa.

"It's not just my area, which you probably know is cybersecurity and infrastructure security. The problem is rampant throughout other parts of Homeland, which includes Citizenship and Immigration Services. And both our secretary and deputy secretary are merely *acting*" —he made air quotes with his hands— "which means there's no congressional oversight of these people."

"I hear you," I said, also putting down my fork. "So what's going down?"

"It used to be just about Red Orbiters, but now the president and his cronies are gunning for everyone remotely associated with the OW Coalition or anyone they deem an alien sympathizer, such as yourself. They're trampling on the Fourth Amendment every chance they get and using intelligence agencies and even the judiciary branch to do so. It's not right." He shook his head.

"No, it isn't. Are you out on a limb on your own? Where's Bart stand on all this?"

"Bart means well, or at least he did at one time. Now I'm afraid he drank the Kool-Aid. It's impossible to know who to trust, with everyone worried about their jobs and families. But I feel like I've got to do something, so here I am talking to you."

And Tim wasn't the only one talking to me, because a voice inserted itself in my ear. "Beautiful, I don't want to spook Homeland in there, or interrupt. Just know I'm outside the restaurant if you need me."

Tim was looking right into my eyes, and he looked alarmed. "Someone's speaking to you, aren't they?"

"Yes, but only to let me know help is nearby if needed. Please don't worry."

"Are the Wilde brothers back?"

"Not yet, but they will be soon. There are forces at work to combat these civil rights violations." I leaned towards him, patting his hand.

"I know, so now I have to ask you not to be alarmed." He placed his hand over mine. "I know you were going to approach Bart and me about this iridescent insect caper going on."

I sat, perfectly still, uncertain what to reveal. What would Win do? What would Luna Moth Woman say? I stayed silent and let Tim continue.

"There's a good reason I went into this line of work. I sometimes hear things too. I had my DNA tested, and my best guess is I hear other human hybrids with similar DNA, predominantly Mercury, Jupiter, and Neptune, although I don't know how I do it." Tim leaned towards me, his eyes intense. "I'm 84 percent alien and expected to trample on privacy rights of other OWs in my freaking job. I randomly heard your friend George, for whom I have the utmost respect, talking about the new Red Orbiter spacecraft and what you're using it for."

Rose came with a menu she handed Tim. "This is signed by me for your mother, and I hope you will bring her here as my guest."

Tim sat with the menu in his hands, cheeks ruddy and beaming like a kid despite being in a state of agitation.

Roger said in my ear, "Ask him if he'll meet with us."

"Did you tell anyone at work about our plans? Does Bart know?" I asked Tim.

"Hell no. I'm hoping you're successful." He looked up, smiling.

Chapter 43

"Don't quit your job," Roger told Tim. We were seated in Roger's suite, and I was having more of that yummy pistachio-cherry liqueur. "At least not yet."

"Okay, but it's a fine line to walk if I'm not going to blow the whistle on my bosses."

"Let us work that angle. In the meantime, let Rowan meet with you and Bart like she'd planned. Let her tell you all about these potentially dangerous bug creatures and what they might be up to. And then let Bart run with it."

"If you can hold out to the election, maybe you won't have to quit," I said. "Homeland needs guys like you who have a clue to help our nation adapt to the reality of aliens."

"I'm glad to see you haven't totally lost your faith in us government types." Tim smiled.

"You have your uses," I teased. "I'll reach out to you Monday, and we'll go from there."

"Before you go," said Roger, "would you like to see the latest UFO to terrorize the skies?"

"Sure," said Tim, grinning. "Can I see your antennae and wings too?"

While we were out on the Red Orbiter flight deck, my burner phone buzzed in my purse.

"It's Win calling," I said to Roger. "Is he going to be mad because I haven't had a chance to fill him in?"

"No, Oz talked to him. Because I talked to Oz."

"And O.W. talked to you? You guys are worse than Morse code," I said before answering my phone. "Luna Moth Woman here, coming to you from greater Planet Wynne."

"Oz said you had a slight change of plans. All good for next week?"

"Roger that!" I said.

"You did good, kid," said Win.

"Thanks. Don't be sleepless in Seattle!" I might have had a tad too much liqueur.

I got off the phone to hear Tim ask Roger, "Is Oz the astronaut? I *knew* he was a Red Orbiter!"

We returned to Roger's suite, Tim departed, and I realized I still had to drive home.

"Young lady, you have some explaining to do," said Roger towered over me, scowling. "It's not that you met with Homeland without anyone else knowing. I don't want you driving alone."

"But my car's in valet parking. It's fine." I hunched my shoulders.

"I know that. This time. But what about the next opportunity for you to go running off without notice?"

"Once again you make me feel like you're twice my age, or I'm half mine." I moved away from those penetrating eyes. "I'm tired. I feel bad for Tim."

"He's smart, he can take care of himself. And we've got his back."

"I know, but I think he's lonely here in Vegas. Do you have female friends you can introduce him to?"

"Let me think on that. We need to get you home. I'd make you stay here, but I know you won't leave your critters all night. Plus you said you were tired, so you're no good to me."

"Bite me," I said. "And no, that's not an invitation."

We were back outside getting into the Ferrari when Roger's phone went off and I got the strangest feeling in my head, and not because his ringtone was the iconic five-tone audio sequence from *Close Encounters of the Third Kind.*

Roger spoke with the intensity of a drill sergeant. "How many? When? How soon?"

It felt as if fluffy clouds drifted into my mind, about to burst open with rain.

Roger said, "Change of plans. Is your house key in your purse? Come with me."

I was taken aback by his tone but didn't argue because in my head I heard, very faintly, but with urgency, "Danger! Rowan! Home!" in a robotic yet oddly soft voice.

Roger was back on his phone, steering me by my arm to a pistachio craft, and its door was opening as if on a hinge, the lid rising for a ribbonlike ramp to emerge. Or maybe more like a tongue, as it was dark pink. Magenta, my favorite Crayola color.

We hopped onto the tongue, slipped inside, and the cover of the newest Red Orbiter craft closed on us in some kind of anteroom. I followed Roger around to a wall with huge glittery wings. He grabbed them along with a shimmery-shaded flight suit that perfectly matched the spacecraft's iridescent exterior.

And if I didn't feel woozy before, I did now. With his back to me, Roger stripped down to a pair of black briefs, and I thought I might need to sit down. Or pee.

He attached the wings to the back of the flight suit and slipped into it. I could still see the rippling muscle of his arms and back under the fabric.

"Where's your bug mask with antennae?" I asked.

He turned to me. "In the control room. Come this way and I'll explain."

We entered an area similar to Rauc's orb, but larger, with more controls and lots of lights, buttons, and screens with more flashing lights. I held my arms to my sides to make sure I didn't accidently touch anything.

"Pilot's on the way," said Roger, turning to me. And he did indeed look like a giant fairy, albeit a very brawny, masculine one.

I giggled.

"How come you're giggling and not asking questions?"

"You were being kind of bossy-scary, so I figured it best not to." I smirked.

"I'll keep that in mind." He sort of smiled as he handed me two long squishy tubes.

"See the lines in my wings? There's a hole at the top. Slip these tubes into each wing for me." He had to bend way down so I could reach the insertion holes.

"You're going to get to see a bug encounter close up, which I'm not thrilled about because I don't want you in anyone's line of fire. I need you to follow my instructions without question. Are we clear?" Roger's formidable eyes bore into mine.

Yes," I said, stopping myself from adding "sir."

He placed his hands on my shoulders. "Three men are headed to your house from Pahrump. One of them is the guy from the writers group. The White House may not have believed his abduction tale, but his buddies did. And he told them all about you and how your book bashes the president."

Chapter 44

The rush of fear I felt for Bodie and Morris made my knees crumple, but Roger lifted me in his arms.

"It's okay, beautiful. There's a protective magnetic force around your house. They cannot come within several feet of it, and we'll intercept them long before they get anywhere near your street. We've got this."

My throat was so constricted, all I could do was nod as he put me back on my feet but continued to hold me by my waist.

"Listen to me, Rowan. They did not plan to hurt you or your pets. Their aim was to spray-paint your house with a big red *A*, their idea of calling you an alien lover. They did the same to Senator Rojas-Ortiz's place, which now has a protective shield even when she's not there."

"How do you know they wouldn't hurt me or Bodie and Morris if they could?" My lips quivered.

"They're cowards. They won't confront you directly. But when they see me in this getup coming out of a UFO, they'll react and are likely armed because these dudes live for their guns."

I wanted to believe him, but I could think only of my critters.

"This is why you have to stay put. You can watch from in here, but you cannot come outside with me."

"Okay, but can we please go now?"

"I'm here. Let's do this," said a tall redheaded woman striding into the control room.

"Rowan, this is our pilot, Maggie. You'll be happy to know she's a former Marine with combat experience, so we've got backup if needed."

I stared at Maggie as she took control of the spaceship, deciding she was the perfect physical embodiment of my literary Luna Moth Woman, ponytail and all. The masculine planes of her face only served to make her more attractive.

"As Roger said, Rowan, we've got this. You can come sit here by me if you like."

I sat in what I presumed was a copilot's chair and watched Maggie do her thing. A marvel of efficiency and calm, her hands were a blur of activity, and I noticed she wore no wedding ring. Did Red Orbiters have wedding bands?

The pistachio craft was moving, and I steeled myself to feel queasy, but didn't.

I looked at Roger, standing there like a ship's captain on deck in a bracing wind.

I giggled at his sparkly wings, but when he put on the grotesque bug mask, I stopped. Nothing Tinkerbell about that face.

Maggie said, "Rowan, you can watch this screen to see where we're headed."

It looked like we were now directly above Route 95 at the spot where it reduced to two lanes as it passed Mercury, mere miles from the turnoff to Pahrump. Beyond, as I well knew, was the Area 51 Alien Travel Center where Rauc and Rowdy had once dive-bombed Tim Rider's rental car with their orb as he followed me.

Here in Amargosa Valley, there were few travelers at this hour that weren't large commercial trucks.

"I've got the mark in sight," said Maggie, "let's put this baby down."

I could feel us descend with a whoosh.

On screen, it looked like we were headed for collision with a pickup truck, but it swerved off the road, bouncing erratically onto open desert.

We followed, dive-bombing and cutting the pickup off every which way it tried to go until it stopped, headlights shining a path through sagebrush and cacti where we were landing.

Roger nodded to us and headed back to the anteroom, and I kept my eyes glued to the screen.

"I've engaged the audio so you can hear what's going down. First you're going to hear four loud pops as I deflate their tires," said Maggie.

The sound and jolt apparently startled the truck's occupants, who spilled out with what looked like semiautomatic weapons.

I gasped.

"He's protected, Rowan, do you want me to mute sound?" asked Maggie.

"No, it's okay. I just need to remember to breathe." I hugged myself.

We watched Roger disembark, gliding to the ground and charging at the men standing by their truck so swiftly I jumped—as did the men. They also screamed in terror and opened fire.

Roger's wings curled forward, their tips now pointed at the panicking men, a rainbowlike mist spraying straight into their faces, which jerked back at the impact. They dropped their guns and rubbed their eyes, trying to see through the thick fog of bug spray.

I heard them gagging and wailing, vulnerable and afraid. And then they began babbling like Porky Pig.

"I should've just gone to the Hungry Beaver. I heard there was a really hot nasty alien there, because now I ain't got no more bullets, and is that bug taking the spray paint?"

"What happened to my tires, dude? And why's that ugly bug not dead? It should be dead because we shot it, and now we can't go spray that nasty alien lover's house."

"That is one giant mother-fucking bug. Not like those mean little… Whoa! Why's it in such a hurry? Is it gonna grab me and take me off in that shiny thing? Please not again…"

Bug Roger moved in a blur around their pickup and was back inside with us before I could tell what happened.

Maggie blasted the area with light as we ascended, and I saw the pickup clearly on the screen, its entire side covered in words spray-painted in red.

"DON'T BE STUPID!"

I heard, "What's your emergency?" but couldn't discern why.

Roger removed his bug mask and answered, "I'm headed north on 95 just past the Pahrump turnoff, and a pickup driving crazy went off the road and probably needs help."

He disconnected the call with 911.

Maggie said, "Sending footage to media now."

Chapter 45

Really strange dreams left me twisted in my sheets. Too many people talking in my head as I tried to sell them fluorescent fruit. Was it mangoes?

Last night pilot extraordinaire Maggie made clouds form above my house to disguise the pistachio craft while Roger deposited me on my doorstep, kissing the top of my head before buzzing off to be a bug menace throughout the night.

Not enough coffee existed in the universe to clear my head this morning, but headlines came close to startling me from my stupor.

"PRES SAYS INSECT WAR GIVES HIM WARTIME POWERS"

"CAN WAR POWERS BE INVOKED FOR ALIEN BUG ATTACKS?"

"ALIEN MESSAGE REAPPEARS NEAR LAS VEGAS: DON'T BE STUPID"

And one with echoes of dinner with Tim:

"PRESIDENT URGING INTEL AGENCIES TO TRACK OW ACTIVITY"

I checked social media to find Alamogordo61 had weighed in: "Is the president attempting to use NSA to create a virtual reality wherein he is not a scrofulous, bloviating dirtbag?"

Tell us how you really feel, Win. And kudos for using a word I had to look up that sounded like what it was. *Scrofulous* meant "morally contaminated and corrupt."

A domineering voice in my ear said, "Turn on the local news."

"Good morning to you, too, Roger Bugjet Juicer! Aye, aye, sir!" I snarked because he rattled me and sounded as bossy as he had last night. But I did reach for the clicker.

"Hmm...'sir.' I like the sound of that," said Roger, curling my toes.

"You would," I said as local morning news blared on the screen, footage of last night's bug escapade. Roger looked like a rainbow-hued terminator.

"Drunken vigilantes opened fire on an unknown alien species last night. Police say the three men from Pahrump were arrested and booked on charges including DUI, driving recklessly, illegal possession of firearms, and intent to destroy property. All three admitted their intended destination was a North Las Vegas home of a woman they claimed loves aliens and doesn't support the president. It is not known if they will be charged with attempted murder of the unidentified alien, who apparently left the scene by air after being fired upon."

"Way to control the narrative," I said. "At least they didn't say my name. But they should add destruction of desert flora to the charges."

"They're damned lucky they didn't say your name."

"Why aren't you sleeping?" I grumped. "You don't need to bring my car back today. I'm not going anywhere until next week."

"Affirmative. At least not without an escort," said Roger.

"You're sounding all ominous and dominant again. Maybe you should take a nap."

"What bug crawled up your butt this morning? Because I know it wasn't me."

"Take your pick! I didn't sleep well. I'm sick of not understanding voices in my head, or not knowing how to keep them from startling me silly. And I'm probably hungry."

"You left something off that list. Something you definitely need, but I'm too busy to give to you."

I scrambled for a feisty retort and realized Roger wasn't in my ear anymore. I didn't know how I knew, I could simply feel he was no longer engaging.

Maybe I should take a nap. But no way was I going to say it out loud.

Hours later I awoke to the buzz of the burner phone.

"Is there something you'd like to discuss?" said Win when I answered.

"I have to warn you, I'm not sure what day it is." I struggled to sit up as I was sandwiched between Morris and Bodie.

"Doomsday, as usual, if this blasted convention is anything to go by."

"How's that going? I refuse to watch, so you'll have to fill me in."

"You go first," said Win.

"Well, I can unequivocally state that those bug wings do have a fairy sparkle. And also that brainless blowhards with guns exist pretty much everywhere. Oh, and I like what Alamogordo61 had to say about the bloviating bully of a president."

"The buzz phrase bandied about every hour here is how Omni Party members are aliens and should not be able to vote—or hold office. The vice president said in his speech last night that anyone with alien DNA is an afront to God and against natural law. The current and former secretaries of defense are ready to self-destruct over it. Both have DNA off the OW charts."

"Sounds like an issue for the Supreme Court if we could trust the chief justice," I snarked. "But cry me a river! The former sec def is also a former Marine who should've known better than to participate in this travesty of an administration."

"Actually he's a former Royal Marine. From Scotland. And speaking of participation, I'm not feeling warm and fuzzy about your attendance at that writers group. But I know if I tell you not to go, it'll backfire on me."

"I'm not all that gung ho about it either," I sighed. "But if I don't go, I'll feel like a failure. There's a Saturday-morning meeting option. The bigot supposedly doesn't attend that one, and I don't like being around his energy. It makes me more defensive than I already am."

"I guess it wouldn't hurt to keep the cretins hopping. Why don't you tweet about an intention to change meetings, and Roger and I'll keep an ear out? We need to accompany you, though—I agree with him on that. I'll be home tomorrow night and can drive you where you need to go, including your meeting with Homeland."

"But you know I have to appear to be totally unaccompanied going into that meet. Plus, Tim will look out for me."

"Really not willing to negotiate on this one, sweet pea. And I've got to run."

Was Win still in payback mode from those times I hung up on him?

I dragged my butt out of bed because I had to let Bodie out.

Walking down the hall, I jumped at another authoritarian edict issued into my ear. "Open the garage."

"Are you mad at me? Punishing me for some unknown transgression?" I sniped, reversing course in my hallway.

Roger drove into my garage, and his red Ferrari pulled behind him in the driveway, Maggie at the wheel. He unfolded his body from my SUV and handed me the keys.

"We have a meeting at headquarters, so we're dropping it off on the way."

I waved to Maggie. "I was going to suggest we introduce her to Tim Rider, but I didn't realize you two might be an item."

"That would be highly inappropriate," said Roger. "She's my sister."

Chapter 46

I hankered for Chesapeake Bay blue crab (not alien), since it was the season, but being in the Nevada desert, I settled for steamed shrimp (alien) with Old Bay Seasoning that really did come from Baltimore and not another planet.

Win was coming to dinner, having returned last night, so we could prep for both my meeting with Tim and Bart and my next attempt at a writers meeting.

As I tossed coleslaw mix with poppy seed dressing, the sound of Morris crunching startled me as much as voices in my ear. Had he caught a mouse?

No, he was eating Bodie's food. It sounded like cracking walnuts. He'd already puked his breakfast all over the kitchen counter this morning. Was it a hairball issue, or was he picking up an agitated vibe from me? Because I admit to having trouble juggling various facets of my life right now, namely men. Plus my attitude was not improved by the first headline I'd seen upon waking: "PARTY OF LINCOLN CLAIMS OW AMERICANS ARE INFERIOR RACE"

Bodie responded to Morris pilfering his dinner by making his latest high-pitched squeaking noise. Kind of like a spurt of steam from a teapot, or the squeal of car brakes, but softer.

This bizarre emittance was yet another verification that dogs were from another world, that being Sirius. Was Bodie communicating with other canines or with the cat when he made that sound? Because that was a great deal of what his barking was about, for sure. And why did he cower away from some yapping dogs in yards when we walked, yet others he practically yanked the leash from my hand to lunge at them? Was this a breed thing? A gender issue?

Speaking of gender issues, a text came in today from Mom, about Dad: "Your father asked if I'd responded to you about coming for Christmas. He couldn't remember if he responded, and I thought I did. He may have ears that can hear things like you do, but he can't remember to bring me my second cup of coffee. (two hearts, hatted birthday face, lips, mushroom, sunflower, pink flower, red tulip, quarter moon, three-quarter moon, full moon, quarter moon, full moon, three-quarter moon, full moon, shooting star emoji)"

Mom had outdone herself on number and repetition of emoji, their sheer randomness, and an utter wackadoodle lack of applicability to her text—which was uncannily about memory issues. And neither she nor Dad had responded to my Christmas inquiry.

I called my sister.

"I think Mom's losing it. She doesn't seem like herself. I wish I'd asked Rauc if Red Orbiters have knowledge on prevention of memory loss. Although I think for humans it's more about selective memory. Like conveniently failing to recognize who was in America before we Pilgrims arrived. And whose side Lincoln was on in the Civil War. And not just memory issues. There's also the pervasive, persistent problem of certain folks not accepting inconvenient facts not fitting into ill-conceived idiotic notions of identity. Like alien DNA."

"You're making my brain hurt," said G. "What's really bugging you?"

"Is that supposed to be a bug pun?"

"Are you worried about Rauc returning? Maybe it's you who's afraid of memory issues, trying to deal with three different men, two of them alien, two of them spies. I'd for sure have trouble keeping track of what I said to whom, and what they said to me."

"Well, this isn't helping."

"I'm sorry, I wish I were more help. But *your mother* has decided she needs to go the Democratic convention to, and I quote, 'Make sure they stick it to the jackasses and don't foul this up.' She expects me to arrange a plane ticket for her, claiming she can stay with old friends in Virginia, all of whom are pushing ninety and having memory issues themselves, none of whom drive anymore. Plus, the convention isn't in Virginia."

"I guess I should be glad she's not gunning to go to the Omni convention too."

"Yes, and if you dare stick that bug in her ear, Phil says we will send her to you on a one-way ticket, and I'll change not only my name but also my phone number. It's bad enough I have to deal with the logistics of getting us all there for Christmas."

I was going to ask my sister if she was changing her name to Scrooge, but didn't want her to refuse to ever speak to me again.

Once off the phone with G, I checked breaking news of the day.

"FORMER DEFENSE SECRETARY CONVERTS TO OMNI PARTY"

"DEFENSE SECRETARY, USMC COMMANDANT, SWITCH LOYALTIES"

"PRES FIRES DEFENSE SECRETARY, HEAD OF MARINE CORPS"

And another text from Mom: "That jackass president is a disgrace to our nation!!! Wake up world!!! Your father is very upset with news today too. Weather cloudy here. Ugh. How is your weather??? Hug my grandanimals for me!!! (donkey, frowny face, flipped bird, cloud, dog, cat, kissy face emoji)"

And unfortunately one more: "I'm worried about this Omni Party taking votes away from Democrats!!! We can't afford to lose votes and let those tacky jackasses steal the election again!!! (donkey, frowny face, flipped bird, flag, heart emoji)"

At least Mom was back to normal. Or her version of it. But I might be in deep doo-doo.

***

Win and I peeled every last shrimp and were finishing a bottle of Oregon rosé he'd brought, made from pinot noir grapes, my favorite.

"I was kind of wondering why you didn't tell me you'd be meeting with Senator Rojas-Ortiz on your trip."

"For the same reason you didn't tell me you were meeting with Homeland Security—it was a last-minute thing. She invited me to hear her announcement, and to keep her apprised of ongoing plans."

"She's just so beautiful and brilliant." I moped.

"Yes, she is. As are you. I have great taste in women. But I'm the one who should be worried here. You secretly snuck off to dinner with a much younger man who's not hard on the eyes and has a history of dating older women."

"You have a file on Tim Rider too?"

"I have a file on everybody, sweet pea. And so does your Red Orbiter pal Roger. If you don't think he knows everything from what you eat for breakfast to your most intimate bedtime fantasies, you need to wise up."

Chapter 47

After our altercation last night, Win and I didn't end up between my sheets, so no bedtime fantasy for me. Good thing shrimp weren't considered an aphrodisiac like oysters, or I'd have been left high and dry.

As it was, I didn't know what to feel. Alienated? Rejected for having one alien lover and lusting after another?

Actually, it was I who rejected Win over being told to wise up. I wasn't some twentysomething, wide-eyed college student manipulated by a sexually seasoned sugar daddy.

Which is why I also deliberately told Win a false time for my meeting with Tim and Bart today, scheduled for three, not five o'clock. Maybe he'd better wise up and not think he could control my every move.

I picked the Galaxy Grog bar in Planet Wynne because it was familiar and I could use valet parking. Roger wasn't a problem because he thought my meeting was at the Las Vegas Homeland Security office and that Win was driving me. Plus, I'd done a little sleuthing myself and learned Roger should be sleeping at that hour of the afternoon in preparation for another night of alien bug marauding. O.W.'s gossip tendencies proved useful.

And yes, it rankled what Win said about Roger knowing my innermost secrets, so I was steamed at the young Red Orbiter for potentially knowing way too much about me.

I was also seriously considering going to tonight's writers meeting instead of waiting until Saturday morning. You bet I was wising up. I was in command of my own life. Luna Moth Woman takes charge!

Now as long as I didn't take the wrong exit from I-15 to get to Planet Wynne, I'd be cooking with gas. Kicking butt and taking names.

We were seated at a table in the vicinity of the main bar. Bart Reynolds ordered a lite beer, and Tim stuck with club soda. I went all in with a "Space Spritzer" made with that liqueur Roger served me in his suite, which came with spherical ice and a lime slice.

"Before we get started, Mrs. Layne, ma'am," said Bart. "I know you don't like to be called ma'am, but that's how we do things around here, and that's how I roll."

"Around here? We're in a bar, Bart, and Mrs. Layne is my mother. I'm not married. Because that's how I roll."

There was an emboldened edge to Bart I had not previously observed.

"Okay," intervened Tim. "Let's focus on what we're here for. Ms. Layne, would you explain to my partner what you told me over the phone?"

"As I said, Mr. Rider, what I'm hearing sounds like it's payback time. There are aliens out there who are pretty ticked off at being disrespected by this administration." I turned to face Bart. "But I don't have formal names. They don't sound the type to go by mister or missus."

Bart's pronounced Adam's apple bulged spastically, something I did remember well.

"Lowlifes," he scoffed. "Sounds like the president needs to teach them a lesson. Lower the hammer on these invading aliens."

"I don't get the impression these entities think the president or anyone at Homeland has jurisdiction over what they do," I said, sipping my cocktail, which was refreshing. "And I believe the expression is 'lower the boom.'"

"If they're on our soil, we've got jurisdiction." Bart puffed.

"Negative on that too," I countered. "They definitely don't recognize this as our land. I heard them saying they've been here long before the likes of any of us."

"Are these slimeballs waging war on us? Thinking they can charge in here and take over? Because we will fight back!" Bart slammed his fist on the table, sloshing my drink.

I glared at him. "I'm not sure that's your bailiwick, Bart, but I'd say they're showing some pretty ominous signs of aggression from what I'm hearing. We've drawn first blood is the way they see it."

"Were you able to discern anything tangible about their plans?" asked Tim.

"No specific details, Mr. Rider. Just phrases like 'avenging those who've been denigrated.'"

"They sure do use big words and fancy concepts for bug creatures." Bart sneered. "If that's what we're talking about here."

I shrugged and took another sip of my drink. "Couldn't say for sure. I don't see them when they speak. But they clearly don't see us as a worthy adversary. More like an annoying gnat to crush." I stared at Bart.

As I spoke, I noticed a group of guys at the bar. There was something about them, like all that was missing were HUMANS FIRST! ballcaps. They seemed all fired up. And one of them looked over at me with a sneer.

"Why are you telling us this?" asked Bart, jutting his weak chin. "You chose an alien bar to meet in and are known to pal around with Red Orbiters. And they sure like to hang out here." He leaned toward me. "Do you think some of those aliens you're hearing could be here?"

"It's possible. But is this bar really an alien hangout? Seems like an awful lot of tourists in here right now," I said, looking directly at Tim while tilting my head toward the bar.

Tim caught on and looked that way, but the guys were paying their tab just as Tim was taking care of ours. The men soon left Galaxy Grog.

Bart said, all smarmy, "We'll be in touch when we require more information."

I stood and leaned down to him. "I came to you. You will not contact me, and you won't hear from me again if I have to deal with this belligerent, bigoted attitude you're copping. I'm very disappointed in you, Bart."

Bart's Adam's apple did a tango.

I turned to Tim. "Mr. Rider, thank you for your time and your professional demeanor."

I exited hearing Tim say, "What the hell was that Bart? The lady contacted us offering to provide information, and you treat her like she's some sort of suspect. You ought to apologize, but she'd likely spit in your eye. And I wouldn't blame her."

Bart whined, "Why was she calling you Mr. Rider but never once called me Mr. Reynolds?"

Chapter 48

I walked out the main entrance and handed my ticket to a valet while watching for the tourists from the bar. I didn't seem them lurking anywhere.

The sound of squealing tires assaulted my ears as a large brown pickup truck careened into the circular driveway, window rolled down with a guy leaning out from the passenger side.

In his hands was a gallon can of paint, some of its red contents spilling to the ground as he wrestled with control in the fast-moving vehicle.

"Nasty alien-lover bitch!" he yelled.

I stepped back as he clearly intended to splash me with paint. At the same time, a blur of movement and a whoosh of air separated me from my attackers.

One minute I was standing on the sidewalk; the next I was launched in the air held by Roger, who was quite possibly naked. I knew this because I was eye-to-skin with his formidable chest, in the middle of which was a Superman tattoo—the iconic yellow shield encompassing a red *S*. Unmistakable.

Screaming on the ground rose up to pummel my ears.

"Mother fucker, I've got paint in my eyes!" yelled a voice, receding as tires squealed with the rapid departure of the pickup.

"Your eyes? What about my truck? It's covered in paint, you asshole!"

Roger and I did not have one speck of red paint on us as he landed with me on the second level of Planet Wynne. We moved in a blur through double doors toward his suite.

It turned out Roger wasn't naked, though he was wearing nothing but clinging red boxer briefs. They perfectly matched the *S* in the Superman logo.

As he lowered me to the floor in his living room, I touched that *S* murmuring, "Nobody's Superman."

"You sure about that?" said Roger.

"Oh, please," I said, trying to get my bearings and not gape at his muscles rippling as he raked a hand through spiky blond hair.

"It wasn't all that long ago most people didn't think aliens were real. But everyone loves Superman, who happens to be a comic book alien," he said.

"How is it we don't have paint on us?" I asked, trying to catch my breath but not taking my eyes from that tattoo.

"A repelling force. It protected us and reversed course on the paint. Couldn't have you splashed in this sexy, slinky red dress of yours. One hot mama."

"I wore red for battle, and I think I need to sit down." I stumbled to Roger's couch.

"Good idea. Sit while you still can," he said, his tone ever so soft but menacing.

"What's that supposed to mean? I've been intending to address this older woman fixation you have. Is it some sort of mommy fetish?"

"Quite the opposite," he said. "In fact—"

"Don't you dare say 'Who's your daddy?'!"

"You're overly fixated on age, and you have a very bad habit of interrupting, not to mention telling whopping fibs that get you into trouble, don't they?"

"Or maybe I have an excellent habit of not suffering fools," I sniped, wishing Roger would put on some clothes, or stop standing there backlit by the sun pouring in from the windows looking like he was some sort of god.

"The thing is, beautiful"—he strode toward me, taking his sweet time—"age doesn't matter when it comes to most things."

I had a clever retort formulating, but it flew right out of my head when Roger crouched down in front of me.

"For instance," he drawled, green eyes boring into mine, "you being older than me doesn't prevent me from feeling an intense desire to turn you over my knee and make you think twice about lying to me."

"So now you're threatening me?"

"You know better."

"You sound like a sexist throwback from the fifties." I huffed.

"You sound flustered."

"Can we talk about this Superman tattoo?" I looked away from him.

"Why? Do you want to touch it again?"

"You're exasperating!"

"As are you, beautiful. The only reason I'm not tanning your hide right this very minute is I know you'd enjoy it too much."

The burner phone buzzed in my purse, and I thought I might scream from frustration.

"Answer it," ordered Roger. "And then you need to run along so I can get back to my nap."

I answered the phone.

"I'm at your house," said Win, not waiting for me to speak. "I'm with your critters, and you're not here. Imagine that. I just got a call from Oz, who got a call from O.W. And just so we're clear, if you're thinking you might trot off to that writers meeting tonight, go right ahead."

I held my breath watching Roger watch me on the phone with Win. I knew he could hear him.

"You go to that meeting, and I guaran-damn-tee you I will be outside waiting for you," continued Win. "And I will blister your ass, right there in the parking lot, and I won't care who is watching—or listening." Win disconnected the call. Hanging up on me this time.

"Why do all of you suddenly sound like John Wayne?" I asked, feeling small.

"We have a meeting tomorrow at headquarters. I'll pick you up at nine, and you'd better be there, little lady," smirked Roger. "And just so you know, if Win wants his pound of flesh for lying to him, I won't be guarding your body."

Chapter 49

This could be the most awkward I'd ever felt, sitting in Red Orbiter headquarters with Oz, Win, and Roger. If Raucous Wilde suddenly showed up, I might as well throw in the towel.

And I didn't know why it was so taboo for Rauc to bring me here before. It looked like a big flight deck between mountains, albeit on natural terrain, except there was also a vast space not unlike a conference center built into the side of a mountainous bolder.

That's where we were now, and I had to admit to being preoccupied by seething males in my presence. Roger said not one word on the drive out other than to tell me if I spoke, it would be at my peril.

"I paid a visit to the solar warden in Dahlgren to make sure the newest Red Orbiter spacecraft was showing up on their radar," said Win.

"What's a solar warden?" I asked. We were seated around a big conference table.

Roger pinned me with hazel eyes, and I told myself I wasn't miffed they weren't bright green. "Had you been *listening attentively*, you'd know Win just finished telling us it's a Navy program in Virginia that monitors traffic in the solar system, supposedly to protect Earth from 'hostile aliens.'" He smirked.

That sanctimonious look of his had me recalling the last time he looked like that. Yesterday, right before I left his suite.

"Is that some crack about my fourth-grade report card? And how do you even know about that?" I got snippy.

"I know many things," he said, his words so loaded with import, I itched to respond.

Instead, I let the men drone on while I plotted a scene for Luna Moth Woman to save the day instead of mean, glowering, know-it-all bugs. Until I heard my name again.

"You may not have caught this, Rowan, because it happened after your meet with Homeland yesterday and the unfortunate incident that followed," said diplomatic Oz.

"Caught what?" I was thinking I for sure caught hell yesterday.

"At the Democratic convention. Something unprecedented happened that will escalate the current situation into the stratosphere."

Win said, "Had you not been so busy being a femme fatale fool going off on your own, you might have seen headlines. Why don't you take a look now and stop wasting our time?"

I glared at Win, but curiosity won out, and I dug for my phone, pulling up news:

"DEM CANDIDATE PICKS OMNI PARTY RUNNING MATE"

"DEMOCRATIC PARTY EMBRACES OTHERWORLDLY AMERICANS"

"IS A DEM PRESIDENT WITH OMNI VP IN OUR FUTURE?"

"Wow, a two-party ticket," I said. "Who was chosen? Not Senator Rojas-Ortiz? That would be quite a coup to have a woman president and vice president."

"No," said Win. "It's your congressman from North Las Vegas, Warren O'Neill."

"This development will tend to escalate things a bit, in terms of the president's temper tantrums and dangerous rhetoric. We need to ramp up our response because his pansy-assed worshippers are going to lose their collective minds. The presidential candidate's a woman, and her running mate is not only OW—he's also black," said Roger, turning to me. "So do you think you can come back from fantasy land and participate in this meeting?"

"Why don't you take your condescending tone, *both of you*"—I glared from Roger to Win—"and ramp it right up your collective asses?"

"Do we need to step outside?" said Roger, his tone patently paternalistic.

"Okay, I'm stepping in here," said Oz. "You two need to pipe down and leave Rowan alone. She's a valued member of this team, and you should treat her that way. You also need to value your balls, because she looks like she's more than willing to remove yours at the moment."

"Perhaps we should take a bathroom break," said Roger, eyes never leaving mine.

"As long as these two don't think they get to accompany me there as well," I said.

"Keep fantasizing," said Roger.

"Keep dreaming," I replied.

"All right that's it! No one's accompanying anyone!" roared Oz. "Girls will go to the girl potty and boys to the boy potty! Are we clear?"

Win burst out laughing, so I couldn't help but smile too. Until I looked at Roger again. He wasn't laughing, but he did have the most menacing smile.

Win handed me my favorite bottled peach tea as we returned from our break, I suppose a peace offering of sorts. It didn't last long.

"Our plan needs to take into account federally restricted airspace," said Win.

"Yeah, funny how that didn't help matters at the Pentagon on 9/11," I snarked.

Win shot me a *Not now with your crazed conspiracy theories* look, and I resisted sticking my tongue out at him.

"We'll need to create chaos and diversion," continued Win.

"A dramatic weather event?" said Roger.

"Well, it's the perfect time of year in the DC area for a booming-loud lightning storm, and you Red Orbiters could rock those thunderhead clouds," I said, beaming at Roger. He didn't smile back.

"On it," said Oz. "We've got the cumulous clouds covered, but it would be nice to have the whole shit show. Thunder, lightning, wind." He sighed. "Pain in my ass, but we need help from Greens. Win can you—"

"I'll do it!" I interjected.

"You'll do what?" said Win, voice like a whipcord.

"I'll work with Greens on the weather angle."

I didn't expect total and complete silence from my offer.

"What? No autocratic edict on how I'm not allowed to take initiative on my own?"

"I'll just wait for you to run off again. So I can save your ass. Again," said Roger.

"Okay, guys, you're clearly never going to get over this. How about I include you in whatever plans I arrange?" I said, ever-so-sweetly.

"And will that involve an accurate time for the meeting, or more deception?"

"Damn it, Win! I was peeved at you for telling me to wise up, okay? I've had it with domineering mansplaining. I'm not some girl for y'all to jerk hither and yon!"

"Hither and yon?" said Roger. "What was it Win told you to wise up about?"

"Here we go again," said Oz. "Rowan, dear, I appreciate you've built up a rapport with Greens, but can we table this until all of our flying teams arrive and are ready to roll?"

"But the Omni convention's in two weeks. Shouldn't I put out feelers now?"

"How do you plan to do that, exactly?" asked Win.

"I—I don't know. I could write a scene and present it at the next writers meeting."

"When's this meeting?" asked Roger, looking too smug for words.

"This Saturday morning." I huffed. "Hopefully while you're getting your beauty rest and not spying on me."

"Rowan hear me out," said Win. "It's risky for you to write about an alien species that screws with weather to mess with humans. Greens would object, don't you think?"

I sighed. "Then I guess it's up to you to somehow share our plan with them. You can interpret their language. Send them a message. Don't work so hard at shutting them out."

I was looking straight at Roger when I said it.

Chapter 50

Driving home was excruciating. Testosterone positively simmered from Roger.

"I appreciate you rescuing me from being doused in red paint."

"I don't want to hear it," he said.

I turned my face to the window, staring out at the open desert on the winding road before we reached I-15. "Why are you so angry?"

Roger jerked the Ferrari off the road, making dust fly up around us.

I stared at his eyes, watching them turn green and feeling mine fill with tears of relief.

He stared back, breathing slower. He unlatched his seat belt.

His lips were hard, but softened, like the grip on my jaw and in my hair.

Deep, devouring, drugging kissing. Not coming up for air, and not caring.

I wanted this man so badly. Like I was back in high school with hormones raging and angst radiating the deepest core of my being.

This made no sense. But felt so consumingly good.

Roger pulled away, raking a hand through his hair. "There's things you don't yet know. Things I'm not authorized to tell you about. But when the time comes and all is revealed, I don't want you to hold it against me."

"It's about how you age, isn't it?"

He stared at me so long, I felt my eyes sting again.

Roger reached out and stroked my face, wiping tears away, caressing me with those mercurial eyes.

"I want to drink you in and can't slake my thirst. I haven't felt this way in so long."

I reached out and touched that stunning profile, feeling his jaw clench and release.

"I want to fill you with my flesh, Rowan. And show you what it's like to fly."

He fastened his seat belt and drove back onto the road.

When we reached my house, he walked me to my door but didn't kiss me again.

"You make me feel young," I said and slipped inside to my critters.

I spent the afternoon unpacking boxes I'd procrastinated on and told myself I was glad my burner phone wasn't ringing and no voices were popping into my ears.

When my phone rang, I hoped it wasn't Mom or my sister. It wasn't.

"Hi, George. What's up? Everything okay there at OUTWARD?"

"Things are crazy busy here. I called because I'm worried about you, Rowan, and I want to know how you're holding up. I'm angry about what happened to you. This is not worth it if we're putting you in danger."

Hot tears sprang fast, and I struggled to hold back a flood.

"To tell you the truth"—my voice hitched—"I haven't had much of a chance to process it, what with the machismo element all ticked off at me."

"Men are hardheaded. No doubt about that. But I know they're worried too."

"I'm hanging in there. My sister comes next week to be on Rose Bergin's cooking show, so I think I'll lay low until then."

"You've been going gangbusters. You deserve to take a breather."

Next call was Tim Rider on his personal phone. "Rowan I just heard about what happened to you after our meeting, and I am so sorry."

"That's what I get for using valet parking! But I'm fine. No paint, no gain!"

"I want you to know Roger's working with me to find out who they were. I've got a friend working hate crimes at the bureau."

"Hate crimes? That's really what it was, wasn't it? I didn't used to think I'd qualify for that, but nowadays—"

"Nowadays the president incites hate crimes on a daily basis."

"True, but there are so many much worse off than me. And they were long before this alien revelation rocked our world."

"I know what you're getting at Rowan, but that doesn't mean we can't address what happened to you so they don't keep racking up victims and getting away with it."

"Thank you, Tim. I appreciate that."

"And I appreciate you. Which is why I'm calling. Roger asked if I'd be interested in meeting his sister. I know I have you to thank for that, so I suggested we make it a double date."

"No way am I going on a date with Bart," I joked.

Tim laughed. "I think Roger was afraid you might say the same about him. He said it was up to you, but I had to ask you."

"Did he say I was prickly?"

"Something like that. But cacti are very resilient, you know. And he and Maggie have Saturday night off, so what do you say? I think I'll be a lot less nervous if you're there. This woman is a total badass who used to be a Marine pilot. Did you know she was one of the two who flew the spaceship into Monterey Bay?"

Chapter 51

"Now that I know you were the pilot in Monterey, Maggie, I'm dying to ask. What went down with that awful White House punk?"

We were dining in Planet Wynne again for privacy purposes, this time at a restaurant with Italian fare called Oregano Wortnik. The herb hailed from the star in its name and happened to have the same initials as Octavius Wynne.

The man himself greeted us when we arrived, saying he hoped we enjoyed our meal at his fabulous bistro he likes to call O.W.

"Oh my gosh, what a worm," said Maggie of the flunky sent from the White House to represent our nation during the historic spaceship landing in Monterey Bay. Mom had not approved of his tacky pink turned-up collar, among other things.

"You're being too diplomatic," said Roger. "I thought I was going to have to kill the guy, but she didn't need my help." He smiled at me.

I was glad to see Roger smiling again.

"He kept asking if I was an alien," said Maggie, rolling her eyes. "Drooling at the thought of it, and over his fantasy that I must be packing heat, insisting we could fire up heat of our own."

"He was obsessed with you being an armed alien? Sounds like Bart," said Tim, who hadn't taken his eyes off Maggie since we sat down.

"Before our last meeting, I'd have said Bart had a long way to go to be as big an ass as that guy, but there's a pandemic among those exposed to this administration's attitude."

"My sister adjusted his attitude quite effectively," said Roger.

"What did you do?" I asked Maggie.

"After his numerous thwarted attempts to search me for weapons that might be hidden under my flight suit, I took the opportunity to return the favor. When he reached for my inner thigh to see if I had a strap-on tool, as he put it, I reciprocated."

"She had his balls in a vice grip until he apologized," said Roger.

Poor Tim spit wine, making me think of Mom.

Maggie turned to Tim. "That is not something I generally do with men who show a healthy interest in me."

"Glad to hear it," said Tim, taking a hearty swig of wine.

Roger laughed, and it was a happy sound.

Once I finished my eggplant parmesan (yes, alien, because dark-purple eggs only originate from another planet), I excused myself for the ladies room, and Maggie followed me.

"Were you assigned to escort me to the bathroom?" I asked, wishing I had her long legs and lean look.

"No, I have to go too. Is my brother being overbearing with you?"

"You have no idea."

"Oh, yes I do, but I've never seen him like this. He can't take his eyes off you, and he's grumpy a lot."

"Tim can't take his eyes off you either." I laughed. "But was Roger ever really little? And if what I've experienced is merely grumpy, I don't relish seeing him furious.'"

"Roger would never hurt a hair on your head, but those who try would have cause for concern. Though he has more self-control than anyone I know, certainly more than I do."

"You look like the epitome of composure to me. I want to be you when I grow up. But does it bother you Tim is younger?"

"Only by a few years." Maggie shrugged. "And in my male-dominated profession, I learned a long time ago that maturity level has nothing to do with age."

"So true," I said. "Tim is definitely the oldest thirty-year-old I've ever seen. He deserves to have some fun, and he's under a lot of pressure."

Maggie smiled. "Information received and noted. You'd have made a wonderful mom."

"Yikes! That's what I've been worried about when it comes to Roger's interest in me."

When Maggie laughed, she sounded exactly like her brother. "Let me tell you a story." She put her arm around me as we left the restroom. "When Roger was about sixteen, he was cocky and rebellious as hell, as you can imagine."

"And how is that different from now?"

"Right, good point," said Maggie. "Back then, our dad was gone a lot, as he's a pilot like me. Mom had her hands full parenting Roger. One night they were arguing because he wanted to go out and was challenging her authority."

"I'm shocked," I said.

"She finally moved to physically block him from leaving the house. My giant of a brother took our mother by the shoulders and lifted her off her feet, moving her out of his way, setting her down gently across the room while assuring her he'd be fine. Then he told her she should go to her room and calm down."

We reached our table, and I knew Roger had heard every word, smiling in a way that made my toes curl in the high-heeled wedge sandals I was lucky I didn't stumble in—I'd been foolhardy enough to wear them to compete with the sky-high stature of my dining companions.

Roger stood and pulled out my chair, and I ogled him in his well-fitting pants and silky t-shirt. Mom would applaud the all-black ensemble. He looked better than dessert. Problematic, because I was driving home alone with him.

He and Maggie had picked me up in an SUV because we wouldn't all fit in the Ferrari, but she was going off to spend some alone time with Tim.

Once on the road, Roger said, "We didn't want to talk shop at dinner, but Tim told me the pickup's license plate number provided by the valet proved illuminating."

"Please tell me it wasn't vigilantes from Yearntown that tried to dump paint on me."

"No, this is a fringe group of the Everlasting Evangelicals that calls themselves Armed Evangelicals, so they're also NRA knuckle-dragging, wannabe warriors."

"I like that phrasing. Can I use that in my book? And it sure sounds like Yearntown. But if they're such teetotaling Christians, what were they doing hanging out in a bar?"

"Their idea of covert intel. They think they're sniffing out subversive aliens who seduce good Christian nonalien women in bars."

"Instead they got me. With two guys from Homeland Security."

"They're not smart enough to recognize government agents who aren't tricked out like ICE enforcers. *Like* only comprehends *like*."

"Speaking of that, did you see the president is attempting yet another executive order to block all alien immigration he claims is coming across the border to steal jobs and guns?"

"All those Martians and little green men slipping in from Mexico are so terrifying, are they not?" Roger smirked as he pulled into my driveway. "But no aliens whatsoever coming from Canada. Funny how that works."

"And that Second Amendment right to spray aliens with bullets only applies to good, decent Christian folk."

"Yeah, those folks would never do this," Roger said, taking his hands off the wheel, reaching out to grip the back of my neck.

I tensed, prepared to spontaneously orgasm, but the kiss he bestowed pretty much had the same ecstasy-inducing effect.

Chapter 52

I woke Sunday morning thinking maybe I should go to Mass to atone for my sins, except I wasn't a practicing Catholic and hadn't been fornicating. In fact, I was as frustrated as a lovestruck teenager, rendering me less than gracious when I answered the burner phone.

"I didn't go to that writers meeting yesterday, so save your threats for someone who likes overbearing boorish men."

"It wasn't a threat, it was a warning of intended reaction to your possible course of action," said Win, sounding too damn chipper.

"I have not yet had coffee, so you might want to quit with the wordplay."

"That's not all you haven't had, if your mood's any indication. I admit to being delighted."

"Do you want me to hang up this phone? Because third time's a charm."

"I've been meaning to address how rude that behavior is. And my displeasure at it."

"What are you, James Bond? You sound so properly British this morning."

"Maybe that's because I'm in Great Britain. Edinburgh to be exact."

"I love that city." I sighed. "Is heather blooming in the Highlands yet?"

"I don't think so, but I did have salmon in my eggs for breakfast. Now I'm sipping Scotch and thinking of you."

"Are you drunk?"

"Not yet. You know the secretary of defense who resigned months ago after the president bashed the Marine Corps for originating on Mars?"

"Red MacLeod?"

"That'd be the one. Like I told you, he was a Royal Marine back in the day, originally from Scotland but also Mars. He's our newest member of the OW Coalition and Omni Party and is also one pissed-off member of the warrior class."

"Oh, aye, that I am," said what had to be Red in the background.

When people got confused about how we could have a "foreigner" in the cabinet, I remind them about that German guy who was secretary of state for Nixon, who supposedly was highly frustrated he couldn't run for president. You have to be born here for that, per the Constitution, but not for any other position. The Founding Fathers sought to ward off disloyal presidents who would seek to be king. Who'd have thought it could happen anyway?

Win said, "I'm meeting with him and some of our buddies in the business because it looks like Britain could be headed for its own Iridescent Insect War."

"Aye, but we need to change that name."

I giggled.

"Anyway, Red says hi. He's a fan of yours. And he looks forward to meeting you at the Omni convention. I'll be back next week if you might be looking forward to seeing me again, or even if you're not. Will you please stay safe until then, sweet pea?"

"Okay. Have a cider with black for me, and some scones and cream. I'm envious."

I got off the phone and called my sister. "New development."

"Not another one."

"I haven't actually met this one yet, but we both sort of know who he is."

"Lay it on me, sister."

"Redheaded Scotsman, my age, former Royal Marine, former US secretary of defense. Currently likely a spy, possibly for MI6 and us, and if he has a degree in physics from the University of Edinburgh like Dr. Bruce Robertson, I might have all boxes checked."

No laughter.

"Are you still there?"

"You're making this up." I could practically see G's brow furrowing, lips pouting.

"No, I'm not. It's Red MacLeod. He was recently in the news, calling the president a cockwomble for firing the secretary of defense who replaced him, as well as the commandant of the Marine Corps. And he just switched to the Omni Party. You might have seen that headline."

"Seriously?"

"Oh and, just to make it extra spicy, he's also best buddies with Win."

Chapter 53

"Have a crazy culinary time, sis. You'll make the best sous chef ever!" I told G when I dropped her off at the production room door for Rose Bergin's cooking show. Luckily, it was on the same level in Planet Wynne as the Galaxy Table restaurant, so all I had to do was trot down the escalator and cross the casino to the self-park garage.

Yes, I'd used self-parking after picking my sister up at the airport, but who could blame me for thinking it less risky?

Coming down the escalator, I rummaged in my purse for keys and looked up to see Raucous Wilde ascending in the opposite escalator. He didn't see me, but the attractive woman with him did. We had nearly identical long curly red hair, mine being the reason Rauc called me Copper.

I felt gut punched as I stared across at Rauc with a Red Orbiter Barbie who looked barely old enough to be legal, so I grabbed the escalator handrail to keep from tumbling on top of those riding down in front of me.

Feeling in desperate need of air, I made it to the bottom and headed for an exit onto the Strip. But not before my mouth took over my mind.

"Raucous Wilde, you could have at least sent me a message in a meal to let me know you returned! But I see now why you didn't!

Have a nice life with whomever she is!" I yelled at the entrance to Planet Wynne, tears stinging my face as I plunged outside to furnace-like heat, fleeing this bitter betrayal.

I dodged crowds of tourists who never looked where they were going and dashed onto an escalator leading to a skywalk that would take me to a casino that hopefully had no association with Red Orbiters.

Weaving my way around six various-sized strollers and numerous visitors taking selfies smack dab in the middle of the skywalk, I felt lightheaded from the heat and my hyperventilating heart. I stopped and made my way to the railing, looking down at more hordes of tourists and clogged traffic, horns honking. I turned, needing to be back indoors, away from this chaos.

That's when I saw them, or they saw me. The Armed Evangelicals of red paint infamy.

"Well, if it isn't the alien whore!" said one as the three of them lunged toward me.

"You owe me a new truck, alien bitch!" said another who pointed at me, his finger now a foot from my face.

Out of the side of my eye, a flash of rainbow glitter manifested as a tall—though not tall enough to be Roger—bug creature landed on the skywalk, wings curling to point in our direction.

"Whoa!" I yelled, causing the men to scatter when they saw the invading insect, their screams so painfully high-pitched I covered my ears.

They didn't move fast enough.

And I should have covered my face, because I was in the path of the bug juice spraying the three men.

Now it was a thick mist that took my breath away, and I willed myself not to panic as the bug stepped forward, swooped me up, and ascended into the air.

I twisted about to look up at the top of Planet Wynne and then looked down. "Wow, this is pretty cool." I sounded like Porky Pig. "What the hell!" I yelped at the sudden searing whack on my rear end.

"Stop squirming or I'll drop your ass," said Raucous Wilde. I'd know that delectable voice anywhere, even with a bug mask on.

He whacked me again.

I glowered at his grotesque bug face. "I don't know why I ever thought you were too nice for me."

Another whack, and I began babbling in an awful, goofy voice as we landed on the flying-saucer level of Planet Wynne. "I'm sorry I didn't wait for you, but apparently you didn't wait for me either! At least I haven't had sex with Roger Ramjet. Except for that one orgasm that really shouldn't count, and I don't understand why you didn't tell me about being able to do that because—Ahhh!"

Intense waves pulsed through me as he swiped the back of my neck.

I convulsed in Rauc's arms as we slipped into a sparkly craft parked on the flight deck.

"Yep, opens up just like a pistachio," I said, now sounding more like myself. "And you do kind of look like a gay fairy when the light hits the purple in the rainbow. It's sort of pretty, but that mask is awful, and those antennae make me think of giant glittering turkey legs. Can you touch the back of my neck again? And where's Rowdy? What happened to Rowdy?"

"I'm not far away," said a familiar snarky voice in my ear. "Can you try not to piss off my brother, Rowan? He's seconds from paddling your ass, and then he's going to feel all guilty about it, and I'll never hear the end of it."

"No, I don't think I will feel bad, so butt out, bro. This is going to be a private discussion," said Rauc, who put me down inside the anteroom, twisted me around, and walloped my bottom a few more times before taking my arm and pulling me into the control room.

"Jeez." I winced. "You try to have one little kinky sexual fantasy without the whole world finding out about it, not to mention how most guys never get it, or understand me, and now—"

Whack!

"Getting a little heavy-handed there, Red Orbiter? That one sounded worse than it felt!" I yelped but sensed an overwhelming anxious concern sweeping into my brain like a thick, bilious cloud. My ears beeped erratically, a crazy electronic version of panic.

"What is that?" I murmured.

Rauc said, too loudly in my opinion, "Pipe down! I'm not going to hurt her—much! And no, I'm not going to bring her to you. So chill out!"

"Who are you talking to? Roger?"

Rauc shot me a look that made me think dealing with Armed Evangelicals might be easier. "No, not Roger," he spit out. "Greens."

"Greens are worried about me?"

"Apparently. Our plan is to abduct particularly problematic bug-juice-blasted humans and hand them over to Greens to do their thing. They think I took you for sinister purposes."

"Didn't you? And what is their thing, exactly? You somehow neglected to mention Greens, along with a great many other things,"

I said, glaring at Rauc's face, normally beautiful without the bug mask, but now leaning down toward mine with anger, almost as menacing as the mask.

"How is it you not only have Roger and Win and who knows how many other poachers sniffing around you, but now Greens are sweet on you too? I've been gone mere months, and now all hell's going to break loose because I just snatched you in the middle of Las Vegas Boulevard and we were supposed to keep you out of the public eye!" Rauc roared, his volume and tone rubbing me the wrong way.

"Well you sure screwed the pooch on that one, didn't you?" I said, looking up at him, hands on hips. "And just what are you implying about poachers?"

Rauc's hands landed on my hips as he sat down in the pilot's seat and hauled me facedown over his lap.

"This is a John Wayne movie. I'm Maureen flipping O'Hara in a macho-man flick," I muttered.

Chapter 54

In between swats to my smarting behind, Rauc let me have a piece of his mind. "Yes, I was mad and should have chased after you instead of donning that bug getup so I could take you away and talk some sense into you!"

Whack!

"Where is the phone I gave you?"

Whack!

"I called your ass this morning to tell you I'd just returned and was going to pick up my bug wings and then I wanted to see you!"

Whack!

"And that redhead you saw me with is my copilot!"

Whack!

"She's Bruce Robertson's sister! And you go off like she's my girlfriend, but you know who's woman she used to be?"

Whack!

"Roger Rogers. How do you like them apples?"

Whack!

I yelled, "Why didn't you just talk to me out loud instead of phoning me? That phone hasn't worked since the minute you disappeared without a word!" I sounded funny because all the blood had rushed to my head.

Rauc lifted me from his lap. "I didn't want to zone in on you and surprise you—in case you weren't alone or didn't want to speak to me anymore."

I wrapped my arms around his neck and kissed him for all I was worth, and for all those times I couldn't.

Two hours later we came up for air in the enormous bed inside the pistachio craft. And Rauc had definitely been holding out on me.

"Why didn't you do this on our trip to Monterey?"

Rauc's hand stroked up my thigh. "I didn't want to overwhelm you or scare you away. I was your first alien, and it had to be a lot to take in. Now I realize how stupid I was." Rauc's other hand lifted my chin, teal eyes penetrating every bit as effectively as his body had. "You're the bravest human I know. And to think you were my first."

"You're not stupid, just considerate," I said, kissing and nuzzling his neck. It smelled as good as his voice sounded. "And what do you mean, your first? No way you were a virgin."

Rauc laughed. "You were my first human hybrid."

"Well, no wonder you handled me with kid gloves. But I have another question."

"Of course you do." His lips twitched.

I finally got to kiss those sculpted lips again, running my fingers through dark red hair the color of rocks in Valley of Fire.

"Why did you not take me into Red Orbiter headquarters when we went to Valley of Fire? Security concerns?"

"Somewhat, but not enough to keep you out. Fact is, I didn't want to share you. Plus, I spared you scrutiny." He smiled. "I didn't figure you'd want to answer more questions than you could ask."

"Speaking of that, I have so many things I never got to ask you. I've been writing them down when I thought of them, on scraps of paper all over my house—except my cat chewed some of them—and on a pad in my purse." I stopped talking because Rauc was laughing and reaching for the back of my neck. "Do that too many more times today, and I might get brain damage," I said.

"Copper, it's good to have you around to make me laugh again."

"Seriously, though, what are you—"

Rauc touched the small of my back, just above my tailbone.

"Oh…my…gosh."

"You said we still have an hour or so before your sister's cooking show finishes, so I thought I'd address this John Wayne movie reference you made."

Waves of pleasure coursed through me as I sank back into the bed, Rauc leaning over me.

"You don't even like John Wayne. He's not a redhead, and I know he could never do this."

***

"Situation contained," said Rowdy's voice from the ether. "And sorry to interrupt, but we have another issue you need to know about, and Rose is almost done with the show. Your sister's a cutie patootie and did great, Rowan."

"We'll meet you at the bar in five," said Rauc.

It was weird to see Rauc dressed in non-Wrangler clothes, instead wearing white jeans and a teal-blue t-shirt that matched his eyes. Once inside Galaxy Grog, I saw Rowdy was wearing typical tourist garb—baggy jean shorts below the knee and an orange Hooters t-shirt.

"Seriously?" I said, and he grinned lecherously in reply.

"Got to blend in around all these wankers," he said, standing to give me a hug.

"Did you check to make sure there's no Rambo wannabes lurking about?" I asked.

"There would have been, had we not intercepted them," said Rowdy.

"So are the guys from the skywalk with Greens now?" asked Rauc.

"Sure are. And they'll have no memory of seeing Rowan Layne at all, much less seeing her abducted by a bug on the Vegas Strip," said Rowdy. "But before that, they sang quite a song. They parked their truck at another hotel because the wimps were even more paranoid by then, and were on their way to meet up with their new buddies from Pahrump at this bar. Seems they've joined forces against a common enemy, the terrifying bug-juicer aliens."

I snorted.

"Problem was, the Pahrump dudes did park in this hotel, where they happened to recognize a certain vehicle that should not have been self-parked," said a voice I never dreamed I'd dread hearing so much. Roger sat down at our table, and I thought I might choke on my cocktail.

"Well, it's not like valet parking worked out so well for me last time, did it? And is my car now covered in red paint, or painted with a big A?" I cringed.

"Your car's fine. They were spotted on security cameras, so a big scary bug descended on their asses once again before they could inflict damage. And now they've been arrested, one more time. The security tape footage was given to the police. And also to the media."

"Thank you," I said.

"What's it going to take to get you to not run off on your own?" said Roger, his voice deceptively soft.

"I was with my sister. I picked her up at the airport and—"

The burner phone buzzed in my purse, and I wished teleporting to another universe were possible.

"It's the phone Win gave me." I winced. "I should probably answer it."

I didn't look at Rauc, but I heard him, and his voice was also way too self-contained. "You mean to tell me you have his phone with you and not mine? I so want to blister your butt again."

"Get in line," said Roger.

"I'm upstairs with your sister," said Win when I answered his call. "I figured somebody ought to look out for her while everyone else was busy saving your bacon again. Shall we come down and join you?"

Chapter 55

I didn't need to introduce G to Rauc, as they'd met in Portland when he dined with my family. But she'd never met Rowdy, and my sister had really pretty blue eyes, but they popped out like a bug mask when she saw Roger.

"O.W. gave you the suite next to mine, so if you need anything while you're here, let me know," he said, taking her hand. "Rowan, I need your keys so your car can be moved. It'll be parked up by mine, and I'll help you get it down in the elevators when you're ready to go."

"I'm going to bow out now too, so you and your sister can have time together. It was a pleasure to meet you, Gwynne. Rowan, I'll be in touch about the convention," said Win.

"It was great meeting you," said G. "Thanks for coming to get me after the show."

"Come on, Rowdy. We need to talk to Oz, as I'm sure he wants an update," said Rauc.

"Yeah, we should bug out," said Rowdy, winking at me. "You must be exhausted, Rauc."

"Zip it, Rowdy," said Rauc, turning to G. "Once all this craziness is over, I hope to see your family again. Tell your husband I have a new watch for him to check out. Rowan, things will be hectic the next couple weeks, but I'll be in touch." He leaned down and kissed me.

G watched Rauc and Rowdy walk away and said, "Well, I spent the afternoon cooking otherworldly tastiness for TV, and it was a total blast, but I'm thinking you must have had an even more interesting day. All three men plus the crazy brother. How do you do it, little sister?"

"It's not like I had sex with all three of them today, and oh my gosh, do you think the sodium pentothal didn't wear off?"

"What do you mean?" My sister looked frantic. "Is the CIA torturing you now too? Is it Win? Is he really a bad guy? Because that would be a total bummer."

"No, I'll explain. And I wish you weren't allergic to Morris so you could come stay at my house." I sighed. "I'm exhausted, but I want to hang out."

"I'm sorry I'm only here for one night. Let's go up to my suite. I'm not hungry after eating everything we cooked today, but we can order you something."

"Roger?" I said, hands on hips. "If we go upstairs, will you promise not to be a snoop?"

"You can't ask me any nicer than that?" he drawled in my ear. "But yes, beautiful, I will refrain from listening to you and your sister."

"That is beyond creepy," said G. "Did he answer you?"

"Yes, and we're good to go."

"My sister really is Luna Moth Woman," she muttered as we left the bar.

"Wait till I tell you about the past week. Rauc is amazing, and Roger thinks he's Superman."

"Roger looks like Superman," said G.

After I told my sister about being twice rescued by bugs and after she stopped laughing when I told her Roger's full name, she said, "I'm worried about you. But at least you no longer live in that town and have plenty of protection here."

"I'm hoping to stay so busy writing for the convention I don't have time to think about it. It's like I'm seventeen again, with crushes on three different guys."

"How do you feel about Rauc being back?"

"Ecstatic. And scared. Relieved he gets me when I wasn't sure he did."

"And Win and Roger?"

"They get me too, though I don't know if that's a good thing. And I didn't tell you before, but Roger's only thirty-three, though usually I feel like I'm nearly a quarter century younger."

"I just want you to be happy, Rowan. You're already in a much better place than you were, even if things have moved pretty fast here in Vegas. It's exciting you're going to be participating in the Omni convention."

"Yes, and when do you consider it safe for me to tell Mom? After the fact? Never? You tell her so I don't have to! Because she's going to text me that flipped bird emoji."

***

I leaned against my car with Roger looming over me, my keys still in his hand.

"I'm not willing to step aside, nor will I simply let slide how you got yourself in hot water again today."

"Look," I placed my hand on his chest. "I don't want to seem ungrateful, but I didn't bring all of this on my own. Are you sure you're not madder at yourself than you are me?"

Roger gripped the side of my face and kissed me so swiftly, I swooned.

Possessive didn't begin to describe it. Potent. Powerful. Probably would land me in more trouble.

"Get in your car, and take your infuriating butt out of here before I throw you over my shoulder, fireman style, and bring you to my cave."

Chapter 56

The week leading up to the Omni National Convention was one of daily insanity, in the form of turbulent tweets and histrionic headlines.

"I have instructed Space Force to shoot down and destroy any and all alien spacecraft harassing Americans. HUMANS FIRST!" tweeted the president.

And because every word was spelled correctly, it was assumed he had assistance writing it, which was downright chilling. Especially because we currently had no secretary of defense. Who was running things? His little brother?

Once breaking news revealed the colorful insect aliens hailed from Uranus, Calamity weighed in on Fox: "The president has declared war powers in the Double-I War, and he can and will shoot down these flaming cowardly bugs with toxic fairy wings from Uranus! A terrible planet for sure, one seeking to destroy us and our way of life! We must defend what is ours, take up arms against this scourge to all we patriots stand for. Because the only thing they will understand is the spray of bullets bringing them to their alien knees! Guns and God will protect us, will protect you on this mission for liberty! HUMANS FIRST!"

Easy for him to say, safely behind the walls of Fox. It took about six hours for the president to follow: "Now we know who has been at these alien abduction and probes all along. Gay fairy bugs from awful Uranus! Who like to do nasty things to humans! They must be annihilated!"

Again, words like *annihilated* used and spelled correctly, making me wonder if the president had indeed been abducted, his tweets taken over by cronies who formed coherent, if pathological, sentences.

Jax Smith of SlayNews wasn't taking this bug invasion lying down, or bending over: "These Uranus anal-probing bug aliens are spraying you with powerful mind-control drugs! That's why you need protection, and we're offering it! We've got a two-for-one deal for just $49.95 for the first month's supply of Bug Blockers! A pill to block their bug juice and a suppository to protect your most private parts from their evil globalist plot to make sex slaves of us all! Patriots, get your Bug Blockers from SlayNews now!"

How long would it take for someone to get the pill and the suppository mixed up? How soon before the sale of Bug Blocker butt plugs?

The Everlasting Evangelical leader took a different tack: "God is guiding our mighty and righteous president to smite this fruity homoalien plague down! Feminazis they fornicate with will rue the day they brought this pestilence to our shores!"

Sure, any chance to stick it to, and blame it on, women. And fixate on fornication.

It took another day for this presidential tweet: "So sad to be from Urranus and have flaming fairy wings. I would never be from such a nasty place. I am 125% human. HUMANS FIRST! Shoot them all down with our stelth plaines they will never sea coming!"

Responses included:

"Better not shoot down those bugs, Mr. President, or they might just rebound those missiles right up Uranus."

And from Alamogordo61: "The president is 25% alien. Minuscule, yes, but that entire amount derives from Uranus. Show the world your DNA results, you barely coherent talking pile of pestilence."

Win was also most likely responsible for the headline that followed: "BUG ALIENS FROM URANUS AND SO IS YOUR PRESIDENT"

I called Win.

"Nice to hear from you, Rowan," he answered.

"I'm worried about all this crazed chatter from a deranged toddler who had to be talked out of shooting missiles at tornados."

"Such touching concern for all of your Red Orbiter men," said Win, which explained why he didn't call me sweet pea.

"Okay, well this phone call was a mistake. Have a nice day." I disconnected.

My burner phone rang.

"Yes, Master?" I snarked.

"Hanging up on people is childish and rude, and you do it so often. I do certain things very thoroughly myself. You aiming to find out?"

"Oh yeah? You gonna put that Vulcan grip on me again?"

Win snorted. "Don't worry about missiles. It's a flailing attempt to divert attention from the Omni convention and the terrifying reality for his party that they're in checkmate."

"What, you don't think Republicans choosing the president's daughter-in-law as his running mate was a stellar idea? I myself particularly liked the headline, 'RUNNING MATE OR PLAYMATE?'"

"And yet nothing's guaranteed," drawled Win.

"Why can't we just have Greens abduct the president, erase what little mind he has left, and replace it with sanity?"

"We don't want him reelected, and that's not the way things work. It's not the job of Greens to save our asses from our own folly. We're pushing it by asking for weather help."

"About that. Do they cause hurricanes and tornados?"

"No, they stick to less-destructive means of self-defense. Their aim is not to destroy us, simply to deter."

"That's our aim too, isn't it? With this bug scheme? Deter not destroy."

"That and sometimes if you give folks just enough rope, they'll hang themselves with it."

"Why do I get the feeling you're talking about me?"

"It's something to think about, next time you feel the urge to hang up on me. Or defy protocol. Which is what we need to discuss. I'm in charge of security for the convention, which means you, my dear—"

"Don't you dare tell me to wise up again!"

"You also have a habit of interrupting. I was going to say you need to start *listening attentively.*"

I hung up on him. I know, childish, but it beat screaming.

Chapter 57

"Doodles, your horoscope says you may feel caught between a rock and a hard place this week!!! Dad says hi!!! He tried on three different outfits to golf with your sister and Phil today. I liked the black one but he picked the blue!!! Sunny here for a change!!! Love to you and critters!!! (smiling sun, kissy face, dog, cat, heart emoji)"

There's a golf emoji but no way in hell would she use it.

And wasn't that a dandy horoscope for the starting day of the Omni National Convention? Could the "rock" be Rauc and the "hard place" the domineering bodies and minds of Win and Roger?

I had to figure out what to wear for three days and now wished I'd told Mom about the convention in time to send me outfits. At least all my work was off-camera, but I'd be meeting a lot of people, including the potential vice president of the United States not to mention a former secretary of defense.

Little-known fact: I once thought I wanted to be sec def. But in hindsight it was more about being mother hen to cub troops. Or queen of my own army.

This morning was also a blast from the past—or maybe my past coming back to bite me.

First I had a private message on Facebook from Cate, my crafting friend in Yearntown.

"I know you're busy having an actual life there in Vegas, but I thought you should know there's been online chatter. Certain individuals decided to blame you for the alien bug attacks and the matter of ammunition gone missing from their stockpiles."

"And here I thought the president said it was guns those evil aliens are after. No guns missing at all? That is just too strange," I snarked.

"Think they'll ever figure it out? We also just had a little excitement at the grocery store involving police, which I suspect you'll be to blame for too."

"Because I have sex with aliens?"

"Because you made them look ridiculous in the newspaper. Not that they haven't done that all by themselves. The good news is we have an OW Coalition member running for county commissioner under the Omni Party, but they're from Silver City not Yearntown."

A beleaguered open-pit mining town unfortunate enough to be situated next to anti-alien Virginia City dwellers who still milked rage at Red Orbiter involvement in the Great Fire of 1875.

I was typing a reply to Cate when my phone rang, and it was my pal "pronounced like the gemstone" Oapule, also in Yearntown.

"Oh my goddess! Rowdy was at the grocery store, and I tried saving him from getting shot by the sheriff, but he saved me, and I was just on the news!"

At the same time Rowdy's voice said in my ear, "Make sure you turn on your TV at noon, channel eight."

"Are you okay Oapule? Was bug juice involved?"

"I'm marvelous! Rowdy and the most beautiful redheaded woman I've ever seen shielded me! Blessed be!"

"Are you kidding me?"

"Well, the most beautiful woman other than you, of course," said Oapule.

"It's Genie Robertson," said Rowdy in the ear that didn't have my phone pressed to it. "She's flying with me now because she doesn't want to upset you after you saw her with Rauc last week and threw a hissy fit."

"I didn't throw a hissy fit! Okay maybe I did, but I was freaked out at seeing Rauc!"

"Why are you yelling?" asked Oapule.

"I'm sorry, Oapule. Rowdy's in my other ear."

"Really? He was just across the parking lot, but I don't see him now. And oh my goddess, the state police arrived and are arresting the police chief!"

"Is it a really tall state trooper?" I asked.

"No, but there was a giant blond guy here a few minutes ago. Kind of reminded me of a cartoon I watched as a kid. All these beautiful men showing up in Yearntown! A cutie in a spiffy blue suit handed me his card and would like to speak to me."

"Does the card say Tim Rider, Homeland Security?"

Muffled rustling rattled my ear before Oapule said, "Yes! Maybe I shouldn't talk to him. You said I should be wary of anyone from—"

"You can talk to this guy, Oapule. I know him. But watch out for that tall blond guy."

"You're fixing to land yourself in hot water, beautiful," said yet another voice in my ear.

"Come on, Roger Ramjet." I put my hand over the phone. "I'm just having a little fun. Is everything okay there? How'd Tim get there so fast?"

"He came with me. Maggie flew us in an orb. Rowdy and Genie were also in an orb they landed at the local airstrip before walking to the grocery store where Rowdy had his truck parked. He was sniffing out a whiff of insurgence with your name as the target."

"Yes, apparently I'm now to blame for all ills in Yearntown. So no bug invasion?"

"No bugs. The sheriff was grocery shopping. A deputy saw the orb land and called him. He came running out of the store to confront big bad Red Orbiters who dare drop in on the county seat. Meanwhile, the Yearntown chief of police was having an early lunch at the pizza place next door. He waddled out and opened fire on Rowdy and Genie, just for grins."

"And Oapule jumped in to save the day?"

"Yes, I did, but who are you talking to now?" said Oapule because I'd taken my hand off my phone.

"The big tall blond guy that reminds you of Roger Ramjet," I said.

"That's *it*! I couldn't think of the name of the cartoon. My stars, he's a stunner," gushed Oapule. "He's even bigger than my grandson!"

"We're going to have a talk about this Roger Ramjet thing," said Roger.

"Aren't you supposed to be playing lord of security with Win at the convention?" I asked.

No response. Probably already headed back in my direction to menace me.

"Oapule, are you seriously okay? I wish you'd come for a visit." I eyed the clock on my stove, and it said almost noon.

"I'm fabulous!" she trilled. "Give my love to Bodie and Morris! I have to go grocery shop now. Blessed be!"

I turned on the news per Rowdy's edict and saw footage of him with Oapule flying into the frame at the sound of weapons discharging. Genie Robertson must have filmed it.

Las Vegas news at noon reported: "A rural Nevada police chief opened fire on an unarmed man and woman in a grocery store parking lot this morning after the county sheriff confronted the two for being Red Orbiters, claiming it was his job to keep the riffraff from influencing the God-fearing populace of his county.

"A Reiki practitioner attempted to intervene on behalf of the Red Orbiters and was uninjured despite also being fired upon. State police arrested the local chief, who claims he did nothing wrong because, 'They didn't die like they were supposed to, and this was all the fault of a nasty media woman who used to write mean lies in the paper, and she's the one who brought aliens here.'"

Chapter 58

The blasted convention center at Planet Wynne just had to be on the top level in the round monstrosity depicting the moonship, right up there with the flipping nine-hole golf course in the top of the sphere.

I yanked out my newest burner phone from Win, shocked he answered. "Look, I know you're probably too busy to help my sorry butt right now, but I could use some Red Orbiter assistance getting up to the third level because I'm not attempting these insane elevators. I'm assuming everyone I know is working security or off being a bug right now."

"Someone will be down in five," he said, cool and composed. Mr. Superspy had everything under control.

I was standing next to a restroom and decided to, as one of my rubber stamps said, "never pass up an opportunity to pee."

When I emerged minutes later, media personnel milled about, one of them somehow recognizing me.

"You're that lady that's supposed to write a book about Red Orbiters!" he lunged at me with his phone out, ready to record. Must have been a desperately slow news hour, as the convention was not due to begin until early evening. "Whoa!" said the reporter, now blocked by an imposing tall blond frame.

"Ms. Layne is working this convention and cannot answer questions at this time," said Roger, taking my arm to lead me away.

"Did you park in valet, or do I need to address that before we go to the top level? And I presume you prefer not to fly outside in this heat?" He looked down at me, and my stomach flip-flopped.

"You know, in that tight white shirt, I can almost make out the red *S* underneath. Such delusions of grandeur. Perhaps you should get some help for that."

A whoosh of air and a tickle in my tummy and I was swept outside into blazing heat.

"I parked in valet, you imbecile!" I screeched as we flew up to the flying-saucer level and landed on the flight deck. "And you need to quit with the Superman act! You are not Superman!"

"You sure about that?"

Another whoosh and blur of movement where my face kind of felt like it was swooping backward and everything was all shimmery because we somehow went from the rim of the flying-saucer level upward and into an empty hallway inside the spherical top level.

I was on my feet with Roger pulling me toward what sounded like sheer chaos. We were backstage at the Omni National Convention, and if I'd ever remotely considered running for office, I was now absolved of that fantasy.

People everywhere in headphones, shouting, darting, yelling, directing. The intense wave of frantic energy hit me like a rogue wind, and I turned and gripped Roger's shirt below the Superman tattoo, burying my face in his torso.

"I'll take her from here," said my very favorite voice on Earth. I turned to see Rauc with Octavius Wynne, aka O.W.

"I thought you were off being a bug," I said, hugging Rauc.

"No, we're grounding them during the convention. There's too much going on with protestors already starting to form out front."

O.W. said to Roger, "Speaking of which, Cassandra's flight lands in a half hour. Bring her and the congressman through our back entrance. I've arranged private press coverage there to cover their arrival."

"I'm off to the airport then," said Roger.

"Are you flying there too?" I said, immediately regretting my snark when Roger's eyes turned gold—and cold. "Please tell the senator I'm here and ready to make any last-minute changes to her speech for tonight, and thanks for bringing me up," I added, sounding like Dorothy, the small and meek.

Rauc said to O.W., "Do you have somewhere Rowan can work in relative quiet? Away from all these people?"

"Come right this way," said O.W., and I mouthed "Thank you!" to Rauc.

We entered a group of small offices, like a business center. Very utilitarian but for the cool moon theme with fascinating photos and a blue-gray-white swirling color scheme. I sat in a fancy ergonomic chair and deep-breathed while Rauc consulted with O.W. outside the door.

My breathing was helping restore some semblance of calm when I inadvertently heard Senator Rojas-Ortiz speaking from what I presumed was her airplane.

"We'll need to get with Rowan Layne for her to write up a speech to introduce you tomorrow night. She's a good choice, as she's now one of your constituents and grew up in the nation's capital region. She's also a former government lawyer and Texas graduate like yourself. She'll look good on camera and will energize the audience."

Okay, so how had I not known my congressman was a Longhorn?

I rustled my phone out of my purse and called my sister.

"What's wrong, sis? Aren't you at the convention? We're just coming off the golf course. Something didn't already happen, did it?"

"Not anything bad, but you need to tell Mom I'm working the convention if she's planning to watch it on TV."

"She is. She's having Dad make popcorn when we get back from golf and intends to open a bottle of rosé for this momentous occasion."

"That it is." I laughed, but it came out more like a croak.

"What's going on, Rowan? Is Rauc there?"

"Yes, I'm here, Gwynne," said Rauc, now massaging my shoulders. "Your sister's a little frazzled right now," he said into my phone. "She's giving the speech to introduce our next vice president tomorrow night. Will you please assure your dad we've got security well-covered here?"

I said to my sister, "Mom will want to know what I plan to wear. I have no earthly idea. And the last time I had a haircut was with Kyle in Portland in March."

Within a half hour I had a text: "Doodles, you have to let Rock fly you up here for Kyle to cut your hair and we can get you a pedicure and an outfit at Dazzle for you to wear tomorrow night. Cloudy here, looks like rain. Ugh. (cloud, kissy face, blue dress, red shoe, kissing lips, lipstick, pink purse emoji)"

We should have waited until tomorrow to tell Mom. But at least she wasn't mad at me.

Chapter 59

Rauc returned with O.W. to my little office.

O.W. said, "We have an appointment in Caesars Forum to get you a dress, shoes, the whole look, at ten a.m. If need be, we'll hit the Shops at Crystals by the Cosmopolitan. At two-thirty your hair will be cut by one of the hottest celeb stylists in L.A., which no one knows is a Red Orbiter, and he's fabulous with long curly hair. At four-thirty you go into makeup."

I tried to wrap my brain around logistics. How was I going to feed my critters dinner? It just seemed like too much, so I was hyperventilating again.

Rauc said, "You're worried about Bodie and Morris, and all that driving back and forth?"

I nodded. "I thought I would only be here a few hours each day and didn't make any other arrangements."

"All rooms are booked for the convention," said O.W. "We could ask Roger—"

"We can use my orb," said Rauc. "It'll be easier. We can walk Bodie on the flight deck. If we get them now in your car, we'll be back in plenty of time for the evening's festivities."

"As long as you don't mind a litter box in the bathroom and we close off the control room. because Morris will climb all over it and no telling what buttons he'll push."

Once we reached my house, I packed quickly, making sure I had plenty of clean underwear and all possible pet necessities.

On the way back, it was weird to have Rauc drive my car, but Morris meow-wailed less in his carrier on the front passenger seat, and I sat in back with Bodie and told him we were going on a grand adventure.

As we transported everything from my car to the orb, Bodie was on his leash, and I barely caught him as he raised a leg to pee on Roger's Ferrari. Rauc was no help—he was laughing.

"O.W. said to tell you he recently had a dog park created next to the golf course on the top deck, so we can take Bodie up there for walks too," he said.

Once in the orb, I was surprised Morris didn't stay hunkered down in his crate like he had for twenty-four hours after we'd moved to Vegas, but Rauc spoke softly, cajoling him.

I said, "While you're at it, can you also tell Morris it's okay to eat the bottom layer of food in his bowl?"

I'd brought a pillow from my bed, so I placed it on Rauc's bed. Morris pawed and sniffed and curled up against it after I pulled the bedspread over him. I gave Bodie a giant rawhide bone and told Rauc to put up anything really important that might be chewable.

Rauc said he had a quick meeting, so I headed back down to my little office area in the convention center, which was getting more hustle and bustle as folks arrived to work in their spaces.

Within seconds, O.W. walked in and handed me a sheaf of papers. "This is the background information on Congressman

O'Neill for you to comprise your speech. The senator said you'll have fifteen minutes to introduce him, and all they ask is that it echo the convention theme of diversity. Otherwise you've got free rein with how you do it."

A sensuous voice slithered into my ear. "I'm rooting for you, beautiful. Think great Texas icon Ann Richards and channel that 'born with a silver foot in his mouth' convention wit. You've got this."

I asked, "So I won't need to meet with the congressman tonight? Because I'm covered in dog hair at the moment. And did the senator say if she needs changes to her speech?"

"O'Neill's schedule is crazy," said Ow, "but you'll have a chance to speak before you introduce him tomorrow night. And Cassandra said she's good to go on the speech, which is fabulous. I heard her rehearsing it a few minutes ago. This is a big night for Red Orbiters. You have done us proud."

I was getting teary-eyed as Rauc returned.

"We're all set. I spoke with Win, and I'm in charge of guarding you from here on out. Rowdy is also buzzing around and can provide backup." Rauc turned to O.W. "So how do we get this lady sustenance so she can work her magic?"

"There are catered meals in the main hall for all convention staff, but Rose wanted to send over a plate this evening from Galaxy Table. It should be ready in a couple hours."

"And I'm here to extend an invitation to a private dinner party tomorrow night," said Win, walking into the office. "It's hosted by Oliver and Olivia Warnock, Oz, and yours truly."

"Wow. I haven't seen my law professor in years. Good thing I'm getting hair and makeup professionally done."

"Yes, but right now you need to get busy writing."

"Always cracking that whip, Win," I snarked.

"Who, me? Never. I'll leave you with a favorite inspirational quote from Steve Jobs: 'The people who are crazy enough to think they can change the world, are the ones who do.' Show 'em how Luna Moth Woman does it," said Win, flashing that scintillating smile.

I was looking up words, taking down notes, scribbling thoughts, and otherwise getting my fingers splotched with ink from pens that always seemed to leak on me. After two hours of intense focus, I was starved and realized the critters were probably wondering where dinner was.

Rauc walked in rolling a cart laden with covered dishes. Whatever it was smelled out of this world.

"I fed the critters, and Rowdy is going to take Bodie up to the dog run in an hour, so you have time to change for the senator's speech after we eat. And Rose made you a special dessert again." He winked.

"I like this a lot better, you personally delivering me food instead of having to translate your messages from outer space," I said after consuming halibut with mango beurre blanc sauce and a cannoli. Its edible pomegranate message said, "Copper, you outshine the stars."

"The handwriting looks different," I said.

"Yes, it's messier. I wrote it myself. Rose is crazy busy and might have bonked my head with a copper pan if I'd asked her to take time to do it."

"That makes it all the more sweet." I bestowed him with a kiss, even sweeter.

Chapter 60

After giving Bodie and Morris plenty of lovey hugs and then showering, I donned the red dress I'd worn to meet with Tim Rider and Bart Reynolds, but it had a low neckline.

"Too risqué?" I asked Rauc. "I wanted to wear red to honor Red Orbiters tonight."

"And honor us you do," he said, his delectable voice sounding throatier.

I wished I had earphones when we got to our seats in the convention center, right in front of the stage. So many voices, too many of which I was hearing inside my ears on top of the sounds of the auditorium filling with people.

"Front-row seats?" I said to Oz, who looked dashing in a blue suit with red tie like Rauc.

"Hi, my dear. You get to sit next to old Oz tonight." The former astronaut took my hand to help me get settled in my seat.

"Look at me, flanked by Red Orbiter pilots. Can't get much better than that." I grinned. "But do you have advice on blocking out voices in my head right now?"

"Give me a minute. I need to greet Red MacLeod," Oz said as he strolled away.

Rauc shifted toward me. "You want to block voices right this very minute?"

"It'd be nice."

"Okay, here goes," he said, moving too fast for me to catch on to his hand at the back of my neck, stroking across *that* spot.

I bit my tongue to keep from making noise, but Rauc made a few sounds of his own when my hand gripped his other hand, crushing his knuckles.

"Bet you couldn't hear voices in your head for a few seconds, right?" he said.

"Rowan, someone wants to meet you," boomed Oz as I struggled to catch my breath.

I turned in my seat to face the large hand reaching toward me. I let go of Rauc's hand and shook the Scotsman's.

"Red MacLeod at your service, you brilliant bonny lass. I'm looking forward to working with you on the next phase of our project."

"Wonderful to meet you too, Red. I learned a new word because of you!"

"Aye, and what would that be?"

"*Cockwomble.*" I grinned.

He threw back his head and roared, which at least made a few voices around us stop.

Or maybe they were dumbstruck by the full Highland regalia, complete with kilt, sporran, and—was that an actual dirk suspended from his belt? There were perks to having your best buddy in charge of security.

"Oh, aye, we'll have you speaking like a Scot in no time," said Red, sitting next to Oz.

Rauc whispered in my ear, "I bet he's a golfer."

I giggled like a kid as lights were dimmed and the convention announcer hired from the Las Vegas Voice Actors Studio boomed from a mic, "Ladies, gentlemen, and all otherworldly participants, I give you Senator Cassandra Rojas-Ortiz from our great state of Nevada!"

The senator strolled onstage with her famous red-lipped smile, waving to us before she stepped up to a podium.

"Welcome to the very first Omnipresent Party National Convention in the United States of America! And make no mistake, we the otherworldly are making history tonight, and from this day on. We've got Congressman Warren O'Neill from right here in Las Vegas representing us on the presential ticket as our next vice president!"

The crowd roared.

"We've got Wendy Orbach from Henderson running for the Senate and a most impressive group of Americans from all fifty states seeking office at the local, state, and national levels. You'll hear from many of them in the next two days, including Olivia Warnock, Senate candidate from Maryland and OW Coalition founding member.

"Our members bring a message of diversity, of collective wisdom derived from variety in our heritage that makes us who we are and what we are meant to be.

"Let us take pride in our diversity, in our striking similarities and celebrated differences, we who are otherworldly Americans. Our diversity will empower us, strengthen us, and send us soaring to new possibilities, new opportunities, and new leadership!"

I shifted in my seat, holding my breath as if I didn't already know her next words.

"It's in the spirit of pride in otherworldly ancestry residing in every one of us that I choose to share this with you today. I, born of Las Vegas and a Nevada senator for the past six years, am not only one of the Omnipresent Party's newest members—I am a Red Orbiter."

When the roar of the crowd died down, Senator Rojas-Ortiz continued speaking.

"Though we originally hailed from another planet long ago, Red Orbiters are, as a species, as a people, not defined by place of origin or birth in the traditional manner of our fellow Americans. Our identities derive not from traits such as race or ethnicity but instead from individual and diverse gifts, and what we choose to do with our unique abilities. I chose to serve my nation in government, but my parents were aviators, as is a special someone you all know, Red Orbiter and Astronaut Oz Walden!"

Spotlights hit us in the front row, and my face froze, trying not to wince at the glaring flashes of light as Rauc squeezed my hand. Oz stood and waved to the audience.

"I didn't write that part," I murmured.

"Oz wanted to surprise you," Rauc said in my ear over the audience cheers. "My uncle decided to come out because of what you wrote."

Oz sat down and patted my arm as cameras kept flashing.

"We are and have always been part of this rich heritage of Earth, of these United States. We are proud to serve as your senator, your astronaut, to be your teachers and your friends. We have much to learn from each other to forge ahead to return our nation to its original promise of liberty and justice for all. We choose to reveal truths long sought by many and denied by those who would decry the very fabric of their DNA. We the people are otherworldly in all its myriad colors and ideals.

"We are the Omnipresent Party, formed of necessity not unlike a Declaration of Independence made on July 4, 1776, stating, 'When…it becomes necessary for one people to dissolve the political bands which have connected them with another, and to assume among the powers of the earth, the separate and equal station to which the Laws of Nature…entitle them,' the inalienable right of equality, of life, liberty, and the pursuit of happiness.

"It is time now to embrace those truths and assume our earthly power, this diversity among us. The Omnipresent Party is the arbiter of the future in which our hopes and dreams may manifest for all of us in acceptance and celebration of that diversity.

"My name is Senator Cassandra Rojas-Ortiz, and I am a Red Orbiter, an American, and a Nevadan. Let us diversify together."

"I wrote that part," I whispered to Rauc.

Chapter 61

With all the excitement, I normally wouldn't sleep well. But Rauc took care of wearing me out, such that Bodie finally gave up his spot on the bed. He and Morris took over a couch in the lounging area, where we found them in the morning, cuddled together.

As I rushed to throw on clothes suitable for what portended to be an exhausting shopping spree, Rauc said Rowdy and Genie were joining us.

"We thought you might want some female input."

"Why do I need so many guards and spies? Isn't that what Genie is? So how come she's flying with Rowdy? Aren't you supposed to pair a pilot observer with a spook copilot?"

Rauc laughed. "For red orb missions, yes, but we recruited Genie for flying our newest craft specifically for this bug deal. She trained as a pilot, so we paired her with someone big enough to don the bug getup, which was me and is now Rowdy. She's kind of petite."

"In what way is she petite?" I scoffed. "She looks like Jessica Rabbit."

"Perhaps." Rauc's lips twitched. "But she's not very tall, and we want all scary bug aliens to appear tall and large—in the *shoulders*. Those wings are heavy, especially when full. Now, do you want me to bring you breakfast so you don't have to deal with hordes of staffers in the convention hall?"

"Yes, please. I'll be here detangling my hair."

Rauc walked Bodie in the dog park while I ate, and then we went to the first level for a Planet Wynne limousine. Rowdy stood like a chauffeur holding open the door. Jessica Rabbit, aka Genie Robertson, was already inside.

"There's whiskey in here in case you need it, what with Rowdy driving," she said, and I loved her already.

Once inside Caesars Forum, we were greeted by a personal shopper who resembled O.W. in demeanor and said his name was Fabio. Not kidding.

He fluttered around me. "Fabulous hair, eyes, and boobs," he said.

"My sentiments exactly," said Rauc.

"So what look are we aiming for?" Genie asked me as we were shuttled off to the first boutique.

"I don't want to look too matronly, but I probably can't handle heels higher than three inches. Nothing sleeveless, and I'd like to be able to breathe." I grabbed her arm. "Also, I tend to go with the first thing I see, so don't let me do that if it isn't right."

Rowdy said, "Are you that way with men too?" Genie swatted him for me.

It only took three shops and four bottled waters, but we found a dress. And who knew I'd end up looking good in a fifties throwback frock?

Teal-blue silk with a high neck in the back, it had a deeply scooped front and three-quarter sleeves. But the best part was the full skirt with a gathered layer of netting underneath to poof it out, falling well below the knee, with a sash of black crystals scattered like stars.

"Don't think for one minute that high collar will protect you from me," Rauc whispered in my ear.

"You look like the original Barbie, but in a good way," Rowdy said.

Genie said, "We need the perfect bra for this."

Fabio agreed and sent Rauc and Rowdy to get more water and snacks.

I obtained the most amazing black bra and panties ever, and Genie was my new best friend for finding one I didn't want to tear apart for digging in all the wrong places.

"Who's paying for all this?" I asked Genie.

"O.W. planned to, but Rowdy gambled last night." She rolled her eyes.

"So now you're my kept woman!" snarked Rowdy, joining us outside the lingerie boutique.

"You couldn't handle her, Rowdy, and you know it," said Rauc, supremely smug.

"Focus, people!" said Fabio, clapping his hands. "We still need shoes and a handbag, and I know the most utterly fabuloso earrings. Off to the Shops at Crystals!"

"Did he say fabuloso?" said Rauc.

"Did he say earrings?" said Rowdy. "I hope he isn't thinking diamonds."

Fabio was on the phone in the limo talking to a jewelry boutique, and I recognized the name as one that loaned jewels to stars for events like the Oscars. "They look like shooting stars with blue-greenish gems. White gold. Yes, those are the ones. Please hold them for us, and we'll be there within the hour."

Rauc and Genie laughed at the look on Rowdy's face.

At our next stop, Fabio went fluttering into a boutique that my sister and mother adored, saying, "I saw the perfect shoe in here last week."

I said to Genie, "Please let it not be open-toed. We don't have time for a pedicure."

Fabio directed a salesperson to obtain my size. The stars were shining on me because it was a black closed-toe pump but not a sky-high stiletto, although it did have a half-inch platform in teal patent leather that matched the heal.

"You could even dance in those," said Rauc.

I also got a black beaded evening bag with little stars on it.

And it turned out those earrings were diamonds. Blue diamonds, to be exact—something I'd always coveted but never dared dream of.

"I'm buying these," said Rauc when he saw me hesitate.

"But it's too much," I said.

"It's the six-month anniversary of the first time I ever laid eyes on you. You're my queen of hearts, and my shooting star."

Chapter 62

O.W. met us as the limo pulled up to Planet Wynne. "You have twenty minutes before hair at the salon," he said, sounding like Mom.

I took the fastest shower of my life and grabbed my speech I'd printed out.

While my hair was washed and snipped and styled into what looked like a waterfall with a clip holding it away from my face, I practiced my speech.

I apologized to the famous stylist for having to constantly tell me to keep my head straight and stop fidgeting, but he said I wasn't half as bad as a celebrity and he really liked my speech.

Next I flew into my new dress and joined Senator Rojas-Ortiz for makeup, where she scanned my well-worn pages and handed them to an assistant to make ready for the teleprompter.

"I've never used one of those," I said to the senator.

"It's easy, and you won't need readers," she said. "And if you pull this off like I think you're going to, you might need to get used to one."

Roger stood guard outside the salon, and I tried not to be thrilled to my toes that his eyes turned bright green when I emerged in all my finery.

Rauc stepped forward with a small black box. My shooting-star, blue-diamond earrings.

Both Red Orbiters wore black suits with muted red ties, and wore them well.

"Are you ready to head backstage?" said Win as he approached with that stealth gate, looking fine in a black suit and a broad grin. "You ladies shame the brightest stars in the galaxy. Truly breathtaking." He spoke into a microphone attached to his ear, "We're walking."

I heard Rowdy say, "Roger that. All clear."

I concentrated on not stumbling in my new shoes and endured the ringing in my ears because it drowned out a multitude of voices. There were many Red Orbiters in the auditorium, whether folks realized it or not.

Congressman Warren O'Neill was already backstage flanked by his own security detail, but he stepped forward to greet me. "Rowan Layne, I thank you for tackling the task of making me sound good." He smiled broadly as he took my hands, his light-green eyes arresting.

"I'm honored to do so, and I thank you for taking on this political challenge of a lifetime. I'm only too happy to support a fellow Longhorn. I hope Washington has treated you well."

"It's been interesting." He grinned. "And it's getting more so. My world has turned upside down, like when I first learned my DNA results. I know you know what that's like." His gaze spoke volumes.

"Five minutes, Ms. Layne," said an unfamiliar voice.

Oh my gosh. I could hear the roar of the crowd over the backstage cacophony.

At precisely six p.m., which was nine p.m. prime time on the East Coast, I walked onto the stage to a podium. I focused on the front row of familiar faces including Oliver Warnock, my law professor, and I began my speech addressing only him, as suggested by Senator Rojas-Ortiz, to get me rolling.

I thought of my professor's precise, clearly enunciated voice, and I channeled it, relying on the teleprompter heavily at first to make sure I got facts and dates and details about the vice-presidential candidate correct. I willed myself not to speak too fast, and to breathe. Just breathe.

"We've been talking a lot about diversity and what makes us who we are. Congressman O'Neill says he got his eye color and compassion from his mom, and his skin color and street smarts from his dad, but both say his lifelong wish to run for office and serve his country he came into all on his own. His parents nurtured him and empowered him to reach lofty heights of his own design.

"By embracing our diversity, the colorful and complicated variety of our existence, we empower and respect each other, appreciating what makes us who we are. The name in our party says it all. *Omnipresent* means 'widely or constantly encountered.' It denotes that which is present everywhere.

"We the otherworldly are present everywhere, and always have been. Warren O'Neill understands this—he embodies what it means to be omnipresent and embraces that which makes him who he is, and who he will be. The next vice president of the United States of America!"

I took deep breaths as the crowd cheered, soaking it in and making it mine. I was in the pocket, relaxing into this surreal moment enough to hear Rauc say, "You're shining bright and knocking it out of the park, Copper! Bring it home!"

"Diversity in DNA means diversity in leadership skills, in problem-solving skills. It means varied and valued perspectives for solutions, for ideas. For years people liked to say, 'It's in his genes,' or 'That's how he was born.' And yet many today deny the core of their identities, their genetic code, that to which they are born.

"Poor Mr. President, who thinks a DNA test is something to pass or fail. Maybe he can't help it. It's how he was born. It's in his genes. He claims his DNA is lacking, and it's true. His lack of diversity renders him lacking in every way that counts. Lacking in leadership, lacking in perspective, lacking in solutions.

"Congressman Warren O'Neill's first job, back in high school in North Las Vegas, was a lifeguard at the community pool at SkyView YMCA. Today, let's all rise with Warren on that lifeguard stand, let's blow our whistle and issue a command, "You! Mr. President! Out of the gene pool!"

I pointed my finger and drew my arm up over my head as if signaling "out of here!" as the audience roared, some leaping to their feet and mimicking my motion.

I shouted into the microphone, "We want diversity! We need diversity! Congressman Warren O'Neill is that diversity. He stands for greatness that resides in all of us. Because as he knows, it's in our genes. And in our hearts and minds. Members of the Omnipresent Party, I give you the next vice president of the United States, Warren O'Neill!"

Chapter 63

At the private dinner feeding a number of us at Galaxy Table, I was situated between my old law professor Oliver Warnock and Red MacLeod. I think Win had a hand in the arrangement, as he was on the other side of Red with Oz, but Rauc was across the table and a ways down from me seated next to Olivia Warnock and her husband, Ogden West, who was next to Roger, who of course was with the senator and congressman. The other diners were unknown to me.

Before we sat, I quickly read and responded to a text from Mom that had come within seconds of my speech finale, though I hadn't had a chance to see it until now: "Bravo Doodles!!! (handclapping, face with stars for eyes, heart, kissy-face emoji) We are so proud of you and Dad said you looked stunning!!! We loved your dress and hair and makeup!!! That congressman is very dashing and with it!!! He will make a great vice president and president someday!!! No rain today!!! (smiley face emoji)"

As various appetizers were passed around the table, Olivia Warnock stood to welcome us. I liked what she had to say about the owl being the symbol of the Omnipresent Party: "Owls have cultural significance transcending geographical boundaries. In the classical Greek tradition, an owl often perched on the shoulder of Athena, goddess of wisdom, and owls were seen as warding off bad luck in

Roman lore. But in Native American mythos, owls are patient messengers, bringers of information, and holders of wisdom, capable of seeing the unseen. We have many among us tonight who fit that description, who embrace the otherworldly within and now seek to share that wisdom, knowledge, and vision."

"So why aren't you sharing your knowledge and practicing law?" Oliver Warnock asked me during dinner. Inevitable, really. He was the man who'd taught me all about constitutional criminal procedure under the Fourth Amendment.

"My heart isn't in it anymore. I've also come to realize I loved learning the law a great deal more than I enjoyed its practice."

"Teaching might be a good fit," he said with his clipped diction.

"Perhaps. I've tried to do a bit of that in my writing."

"Good for you, Rowan. You are a compelling writer."

"Aye, that she is. A hard act to follow for me tomorrow. I don't relish the thought," said Red MacLeod seated to my left.

"Are you running for office?" I asked.

"No. Just giving closing remarks for the convention, as it were. Newest member of the Omni Party and all that."

"So you made the switch too? At least now my mother approves of me doing so, especially since I'm still voting for a Democrat for president."

"Aye, it'll be a first for me," said Red.

My professor now engaged in conversation with the person on his right, so it was a good opportunity to lob a few at the former secretary of defense.

"Speaking of that, what were you thinking working in this administration? Seriously? Even as a Republican, there's just no excuse."

Red eyed me with ire in his eyes. "Win warned me you had quite a mouth on you, lass. Wasn't it not all that long ago you were a Republican as well?"

"A long time ago. 1991. I was in law school, and watching how Anita Hill was treated was the last straw, clearly delineating how the party felt about women. I never looked back."

"And yet you still worked for and supported the military."

"Yes, but I never supported the idiocy of voting like sheep, especially against their own interest with this administration."

"Aye, that's true enough, I suppose. I, like others, thought I could still do some good."

"Well, at least you came to your senses," I said.

Win joined our conversation. "I told you. Gets under your skin, doesn't she?"

"You know what I'm saying is true," I said.

"I will endeavor to redeem myself with my speech tomorrow night. You have inspired me, lass," said Red, although I wasn't sure if he was being snarky with that Scottish brogue.

He wasn't. As I sat listening to him the next evening, I realized I might have alienated a man who shared the very essence of the core of my being. Plus, he started with humor Dad would surely appreciate even if he didn't know who Alice Cooper was:

"A famed American rocker who knows a thing or two about embracing individuality, no matter how bizarre it may seem to many, once said, 'What most people don't understand is that UFOs are on a cosmic tourist route. That's why they're always seen in Arizona, Scotland, and New Mexico. Another thing to consider is that all three of those destinations are good places to play golf. So there's possibly some connection between aliens and golf.'"

Laughter reverberated throughout the audience.

"I hail from Scotland, but my genetic origins are from Mars, as it turns out, so I know a thing or two about golf. And as a former Royal Marine, I know something about battle and engaging with the enemy. And lately it has become increasingly clear who that enemy is.

"When I became secretary of defense, I took an oath—the same oath sworn by all military as well as civilians working in government. And in that oath, I vowed to uphold the Constitution against all enemies, foreign and domestic.

"All enemies, foreign and domestic. Think about that for a minute. Aye, I have thought about it a great deal in the past year. And I am here to tell you, this president and those who enable him are the greatest enemies this nation has ever encountered."

I was on my feet, roaring along with the rest of the audience.

"As an American citizen not born here, I may have come late to the game, but I know when that game is played by a liar and a cheat who would deny Americans their very right to compete in democracy, to engage in the democratic process. Because inherent in the Constitution I took an oath to uphold is the fundamental right to vote in American elections.

"As we have gathered here to engage in this democratic process these past few days, the president has repeatedly vowed to prevent Americans from voting. He claims those who are otherworldly should not be entitled to vote or to hold office, and yet who among us does that not include?

"The Constitution bestows the right to vote on US citizens from all walks of life, and all forms of life. It doesn't matter when you got here or where you came from, or why. Whether you choose to serve this nation by wearing a uniform or launching a run for office, or by casting a vote for the candidate of your choice, you are an American who deserves to be respected and appreciated by the nation you serve.

"That is why I am now a member of the Omnipresent Party, and I am not alone. I am joined today by two likeminded individuals who also know a thing or two about battle and engaging our enemies. Please welcome to the stage and to the Omni Party, the latest former secretary of defense and commandant of the United States Marine Corps!"

Chapter 64

In the initial weeks following the convention, Rauc and Roger were off engaging in a bug blitz across the nation and, it turns out, in Great Britain, where the prime minister and too many members of parliament from the Conservative Party were advocating the otherworldly should not be entitled to citizenship. None of which had anything to do with me, except it could not have been a worse time to lose my personal protection.

Overnight I went from a few thousand followers on Twitter to a couple hundred thousand and counting, despite not tweeting a darned thing in almost a month. My name and face were instantly recognizable to anyone who'd watched the convention or the news, or who were prone to political chatter on social media. "Mr. President, out of the gene pool!" was currently a wildly popular meme, though decidedly unpopular with the HUMANS FIRST! contingent.

"How am I supposed to grocery shop? You can't always be available, and it's still too hot for a disguise with a wig," I told Win when I called him.

"You need something more subtle to blend in and not be noticed," he said. "That is, if you're hell-bent on not waiting until I can accompany you."

"Have you met my cat, Morris? Don't get me started on what it'll be like if I run out of canned food or kitty litter!"

Now a week later, I realized Win was right about one thing. Given how I'd been on TV with elaborate hair and makeup and fancy duds, the best way to blend involved letting vanity lose out to frumpy anonymity. This meant no makeup and putting my hair either in a ponytail with a ballcap or piled up under a big straw hat. And I started wearing readers at the store, which helped with seeing prices in ridiculously small print anyway.

It also helped that people in low places were increasingly preoccupied with daily happenings, because our iridescent insects in their flashy spacecraft were busy-ass bugs indeed. They needed to be, what with armed idiots storming statehouses in protest of the mere existence of the otherworldly, intending to besmirch and intimidate members of the Omni Party.

It unfortunately started in Carson City, thanks to the convention held in Nevada, but proceeded like dominos dropping to Michigan, Georgia, Florida, Alabama, Indiana, Iowa, Arkansas, Idaho, Wisconsin, both Dakotas, Louisiana, and (very sadly) Texas, all of which joined in the humiliation of looking ridiculous on national TV with crazed constituents sprayed by bugs and babbling like Porky Pig.

The president doubled down, tweeting the usual, "All aliens are evil and must be destroyed," learned from too many movies created by guess who? Pathologically projecting humans. Headlines that followed:

"PRESIDENT: MY OPPONENTS ARE NASTY ALIENS OUT TO GET ME"

"ELECTIONS ARE BAD FOR AMERICA, TWEETS PRESIDENT"

"ALIENS WILL STEAL AND CHEAT ELECTION, SAYS PRESIDENT"

The next wave of the Iridescent Insect War commenced after the president proclaimed the armed and violent hatemongers to be "proud patriots doing good," saying police shouldn't intervene because they support him and not "nasty aliens and alien lovers."

At dawn's early light on Friday preceding Labor Day, when it was especially cloudy because everyone knows it always rains on three-day weekends, a message was first detected on the White House lawn, followed by the same words appearing in the inner courtyard at the Pentagon, on the outer lawn at Homeland Security headquarters, and on the sidewalk in front of the Department of Justice outside the AG's office. Next up was Fox News headquarters as well as Calamity's front lawn, all either burned into grass or lasered onto concrete with the message: "DON'T BE STUPID."

And not just in any old color. The warning was iridescent, sparkling in boldly bright colors of the rainbow.

The Everlasting Evangelical Ministry leader commenced crowing about God having miraculously protected his front lawn from "evil aliens who fornicate with feminazis." Problem was, he couldn't see the message laser-painted onto the roof of his home and that of his broadcasting headquarters. Footage was soon obtained via media drones, airing repeatedly on the hour up to and during his Sunday-morning tirade about how "God hates all aliens so we must smite them down!"

I called Win. "Why no peep from Jax Smith at SlayNews?"

"Rowdy ran into a snag, namely Jax drunk and ranting in his backyard all night. By dawn they decided to go ahead and laser his front yard, figuring he'd pass out soon enough. He didn't. And he was also armed with a pistol he knew absolutely nothing about using and began erratically firing in all directions."

"So Rowdy hit him with the bug juice," I said.

"Yes, but Genie also came out to protect the neighbor's dog, who was barking and in the line of fire. So they had to take Jax with them, whereupon he babbled the reason he was raving drunk all night in his yard. Something about a little blue pill not working. And when he saw Genie, he asked her if she was the bimbo who starred in his favorite porn film."

"Is he still alive?"

"Yes, but he'll walk funny for some time, I expect, and no patriot pill or suppository will help. He's also in the care and custody of Greens, so he won't remember seeing Rowdy or Genie, among other things."

"Other things?"

"As far as I can detect, he will not remember the past two years."

"He won't know about the great alien revelation?"

"No, but everything's fake news or a conspiracy, right? So he'll be back where he started."

"Where are you now?" I asked.

"In Washington. The Sunday-morning talk shows will have a field day with this."

"And you're providing them with as much information as possible."

"Me? How would I do that, sweet pea?"

Chapter 65

On Saturday morning when I walked Bodie, my neighbors Darius and Eddie were out working on cars. When Darius saw me, he said, "I've never lived next door to a celebrity!" Eddie's wife, Wanda, came flying out her front door saying, "Out of the gene pool!"

We had a little meeting in the middle of the street, which Bodie milked for belly rubs.

Eddie asked, "Do you have any inside information about these insect aliens? We try to keep an eye out in the neighborhood, but I've never seen one of their spacecrafts."

"I have, coming home from work," said Wanda. "They really don't look scary."

"No, they don't, and from what I know, that's not who we need to worry about. I've got bad guys in the town where I used to live who aren't too happy with me. You might want to keep an eye out for trucks or cars with HUMANS FIRST! stickers or flags."

"Like those dudes that protested at the state capital?" asked Darius.

"Exactly. I only have a few people who visit regularly at this point."

"That huge guy in the red Ferrari?"

"Yes." I grinned at Wanda's expression as she pictured Roger. "And there might be a jeep or a burnt-orange pickup."

"That F8 Tributo must be one sweet ride," said Eddie.

"Is the driver a Red Orbiter? What are they like?" asked Wanda.

"They are fascinating and good people. Also very protective of me, so they're protective of this neighborhood."

On Saturday afternoon I received two phone calls. First I heard from Rauc on the phone he gave me, now working again.

"Why don't you just shout out to me with your amazing voice?" I asked.

"I'm trying to respect your space, Copper. Especially since I haven't been around to help you learn how to manage your skill. And can I just say how bummed I am to have also missed most of the baseball season? I'd like to suggest we go to the World Series in October, but the way things have gone, I'm afraid I'll jinx it by asking." He sounded so sweet and tired.

"I'm always happy to hear from you any way you choose to reach out," I said.

"Glad to hear it. I'm back in town but exhausted. I know I'll see you at our post-op meeting at headquarters Tuesday, but I'd like us to get together tomorrow. We can go wherever you want, do whatever you want—I just want time with you. And I'll sweeten the offer with the chance to ask me one big question that's been eating at you. Maybe two."

I was tempted to suggest dashing off to Monterey Bay, but Monday was Labor Day, and my Red Orbiter pilot might need a break.

"Do you have a favorite spot you can pick up a pizza from and come to my place? I can put together a salad and open a bottle of wine. And I bought some pistachio gelato the other day. We could watch movies and talk and avoid hundred-plus temperatures and crowds."

"Sounds wonderful. Any John Wayne movies?" he teased.

"Maybe just one. And definitely *Bull Durham* and *Hope Floats*."

The next call was not pleasant. Tim Rider warned me to expect to hear from his partner this week, but Bart jumped the gun and called over the holiday weekend.

"This is Bart Reynolds from Homeland!" he barked into the phone, notably not addressing me at all. "We need to meet Tuesday at our office about the recent alien aggression in the Double-I War."

"Are you certain you've identified the aggressor accurately? Is the government at all concerned about armed domestic terrorists threatening American citizens in state capital buildings? And I'm not available Tuesday."

"We have information that puts you in the middle of this bug activity, Mrs. Layne!" His Adam's apple had to be bobbing to beat the band.

"Who's 'we,' Bartholomew? And by what possible lawful means did you obtain this alleged information?"

"My mother is the only person who calls me that, and you are not at liberty to know how we obtain our information!"

"My mother is Mrs. Layne. Would you like to speak with her? Because I am *not* Mrs. Layne. And you called me. Demanding to meet. Show a little respect for your job, and exercise some civility and decorum. I can meet Wednesday, five o'clock, same location, and I will not be alone nor should you be. None of these terms are negotiable, and all will expire in ten seconds if you say anything other than thank you."

I disconnected from that call after receiving the proper, if not grudging and sullen, response, and I called Win. "Homeland meeting set, so add that for discussion Tuesday. And I hope there's still a protective shield around my house because Bart is not a happy camper and neither are the dudes in Yearntown. I'm staying off social media, but that doesn't mean I don't have friends telling me the vile things they're saying."

"You're protected, sweet pea. When we talked yesterday, you said you had everything you needed to hunker down for the weekend. You still good? I don't fly back until Monday."

"I'm good." No way was I telling him Rauc was coming over. "Can I ask you a question?"

"I happen to know you can, and are very capable at asking questions."

I rolled my eyes. "Are there Greens in DC?"

"Abrupt segue there, counselor. But not generally, as this is not a hub for them. But if you're asking if some are here right now, yes. It's been quite stormy."

"So they've traditionally preferred remote locales."

"It would appear so, especially these days. Can you blame them?"

Chapter 66

Rauc and I spent four hours on Sunday watching movies, and three more hours in bed. We were now eating the remains of two pizzas, both of which had garlic and one had Oregano Wortnik and a hybrid basil with three kinds of extraterrestrial mushrooms.

"I'm shocked at your restraint. You haven't bombarded me with questions," said Rauc.

"I can't decide whether to focus on Greens or Red Orbiters."

"Why don't you start with Greens and we'll take it from there?"

"Okay, but first, Chaco Canyon. What the heck happened there?"

Rauc laughed. "Not anything having to do with Greens or us. They returned to the star of their origin, in a cluster you know as Pleiades. Hybrids born on Earth chose to travel with them. Similar to many ancient civilizations here, not everyone chooses to remain indefinitely."

"Are Greens like that?"

"Greens are not from any planet or star in Pleiades. And before you ask, I can't tell you, as it's their story to reveal. They're very secretive out of self-preservation, and it's served them well. Compared to the human hybrid population, their numbers are few."

"So what can I know? Do they exist elsewhere on Earth? How do they reproduce?"

"Yes, they exist elsewhere, such as Great Britain, and there is much lore surrounding their identity. But they don't reproduce like humans. When and if one of their number dies, its inner core, what humans might call a spirit, gets reborn into a new body. A body produced much like a butterfly."

"And like Luna moths, they don't have mouths. Creepy correlation." I shook my head. "Can you tell me what happened in Roswell? Were Greens taken to an Air Force base in Ohio?"

"What I tell you cannot be reported." Rauc's teal eyes bore into mine. "Three of them were taken from the crash site, two alive. Greens were easily able to escape their military captors when they chose to do so, and they took the inner core of their dead compatriot with them, leaving the body, which was photographed and studied."

"Why would they leave the body?"

"Greens knew there'd be a government cover-up and also knew no pertinent information could be gleaned from the body, other than their existence, which would not be revealed or would be adamantly denied if questioned."

"They wanted a cover-up!" I stood abruptly, pacing with a slice of pizza in my hand. "They use the government's patriarchal protectionist tendencies to their advantage. And you said they escaped when they *chose* to do so?"

"Of course." Rauc grinned. "Why waste a stellar opportunity to gather situational intelligence inside a very large military installation, as well as obtain information directly from the minds of anyone and everyone operating there? Not to mention their talent for mind manipulation."

"Keep your friends close and your enemies closer. They've been inside Area 51, haven't they?" I sat down and took a bite of pizza.

"They've been everywhere. And the vast majority of UFO sightings other than orbs are their crafts. Something else you might get a kick out of is they create cloud cover just as we do. Part of their weather manipulation repertoire. Although they tend toward stratus not cumulus, including those thin, saucer-shaped clouds I once heard you remark upon. Excellent camouflage." He winked. "I think they've created clouds that look like the Starship *Enterprise* just to screw with humans."

"Speaking of screwing with humans, when were you going to tell me your real age?" I twisted towards him, eyes squinting.

Rauc eyed me back, and his lips weren't twitching. "Would you like to rephrase that in a tone that doesn't imply I've been deliberately keeping something from you? Or I could answer you with an attitude adjustment."

"Attitude adjustment?"

"Tossing your sassy ass over my knee again."

"I've been wanting to ask you about that too, but this age thing is bugging me, and it isn't like you didn't keep other stuff from me." I moped and also squirmed, sipping my wine.

"If I remember correctly, I explained why I did not share certain things with you. Right after I tanned your behind, which I greatly enjoyed doing. It's excellent stress relief, for starters. Does that answer anything you'd been meaning to ask?"

"I didn't mean to make you mad." I looked down at my hands, wanting to bite my nails.

"I'm not." Rauc lifted my chin, cupping my face in his palm. "But it isn't good to let you walk all over me. Instinct tells me you wouldn't respect me much if I did."

"Instinct? Or was it research you did on me like your spook brother and Roger to learn private things? Just part of your observation process?" I pulled my face from his grasp.

"I am not Rowdy or Roger, and whatever they know, they didn't learn from me."

"But I thought the whole John Wayne–movie-scene thing meant you knew about me."

"If I did, it was merely instinctual. In my professional life, I've had to be passive, measured, and controlled. That control serves me well, but in private I'm less inclined to passivity. Although for a long time, I've suppressed that side of me."

"So you're just naturally dominant as opposed to merely kinky?" I taunted.

Rauc laughed. "You bring it out in me, and when you threw a fit about me withholding Red Orbiter skills, I decided what the hell? I'm not holding back anymore."

Chapter 67

We were back in bed, and when I got up to turn on the ceiling fan, Rauc remarked on what "nice red orbs" I had.

"So it's a Red Orbiter thing, this dominant tendency?" I asked, feeling my face flush.

"It does seem to run strong with our kind." His lips twitched. "Some more than others, though. Just like human hybrids."

I lay in bed, my toes curling at this titillating turn of events.

"I can feel you forming questions," said Rauc.

I rolled my upper body onto his chest. "I can't help but want to know as much as possible about such fascinating creatures."

"Enough with the flattery." He swatted my butt. "As I told you before, in your years I'm nearly fifty. But it's not the whole story, and it's not up to me when you get to know, kind of like the origin of Greens. How we age, or more specifically, how we die or can be killed, is closely guarded information for obvious security reasons."

"You don't look anywhere near fifty." I sighed. "I suppose it also can't be revealed in the Red Orbiter book I was supposed to write? Am I still writing it?"

"Yes, you are, Copper, if you choose to. But you're right, certain information will not be revealed. Though this might be handled by stating Red Orbiters don't age in the same manner, or at the same rate, as humans. I'll tell you part of it, as long as you keep it to yourself."

"That's a big responsibility. Maybe you shouldn't tell me." I looked away from him, marvelously sprawled in my bed.

"You can handle it." He rolled in my direction and pulled me into his embrace. "Red Orbiters don't necessarily have to age past a certain point. For the most part, we can live beyond a typical human lifespan if we choose to. The best way to describe it is some of us decide to remain at a particular age for any number of years. We stall at a time ideally suited to performing our specific gifts or roles."

"So you're immortal?"

"Not really. Let me explain what I've chosen, because it involves you. The ideal age for an observer tends to be older, more seasoned. For my role, I've grown into it enough to learn it's best not to be too young but also not too old, in order to perform the physical aspects, which is also true of Rowdy's role."

"Why is Oz so old then?"

"Red Orbiters who choose vocations on Earth in the public eye, such as an astronaut or a senator, must appear to age at some point. They must publicly retire to maintain their identities if they choose to remain here."

"So Senator Rojas-Ortiz is not really in her fifties?" My heart pounded because she wasn't the only Red Orbiter I wanted to ask about.

"Actually, she pretty much is. She chose her ideal age once she was elected to office but will have to age at some point as a public figure."

"And you? What are your plans for aging?" I looked up at him.

"Not all that long ago, I decided to stall at the age I am now, but that changed when I met you. I would like to grow old with you, Copper."

"I…I don't know what to say. Am I worth giving up this age stalling you can do?"

"I don't see it as giving anything up. Quite the opposite. I'm gaining a life spent the way I wish to live it, with someone I choose to live it with. I've already spent a lifetime giving up a great many things."

"I can't imagine what it must be like to get to choose to stay a certain age. When I think about it, I realize I wouldn't want to go through most decades over again. And if I did, I'd redo my forties before I'd go back to my twenties."

"Well, there you go. Plus, for Red Orbiters it's not so much a do-over as it is a honing, a refining of what we've learned through the ages."

"Why go backward if you can move forward doing what you're good at, what you love?"

"Exactly. But there's something else we need to discuss. I'm surprised you haven't asked me Roger's age."

I averted my eyes. "I knew he couldn't be in his thirties. I also knew the situation with him was something you probably knew about. I don't know what to say about that either."

"Then let me say it. First, Roger's age and his story are also not for me to tell but up to him to reveal. I can say he has extraordinarily enhanced physical abilities ideally suited for a youthful age, but his powers also call for restraint that maturity bestows. He struck a balance in his early thirties." Rauc took my chin in hand, making me meet his gaze. "As for the chemistry between you two, don't beat yourself up about it. Women are inherently attracted to him—that's just how it's always been."

I snorted. "And I'm sure he takes full advantage of his appeal!"

"Actually, Roger does not take liberties with human hybrid women, and he doesn't engage with everyone who would like him to. But I'm more concerned about Win. He's been sweet on you for ages, and he's a human hybrid like you."

"You think it's an advantage for him not to be alien?" I pulled back, eyes wide.

"Of course. It's what you know. He ages like you do, his life experiences are not so vastly different from yours."

"Sure they are." I sat up in bed. "The guy was a CIA clandestine operative. Who knows what he's done or capable of?"

"I suppose it doesn't help to note that you could say the same about me, and especially about Rowdy and Roger." Rauc's lips twitched. "And due to current responsibilities, I can't devote my entire focus on us right now even if I'd like to. But I want you in my life, Copper, even if it means sharing you with others. We've got time to figure this out, and when it comes to you writing our Red Orbiter story, I'm the one who will be right alongside you."

Chapter 68

Rauc and I were having coffee Labor Day morning, and I gave him his in a mug with green aliens in a flying saucer. He arched his brow at me.

"I need a Red Orbiter mug. At least the little green men on this one have antennae. Like bugs?" I smirked.

He pulled me to him as if to hug me but smacked my bottom instead. Morris meowed in response and swished his too-long tail around Rauc's legs. Alien colluder.

"Your coffee cup's got a genetic mutation on it," he said.

"I knew it!" I said, sipping from my Texas armadillo mug. I was fixing to ask him about tortoises when my phone rang. "It's my sister."

"Answer it. I don't mind."

I barely got in a hi before G let loose. "Hell has frozen over! *Your mother* is now wearing a pair of Burpinstalks for her eightysomething feet—"

"Wait, what are Burpinstalks?"

"Oh crap. Now she's got me talking like her. *Birkenstocks.* You know, the sandals she's spent thirty years calling other people tacky for daring to give up style for comfort?"

"How'd it happen?"

"It's the only shoe that doesn't bother her freaking toes. Believe me, she tried on twelve pairs of sandals I had to order online, and summer is officially over as far as retailers are concerned. It was brutal. Now I have to mail back eleven pairs. But that's not all! Oh no! She got a wild hair and ordered herself a recliner!"

"Not the tacky, never-will-one-of-those-set-foot-in-my-living-room chairs?"

"You got it sister! It's being delivered tomorrow, and she was not pleased they couldn't deliver it today. So how is your Labor Day going?"

"I think *our* mother was abducted and replaced with an alien of indeterminate species and alternative taste,'" I said, watching Rauc's eyebrows elevate again as his lips twitched. "And speaking of aliens, Rauc is here right now."

And Rauc swatted my butt again for the alien gibe.

"Well, that's exciting. Tell him hi. Dad loves the emails he sent."

"What emails?" I looked at Rauc who grinned broadly.

"He's been telling Dad stories of his Red Orbiter adventures," said G. "Dad told Phil about it. And Rauc said he wanted to take him to a Red Sox game, but he's been too busy."

"Yes, he certainly has been busy." I narrowed my eyes at Rauc. "He's heading out soon for yet another meeting, so let's talk more later."

I got off the phone and narrowed my eyes at Rauc. "One more thing you didn't tell me."

"It was a nice way to reach out once I got back. I thought you'd be pleased. Your dad told me all about his Navy days navigating by the stars."

"I am pleased." I sighed. "Thank you for that."

"And thank you for this wonderful time. I'll see you tomorrow, Copper." Rauc kissed me, lifting me to the tips of my toes while he did so. A heady thrill.

Minutes after he left, my phone rang. The new Mom.

"Happy Labor Day, Doodles! I have a new pair of sandals, and my foot is no longer a triple-A *narruh* because I've gained weight, *dadgummit.* So I'm doing Renee Gregg. They send meals, and I talk to the nicest gal in California about my weight-loss goals. You should try it!"

Mom clearly didn't realize Renee Gregg was a right-wing supporter of the current administration. Was I going to be the one to tell her? I didn't think so.

"I'm trying to eat less precooked packaged food," I said, which was kind of a fib. "So I hear from G you're getting a new chair?"

"Oh yes! But not until tomorrow, which annoys me to no end. They say it's a La-Z-Boy, but I'm calling it my lazy lady! It's nicer than the one your father has in his TV room that's full of cookie crumbs he thinks he's hidden from me, but I know he's eating them while he watches golf!"

When I got off the phone, I said to Morris and Bodie, "I don't know why Rauc would want to grow old. No wonder Roger is staying young. But how the heck old do we think he is? I bet he's never had a La-Z-Boy! Probably not one big enough to fit him!"

"Old enough to appreciate you, beautiful. And young enough to handle that wicked tongue of yours that says the most riling things," said Roger in my ear, making me slosh my coffee, luckily no longer hot.

"Damn it!"

"Just popping in to tell you I'll be driving you to our meeting tomorrow. And before you open that mouth of yours to argue, know that I can be on your doorstep in seconds to impress upon you the importance of not driving alone."

"How about I won't put up a fight if you'll tell me how old you really are?"

No answer. Infuriating.

"I know you can hear me, Roger Ramjet!"

Chapter 69

"I should warn you, I'm grumpy because I didn't sleep well," I told Roger as I got into his Ferrari. "My shower developed a drip every ten seconds, and do you know what that sounds like at three in the morning? Plus, are we ever going to have cooler temperatures, or is it going to be this way until Christmas? And I can't schedule a repairman until Thursday because—"

Roger reached over and stroked his fingers across the back of my neck.

"Ahhh!" I stopped speaking as waves of delicious tremors pulsed through me.

Once I regained composure I said, "You know that could be considered sexual assault."

Roger glanced my way, not smiling. "I can fix your showerhead."

"But that would mean letting you into my bedroom," I said, still kind of panting. Actually, after imagining Roger in my bedroom, I was hyperventilating.

"Breathe, beautiful. Don't you have questions you'd like to take this opportunity to ask? About something other than my age."

"Did you or Rowdy look into my background, dig up dirt about me?"

"Yes, but why would you call it dirt? We needed to know about you."

"But how did you know about…you know…"

"Can't say the word? The answer is books you bought, movies you watched, websites you frequented, blogs you read, people you dated. Do I need to elaborate?"

"No, that's quite enough, thank you." I huffed, feeling flushed.

"You're gorgeous when you blush. Why don't I tell you something about me? Would that make you feel better?"

"I don't know," I grumped, frowning.

"I'm a twin. Maggie and I are twins, though not identical of course."

"Wow. So Red Orbiters have twins."

"Yes, because it's an alien thing. Twins and other multiple births occur in human hybrids due to the existence of alien DNA. It's like a recessive gene."

"So Elvis really was an alien," I said, chuckling.

"Good to hear you're feeling better."

Due to Roger driving a hundred miles an hour and somehow getting away with it, we were at Red Orbiter regional headquarters in Valley of Fire in no time.

As we entered, Oz walked up with a mug in each hand. "Rauc said you wanted a Red Orbiter mug, but we don't have one. It'd just be a cup with a red circle on it. But we do have a new OW Coalition mug, and this other one has an owl for the Omni Party."

"Thanks, Oz. These are great." I hugged him, noting the OW logo was indeed as my friend George once described, a spherical O and an italicized W, the symbol for sound energy density. I particularly liked the color, bright green.

Rauc came to hug me as well, and ostensibly to steer me away from Roger. We took a seat at a large table where Win waved from the opposite side. He was seated next to Red MacLeod, a new addition to our group. Next to him were Genie Robertson and Rowdy.

Oz got the meeting started by noting how Greens came through for us with a hellacious and effective thunderstorm, allowing a pistachio craft to penetrate restricted airspace long enough to leave messages at the White House and Pentagon, along with all other locales in the Capital Beltway area.

"The president and his cronies are obviously running scared that we so easily penetrated their defenses, and they have not realized this wasn't all we penetrated. We're now able to anticipate potential plans prior to their occurring due to incoming intel," said Win. "We have recorded discussions, email traffic, as well as some written documentation thanks to Greens."

"They do like to pilfer paper, don't they?" I laughed, imagining little gray creatures slipping into the Oval Office. But all this talk of penetration had me shifting in my seat. Rauc put his hand on my thigh, which didn't help.

"Rom," said Oz, "you want to give us the rundown on how your mission went?"

I looked around, wondering who Rom was. Until Rauc started to speak.

"Wait," I said. "Why did you just call Rauc 'Rom'?"

"Busted," said Win, grinning.

"I guess because he's my nephew." Oz shrugged. "I often use his original name instead of his Earth name. You probably think Oz stands for Olin Zachary, but I had to come up with something more legit than Ozymandias for my astronaut name. I'm not from Ohio either."

"Damn, I liked that about you. Like John Glenn." I turned to Rauc. "So what's your real name, and why didn't you tell me before?"

"It didn't seem pertinent. I told you Raucous and Rowdy were our Earth names. My original name is Romulus."

"Romulus? What's a Romulus?"

"King of Rome. Son of Mars. Except Romans got the name from aliens, of course."

"Are you named for a Roman ruler too?" I asked Rowdy.

"No. My name's Ferus," he smirked. "It's Latin for 'wild.'"

"So your name is actually Wild Wilde?"

"No, because Wilde is an Earth name too," said Rowdy. "But our sister, Ophelia, really is Ophelia."

"And my brother, Bruce, is Bruce. Though my original name is Eugenia, which I hate," said Genie.

"And O.W. really is Octavius," said Roger.

"And you?" I pinned Roger with my gaze. "What's your name? Some sort of ruler too?"

"His name's Domitian," crowed Rowdy. "So yeah, a Roman ruler, among other things."

"Okay, so what else do I not know?" I asked, using my consternation to mask total discombobulation at that *name* of Roger's. "Is this not really Red Orbiter headquarters for Nevada or the western United States?" I floundered.

"Nevada? Why would you think that?" said Oz. "This is regional headquarters for the entire North American continent. And I'm head of it, although getting ready to retire. I want to get back to flying now that we have this new spacecraft."

"How did I not realize all this? I think I need a minute," I said.

"You're not going to get mad at us again for not telling you stuff, are you?" asked Rowdy. "Cause Dom here—"

"Ferus, you might want to rethink anything you're planning to blather," said Roger, his voice a deadly monotone.

"Great," I said. "We've got a Rom, a Dom, all we need is a Com to make this a kinky romantic comedy."

At least I cracked Genie up.

"Why don't we take a lunch break? Because we do in fact eat, Rowan, in case you were wondering about that," teased Oz. "And then we'll discuss your upcoming meeting with Homeland, plus your next foray into reading about Luna Moth Woman at this writers group."

Chapter 70

In the end it was decided Red would accompany me to meet with Homeland to throw Bart off his game, and Roger and Genie would provide security. Rauc wanted to go, but he and Rowdy had known histories with me, a distinct disadvantage for this.

Riding in a rental car put me at unexpected risk due to the Scotsman being a seriously erratic driver, though Red was better than the average Las Vegas resident in that he managed to stop at red lights.

Yesterday, driving home with Roger, aka Domitian, had been awkward for different reasons. He was tight-lipped about his name and background, but at least he came in and fixed my showerhead before leaving me with a breath-robbing kiss to make me regret his not staying.

"So what's your real first name?" I asked Red as we merged onto the freeway and I cringed.

"Colin," he said, switching lanes in a manner that portended whiplash.

"Oh good. I feared it was Duncan and you might be the Highlander."

"No, but according to the story, immortals were aliens from another planet." He grinned at me. "Has Win had a chance to speak with you about coming with us to Washington?"

"No. What about it?" I pressed my hands on the dashboard.

"There's talk of you eventually replacing Warren O'Neill's congressional seat."

"Not interested." I shook my head. "Maybe twenty years ago, but I don't want to have to live there or deal with the insanity."

"Okay then, let's go over the plan. I want to make sure I get it right," said Red.

We arrived unscathed at Planet Wynne, where Roger and Genie met us at the entrance to Galaxy Table looking like total badasses in tight black pants and t-shirts, though Genie's Jessica Rabbit curves defied camouflage.

Bart and Tim were already seated at a table. Red and I sat opposite them while Roger and Genie stood behind me.

"What is this?" spluttered Bart. "Are they Red Orbiters?"

"Good guess, lad, aren't you the clever one? I'm not a Red Orbiter, but the name's Red."

"You're the former secretary of defense." Bart gaped.

"Aye, that I am," said Red. "But unlike your bosses, I was actually vetted and confirmed by Congress."

"Hi, Tim, good to see you," I said. "I was afraid your so-called partner here would cut you out of this meeting like he has so much of his recent questionable activity."

Bart's Adam's apple did a dance of distress. "Just what are you accusing me of?" His eyes darted from me to Roger to Genie, where they bulged tellingly before shooting to Red as he began speaking.

"Last week certain members of Congress were provided more than three thousand emails, texts, and vocal recordings by your boss, the acting deputy director for cybersecurity, who clearly knows nothing about keeping his communications even remotely secure—or professional. Contained in his discussions were numerous racial slurs and alien slurs against individuals in Congress, including the vice-presidential candidate, as well as inappropriate and derogatory comments about women, some of a sexual nature, including Ms. Layne and her mother."

"But that's not—"

"There's more, so hold your tongue, lad. Aye, you might want to be obtaining a lawyer." Red warned. "DHS communications about Ms. Layne were based upon her emails and texts, illegally obtained in violation of her First Amendment rights of free speech and association, her Fourth Amendment right to be free of unreasonable government search and seizure, and her Ninth Amendment right to privacy. Did I get them all?" He said to me.

I nodded, staring silently at Bart Reynolds.

"So, Bart, ask yourself one question," continued Red. "Does this evidence, being released to the media as we speak, does it show you willingly participated in this disgusting and disgraceful disregard for civil liberties, not to mention incendiary hate speech? Because you shall not do so with impunity, nor shall you be allowed to undermine and destroy reputations of those with whom you work who do not share your lack of integrity for upholding the rights of Americans."

Roger moved to tower over Bart, saying, "And if you're contemplating retaliation against your colleague or Rowan Layne, don't. It would not reflect well on you. Your boss is not going to protect you, and neither will the president. Man up, and do the right thing."

"I tried many times to tell you this was wrong and wouldn't end well, Bart. I hope you'll listen now," said Tim, shaking his head.

"Were you the leaker?" He asked Tim, belligerent but fading fast.

"No, Bart. I don't have direct access to the deputy secretary's communications. But apparently you do, as your name is involved. They've used you, and it's up to you to decide what to do about it. I'm certainly not going to lie for the acting deputy secretary or anyone else."

"Does it really matter how this illegal activity and offensive behavior came to light?" I interjected. "People are responsible for their own actions no matter who calls them on it."

"Let's go, Tim," said Bart, standing and snarling at me.

Tim remained seated. "I'm having dinner with my girlfriend. Here she is now," he said as Maggie walked into the bar.

Bart's eyes bulged as his throat bobbed. "She looks like a Red Orbiter." His tone was nasty, his eyes spewing hatred.

"Thank you," said Maggie.

"Seriously, Bart? This woman could kick your ass six ways to Sunday," I said. "You need to leave before she, or her brother here"—I cut my eyes to Roger—"takes offense at your sneering presence."

Bart skedaddled from the bar when Roger took a step in his direction.

"One down. How many more to go?" said Roger, smiling.

Chapter 71

This morning as I stepped from the shower I saw the tiniest of beetles on my bathroom floor. No way was I squashing it.

About the same time, a feminine voice slipped into my ear. "Rowan, it's Genie. I didn't get a chance to ask last night if you'd be up for a girls night with Maggie and me. She wants to pick your ear about human hybrid men. She's crazy about Tim and doesn't want to screw it up."

"Okay," I said. "But I'm hardly an expert on human men."

"You're kidding, right?"

"No, but let's wait to meet until after this writers meeting hoedown next Tuesday. The bossy boys don't want me out in public until then."

Genie made a disgusted sound. "Do you want me to speak to Roger? I dated him for a while, and he is by far the most domineering Red Orbiter ever. Sometimes he needs reminding he can't just move us around like chess pieces."

I laughed. "That sounds a lot like Win, actually."

"Well, that's not good news. I find him very compelling."

We made plans for next week, and I wondered if Win could or would resist the charms of Jessica Rabbit. She wouldn't be his first Red Orbiter. And they were in the same profession.

But I needed to focus on Luna Moth Woman and her final move so I'd have it ready for the writers group meeting next week. Except, speak of the devil, my burner phone rang.

I answered, "Jessica Rabbit thinks you're hot."

A silent pause ensued.

"Genie Robertson?" I said.

"Ah," said Win. "Hell on wheels from what I've heard. But we have business to discuss."

"Of course." I snorted.

"Rauc outdid himself zeroing in on every single dipshit in the Yearntown area cursing your name. All residential lawns, meeting places, and sites of stockpiled weapons were sprayed with 'Don't be stupid,' which of course means they will be, because their kind neither read nor heed messages."

"True, unless it's Fox cheering them to go forth and prove the bigger the gun wielded, the smaller minds they exhibit."

"And here I thought you were going to make a dick joke," he said.

"It's not about size—it's about inability to use that which you have. I trust Greens took care of that as well?"

"Yes, they did. Cleaned out of ammunition at all locales hit by Rauc and Rowdy with rainbow graffiti."

"Maybe we should call this the Iridescent Insects Render Asswipes Impotent War."

"And that's why I love you, sweet pea."

Now it was my turn for a pregnant pause. I scrambled to think of something to say. "Hey, what are Greens doing with all those bullets?"

"Recycling metal, ostensibly to use in spacecraft or some other technology, and the gunpowder's also being repurposed."

"Do tell."

"Very soon, storms will come." He paused dramatically. "With ominous clouds portending torrential rains. Raindrops followed by snow flurries will contain a sticky substance dispersed mysteriously only onto certain vehicles, rendering them inoperable until the atmospheric paste is sandblasted off windshields. And damaged wipers are replaced."

"Not a good time to sport a HUMANS FIRST! bumper sticker?"

"It's going to be a hard-luck winter."

"Hey, quick question," I said.

"No such thing with you."

"Ha ha. Red said you wanted me to visit Washington. Was he serious?"

"He wanted you to—I knew you likely weren't interested in moving back in the future. And I can't say I blame you. When this election is over, I'm putting my townhouse on the market."

"You're not moving to Scotland, are you?"

"No, but I'll spend time there. Mostly I'll be setting up OUTWARD's newest satellite office, a Las Vegas location focusing primarily on acoustics. I might even find time to help you learn to interpret a certain alien language resembling Morse code."

"Well, that's exciting. Maybe my pal George will finally come down to visit me. Are you going to be at Bruce and Ophelia's wedding in October?"

"I'll be there."

I felt panic coming on when I realized this posed yet another event in which all three suitors in my mixed-up mess of a romantic life would be present.

"Do you know anything about the 1950 mass UFO sighting in Farmington, New Mexico?" I spit out.

"I told you there was no such thing as one quick question with you," teased Win. "That was before I was born, but there were a lot of similar sightings in the same time period throughout the Southwest and also in Mexico and Central America. I think Greens were having a big gathering and being defiant about it."

"Defiant?"

"After the Roswell crash, which occurred in part because they were flying at night and trying to avoid human detection, they became less concerned about not being seen and more brazen, knowing the government would suppress those who spoke of or reported sightings, or they counted on humans to silence each other. Members of the Air Force in Tucumcari saw it as well. And all of the Farmington sightings took place close to high noon." Win chuckled. "I personally think Greens were being snarky."

Chapter 72

Before I left for the writers meeting, I had a text from Mom, who I knew was watching evening news I'd been avoiding, along with social media. One can only take so many clips of the president whining about how unfair and nasty it was for anyone to run against him.

"That jackass!!! He is worse than a toddler thinking the world revolves around him!!! And he has the tackiest hair I've ever seen, and his ties are too long and he is totally out of it!!! He sounds like he is ready for the loony bin!!! (wacky face, face with tongue sticking out, flipped bird, red devil mask, pile of poop emoji)"

There it was again, the flipped bird. Not to mention the poop with eyes. And not one heart or shoe or kissy face. Good thing I knew she loved me.

Next a text from my sister: "Dad says Mom is yelling at the TV again. How do we get her to not watch? He says she threw a box of tissue at the screen this morning while the president was speaking. (crazed face, angry face, face holding nose, purple devil face, stick of dynamite, volcanic eruption, flame, red meteorite emoji)"

You knew it was bad when G's emoji exceeded Mom's in number and flair.

I texted G, "Surprised she hasn't found the face-with-Pinocchio-nose emoji yet. Hang in there. I'm reading at writers group tonight. (snarky face emoji)"

"You go, sister! Luna Moth Woman has it covered! XO"

I pet the critters and walked outside to my front curb, looking up at cumulous clouds forming over my house and watching Rauc descend from them.

"Beam us up, Rowdy!" I said after Rauc kissed me but before he flipped my torso over his shoulder to take us to the orb.

"What the hell?" I said.

He smacked my behind. "Makes it easier to do that."

"Well, you're certainly getting into this nonpassive new role."

More clouds formed over the casino before the writers group meeting, and Rauc descended with me in a more dignified manner, depositing me at the door. Rowdy zipped off to get ready for the next phase of our operation.

"My goodness, another tall gorgeous man, and a redhead," said Alice, getting out of her car in the parking lot. "Rowan, can we speak before going inside?"

"Sure," I said to the private eye who'd given me nice feedback at a previous meeting.

"Last month," she leaned toward me and lowered her voice, "I was contacted by someone who wanted me to investigate you. They said they were from out of town, pretending to be a government official doing a security clearance, but I knew they weren't because they misspelled *surveillance* in their email." Alice grinned wryly. "I told them no, of course, and wanted to tell you but had no way to reach you, but I saw you on TV."

"That's okay. I appreciate you telling me now. I know who they are. Just so you know, they're likely to show up here tonight. We're prepared, but I don't want you to be surprised."

"Are the Iridescent Insect aliens coming to save Luna Moth Woman?" She smiled.

"Something like that, so avoid the bug juice line of fire." I grinned.

"You did great at that convention," she said as we walked inside.

Win and Red were already seated in the meeting room.

Alice said, "Oh my gosh, isn't that the former—"

"Yes," I said. "He's interested in being an author, at least tonight."

"Aye, that I am, lass." Red winked at us. Win kept a poker face, trick of his trade.

When it was my turn, I didn't bother with introductory remarks, and there was no mention I'd been on TV delivering a speech I wrote, especially from the bigoted blowhard who still had no plot in his misogynistic rants. Was this some sort of passive-aggressive introvert trick, or were they really so unaware of a world in catalytic change?

But I guessed I shouldn't be surprised, as the former secretary of defense also went unacknowledged.

I read my final paragraphs:

> Luna Moth Woman came to the conclusion that these fellow aliens, these masked marauders appearing as iridescent insects, were no enemy of hers, nor the principles she defended. Her crusade for truth was flipped on its ear when she realized the

ultimate enemy of fairness and decency and all that was worth living for on this planet was those who would deny her very right to exist. Those who took up arms to prevent inevitable change, to squelch equality and decry diversity.

She stood before them, defiant in the face of overweening preening emboldened by fellow dastards flanking them, gripping guns as terror leapt within crazed eyes.

"You do not scare me. You who quake in fear and rage at everything you don't understand, everyone who does not seek to demean or destroy as you do. But it is you who defile yourselves. You who long for an enemy at which you can aim and fire and vanquish to assuage a lust for terror. Yet there is not enough firepower in the universe to absolve you of your own inadequacies, your festering hatred for that which you truly detest: yourselves."

I set my pages down and looked up.

"So where's the action? Do they blow the alien bimbo away or what?"

I stared at the bellowing bigot sitting across from me and, unfortunately for him, next to Win, whose barely perceptible movement resulted in a hand on his shoulder. He did a face-plant on the copy of the words I'd been reading.

The meeting proctor was at the opposite end of the table, on the same side, so she didn't witness this silencing of stupidity as she called for more feedback to be lobbed at my person.

"I loved it!" said Alice. "It was excellent commentary on what is happening in our world and how many of us feel."

"Aye," said Red. "Luna Moth Woman is a wise and spirited lass for sure."

A guy who'd not spoken in prior meetings said, "I hope she kicks their idiot asses."

I beamed at him. This might all be worth it.

Chapter 73

The problem was, of course I had to pee by the end of the meeting, a contingency not factored into my security detail.

Five minutes ago Rauc said in my ear, "They're here. Twelve of them, including one woman who went inside and has not yet returned."

"Alice is it?" asked Win. "Would you mind accompanying Rowan to the restroom?"

"No problem," she said, following me out of the meeting room.

As we entered the restroom, a woman with a bad blonde dye job walked out and was startled when she saw me, but she kept moving with an ugly sneer.

I vaguely recognized her. She was, sadly, the wife of a musician in a band with a lead guitarist I'd once dated in Yearntown.

"That woman is dangerously ignorant," I said to Alice, Win, and Red before we proceeded outside, knowing Red Orbiters would hear me. "She once told me it was the absolute truth that the last president's wife was a man, or at least a lesbian, and so was 'that nasty woman who ran for president,' as she put it, and also their children weren't theirs because everyone knows lesbians can't give birth. Her son is one of the idiots who stormed the mine, heavily armed, intent on killing aliens."

The moment we emerged to the parking lot, the crowd of Yearntown vigilantes pressed toward us, the blonde charging forward to attempt to scream in my face, "You alien lover whore! No real man would ever touch you, you ugly redheaded bitch!"

Rauc and Genie stepped from the shadows to block her access to me while Red and Win moved out of the line of fire, taking Alice with them.

"Step away from the alien lover, you mutants!" a man shouted. I recognized both his extremely short stature and his obnoxious voice—the chief of police, heavily armed like the others but not in uniform. "Rowan Layne, you're wanted for helping aliens steal our ammunition! We demand it back, and you'll pay for what we had to buy in Vegas today!"

"Yeah, alien lover bitch! It's your fault aliens came to our town in the first place! Trying to change our way of life! All aliens need to die! Get out of the way before we blow your asses back to wherever you came from! Especially you, you mutant bitch!" He focused his rant on Genie. "You got the police chief arrested!"

That last guy also tried to spit on Genie, but his glob of spittle rebounded and hit him square between the eyes, so he—along with the rest of the jeering mob—were not aware of two pistachio-shaped iridescent crafts landing swiftly behind them while the tires of their assorted vehicles emitted ominous hissing noises.

Then the bleating bigot from the writers group walked outside and shouted, "Look out! We're under attack!"

He didn't mean the armed idiots. He was in gobsmacked fear of three tall—one of them excessively so—sparkly but scary-faced winged bugs advancing behind them.

This made the virility-challenged vigilantes spin about while sloppily firing their weapons, which meant spewed bullets in my direction.

Rauc easily blocked their trajectory as Genie covered me with her body and I was smothered in boobs, thinking many men and more than a few women would kill for this predicament.

At the same time, I felt what could best be described as thick clouds forming in my cerebral cortex, like a sinus clog but not painful, just intrusive, and heard the very faint warning of "Danger!" along with an incoming text ping on my phone. And then I was somehow yanked from underneath Jessica Rabbit and launched into the air.

While in motion I heard Rowdy say, "Son of a bitch! Who dropped the ball on letting the control freaks know we had this covered?" along with frightened wailing followed by Porky Pig babbles that seem to be rising in the air along with me.

Hands were roaming my body, and I was in some sort of room. Two small gray creatures without mouths but huge eyes fussed over me as rapid-fire electronic communication thumped my ears.

"I'm okay. I'm not hurt," I said, realizing they must've thought I'd been hit by gunfire. My phone pinged again. "I need to check my phone. I think my mother's worried about me too."

I was on a table, and the hovering Greens—currently Grays— helped me sit up, one still stroking my arm. I felt my head fill with that cottony sensation and heard, "You. Okay. Mistake. Sorry."

My purse still hung from my shoulder, so I pulled out my phone to read Mom's texts. "Doodles!!! Are you okay!!! Important you contact us!!! Your father thinks something's wrong!!!" And seconds ago, "Doodles!!! Your father says you are in danger!!!"

I typed rapidly, "I'm fine. All okay! Will call later!!!"

I said to my rescuers, "I need to go back. Can you take me, please?"

And just like that, hands lifted me, and I was back on the ground in the parking lot, vigilantes and bugs with their brightly hued spacecraft gone.

Win said, "We'll take care of her, thanks. You go do your thing. Sorry for the misunderstanding."

Rauc wrapped me in his arms, and Genie said, "Don't suffocate the poor woman."

I laughed because it was she who'd almost done that with her boobs minutes ago.

"What's funny, Copper?"

"Well, for one thing, now I can legitimately claim to be an alien abductee!"

"Oh good, I was afraid maybe they screwed with your mind and made you goofy," said Rowdy, appearing from the shadows.

"My goodness, yet another one," said Alice, gaping at Rowdy.

He responded, "I could say the same about you, darlin'. Who's the cute pixie redhead, Rowan?"

"She is a married woman! Paws off," I sniped at Rowdy.

Alice said, "You sure are going to have lots more to write about!"

I froze, realizing Greens might hear her. And she had definitely seen them.

"I can't write about—"

"It's okay, Rowan," said Alice. "I've seen them before. My lips are sealed."

Chapter 74

We were having an impromptu post-op meeting on the second level of Planet Wynne, outside the orb Rauc and Rowdy had flown Win, Red, Genie, and me in. Oz and Roger were waiting for us, removed of wings and bug masks, along with Maggie, who'd flown Roger and filmed the entire event for posterity.

"Greens have all twelve, which was necessary because none of them was especially adept at handling firearms," said Win.

"Not even the Yearntown police chief? I'm shocked," I snarked.

"Don't get me started on him. One of the most ridiculous humans I've ever had to deal with," said Roger.

"Word has it he didn't think so highly of me." I sighed.

"He won't speak your name again," said Rauc, "nor will any of them."

"What? Are Greens wiping their minds of my time in their fair city?"

"No," said Win. "They're being issued an edict to cease all verbal and physical attacks on your person. And to spread the word among their gun-fetish fraternity. Beyond that, who knows? Greens thought they'd shot you." He looked grim.

"Well, someone needs to do something about so many of these warrior wannabes wielding guns they can't handle and aren't trained for," said former Marine Maggie.

"Messages will continue to be issued as needed," said Rowdy. "And I hope they like dust devils. Word has it a huge one did a number on their makeshift shooting ranges last week."

I chuckled, remembering the sustained attacked on Win's RV at Valley of Fire.

"Good to hear you're holding up, lass," said Red. "It isn't every day one gets abducted by Greens and laughs about it."

"I guess maybe now's a good time to tell y'all they've spoken to me?"

"What do you mean, Rowan?" said Win, his voice tight.

"Please don't go all sinister on me." I wrung my hands. "I wasn't keeping anything from you—I didn't realize what it was! They've communicated when they thought I was in danger."

"Are you talking about their electronic language?" asked Win.

"No. Telepathically." I touched my forehead. "I get this cloudy feeling in my head and then hear a faint robotic voice. But oddly soft and pleasant."

I looked at Rauc and Rowdy and Oz, then at Win. All looked stunned.

"You ever hear of anything like that before?" Oz asked Win.

"Never."

"I'm not making it up! I'm not crazy!" I stomped my foot. "Even if I was nearly gunned down tonight by the worst of humanity! How would you feel if the stupidest people alive were after you?" I wished my voice hadn't quavered, and damn it, why did I feel tears coming on?

Roger was instantly by my side, so Rauc put his arm around me and held me close.

Win said, "We believe you. It's just amazing to learn it's possible. I think I'm envious."

"Shocking, actually," said Oz.

"Is there something we're missing in the DNA?" pondered Win.

"Aye, how much of your DNA is Scottish, lass?" asked Red.

Rauc said, "This discussion ends right there. We need to respect Greens and the relationship they have with Rowan. She earned their trust, so let's leave it at that and not mess this up for her. Rowan's still learning how to grapple with her auditory abilities as it is."

"But this is different," I murmured. "I'm sure I wasn't hearing them with my ears. At least it felt completely different."

"I know what it's like to have your abilities doubted and questioned," said Roger. "And most of us can relate to being targeted by ignorance. It's okay to be upset. You've been through a lot, and not just tonight."

"You should have heard her read tonight. She did great," said Win. "The newest guy recruited to attend was freaking out. He's now in custody of Greens too, along with your favorite writer bigot, Rowan."

"Wait, what?" I turned to Win. "Who was at the meeting? And Greens have the sexist blowhard?"

"Yes, they do. He was in the line of bug juice fire when he came outside, along with White House guy behind him. You might not have noticed him. He arrived late and didn't speak."

"Oh, I remember him walking in. He wigged me out. Who wears a leather jacket in this heat?" I scoffed. "I was afraid he was armed, but since you were there, I didn't worry."

"Good thing you couldn't see him smirking throughout the meeting. I wanted to throttle the bugger," said Red. "Except we needed him to report back on what you read."

"So Greens won't be erasing his memory?"

"Only the parts after he left the meeting," said Win.

I started to feel woozy, and then that wooly feeling filled my head. Uh-oh.

"What is it?" said Rauc.

"I think I need to go home. I'm exhausted. And I have to call my folks."

"Yes, and we have a ladies night planned tomorrow, so let Rowan get some rest," said Genie.

"I'll fly you home if you like," said Maggie.

"I'm taking her home," said Rauc. "You can pick her up tomorrow for your evening out."

Chapter 75

It was a three-pod morning with vanilla nut coffee in my OW Coalition mug. My head was foggy with no sign of clear skies. Like a Mom weather report: Cloudy. Ugh. (cloud emoji)

And speaking of Mom, she was at it again. "Martian, glitter bugs, OW? Do we really care who beats this tacky jackass of a president in November??? Now he's trying to get rid of the Post Office so we seniors can't vote by mail!!! Sunny here but readying for rain. How is weather there??? Love to critters from their grandmommy!!! (frowny face, flipped bird, sun, umbrella, dog, cat, kissy face emoji)"

Next up was a private Facebook message from Cate in Yearntown. "Early morning excitement here. Some first thought it was a tornado, even though we've never had one. It was dust devils randomly battering houses and people getting out of their cars at the county commissioners' meeting, including sheriff and two deputies, three commissioners, and head of Chamber of Commerce."

I responded, "What was the meeting agenda?"

"Whether aliens should be allowed to own businesses or work for the county."

"Was the police chief there? Is he still chief after his arrest for attempted murder?"

"He was a no-show. And of course he's still chief. He's put his name in to run for mayor."

"Maybe mayor would be safer than him strutting around with a gun and badge."

***

I was deciding what to wear for girls night when a smooth voice slid into my ear.

"Hi, beautiful. Just checking on how you're doing. And I know you're meeting with my sister tonight, but I'd also like to put in a request for time with you."

"You're requesting rather than scooping me up and away? Wow."

"I see you're feeling more like yourself today," he drawled. "But the scooping can be arranged, if that's your preference."

"No, all this flying willy-nilly into the air makes me woozy, and my head feels stuffed with wool at it is. I'm getting on in years, or don't you know what that's like?"

Roger laughed, and it was a delicious sound. "That's one of the reasons I want to meet with you, this age thing you're so hung up on. What're you going to do if you find out I'm not too young for you after all, beautiful? What happens when you've run out of excuses?"

The thing is, he was in my ear so I couldn't just hang up on him or run away.

"Maybe it's better if I don't meet with you, alone I mean."

"You'd pass on a chance to ambush me with questions and learn all my secrets? That's not the Luna Moth Woman I know."

"No way are you going to tell me all your secrets."

"You sure about that?"

I pondered a good comeback for this phrase I'd heard him utter too many times.

"I'm going to be in and out of town for the next month," he said before I could respond. "Traveling with Senator Rojas-Ortiz, who's campaigning for Omni Party candidates."

"But you'll be at Bruce and Ophelia's wedding, right?"

"Of course. So will the senator. It's a Red Orbiter social event of the season."

"Did you know Ophelia invited my entire family to the wedding? My mother's been planning her outfit for weeks now. And mine." I sighed.

"I'd like to see you before their wedding next month. New outfit not necessary. Nor clothes, for that matter."

The image of Roger's body in nothing but red underwear flashed through my mind.

"You still there, beautiful?"

"Okay, Roger Ramjet, how the hell old are you?"

"One hundred and twenty-five."

Chapter 76

"Your brother is the most exasperating, infuriating, and altogether frustrating creature I've ever met," I told Maggie when she picked me up.

We weren't in an orb—she was driving a VW, a very cute red convertible bug I coveted.

Genie laughed from the backseat. "What was your first clue?"

"Do you realize he had the nerve to get in my head and finally tell me how old he is? Then he disappears liked a popped balloon. I want to strangle him."

"My mother and I empathize," said Maggie.

"Holy cow, I just realized how old your mother must be!"

"She had Roger and me when she was twenty in your years," said Maggie.

"Oh my gosh, you're his twin so you're ancient too. Oops, sorry. No offense!"

Maggie laughed. "None taken. Roger and I decided to stall at roughly the same age."

We arrived at our destination on the Strip, and Maggie took valet parking.

"Your brother would approve," I said.

"Yes, but not of our entertainment choice! Genie picked it. Instead of women servers dancing on the bar like in that movie, it's all men. Serving, dancing, flirting."

"I knew it would bug Roger if we brought you here," said Genie as we walked through the door.

"Great, who's going to protect me if he swoops me away from all this titillation?"

"He's not allowed. Even in your ear. Boys have to butt out tonight," said Genie.

Maggie grinned, which made her look too much like her formidable brother.

I ordered a cocktail that was turquoise and tasted tropical, learning that pineapples were not originally from Earth and were initially blue-green inside until they were genetically messed with. The server's eyes were also turquoise, along with this thong. He had glittery stuff all over his bodybuilder physique, which made me think of the iridescent-tinted bug flight suits.

"Do you like being in your thirties? I don't think I fully appreciated it. I was a lawyer for the Navy and Marines then. Some good times but mostly stressful dealing with other lawyers," I sighed. "And I was married to a Marine, which ended amicably, but I'm not sure I'm the best person for advice about men or relationships."

"When I was a Marine, I never dated any. Didn't want to mix work with pleasure. I have no experience with human male relationships," said Maggie. "But Tim is amazing and thinks highly of you."

"That means he likes mouthy women who challenge him. I wasn't exactly a sweetie pie the first few times we tangled. Also he does like older women, so you've definitely got that covered." I chuckled.

Three nearly naked men danced on the bar to the annoying thump of a monotonous soundtrack.

"The noise is a bit much, isn't it? Let's go to a quieter bar where we can actually converse," said Maggie.

"My bad," said Genie. "I also didn't factor in a preference for brains with our brawn."

We ended up in a staid martini bar, at least by Vegas standards, with a female server and older male patrons ogling Genie. In her tight, flame-red dress, I thought we might soon need to call in paramedics.

"I appreciate you inviting me for girls night. I waited until too late in life to realize how important gal pals are for my psyche and well-being. And my current overabundance of male companions is kicking this old gal's butt. Enjoy it while you're young and can handle it," I said to Genie.

"Hello?" said Genie. "I think Margarida here has a few years on you. And since when did you not have an abundance of men?"

"That's your real name?" I said to Maggie. "Did you two read some file Rowdy or Roger has on me?" I frowned.

"No, I heard Roger muttering something about having to compete with a Secret Service agent," said Maggie.

I giggled, feeling sixteen. "Like Roger ever had trouble competing in his exceedingly long life. What am I going to do about him?" I had to stop myself from chewing my nails.

When Maggie and Genie dropped me off that night, there was a small white envelope propped against my front door. I opened it immediately, much to the consternation of my critters vying for attention. Inside was a card with the Superman logo. The note had nice penmanship, drafted in red ink: "The pleasure of your company is requested at a private gathering in my suite. Friday, 7 p.m. Dress: Casual. Dinner included. Transportation provided. Very truly yours, Domitian."

We'd gone to a comedy show to top off our girls' evening. Lots of cathartic relief for me, though my abdomen muscles were sore from laughing so much. Now I had other muscles, and nerves, twinging. Why on earth did Roger up and use that original name of his?

Was he being formal or indicating a desire to reveal his truths? Or was this his naturally intimidating self? At least he didn't say clothes were optional. But what was I supposed to wear for a "private gathering" with a "casual" dress code? And that Superman shield!

Chapter 77

Forty-two hours later, my doorbell rang. I was in my red dress. Not casual, but I felt good in it, and that's what mattered.

Roger, aka Domitian, was on my doorstep dressed in his uniform of all black.

I pet Bodie and Morris and slipped out the door, not seeing the red Ferrari.

I looked up to see if clouds were hiding a red orb or pistachio craft but saw none, and I was already ascending in Roger's arms. Flying in the direction of the Strat, clearly visible, especially from this altitude.

And yes, I should've felt dizzy or nervous or wigged out, but I didn't. It was like seeing my first UFO. Strange, but somehow not shocking or unexpected. Unless my neighbors were looking out their windows, but would they be surprised?

We landed on the Planet Wynne flight deck and went inside to his suite, Roger holding my hand once he put me on my feet. Dinner was immediately delivered on a cart of covered dishes.

"Rose Bergin?" I asked.

"I'm not much of a cook," said Roger, sheepish, which was strangest of all. "Would you care for a glass of wine or some other libation?"

"Are you having anything?"

"I rarely drink," he said. "But tonight I just might."

"You're the one who's nervous?"

"Is that what this feeling is?" he asked, his face bemused. "It would probably be easier if you'd blitz me with questions."

"How long have you lived as Roger Rogers?" I craned my neck up him.

"Since I was ten and my folks brought us to Earth, to El Paso."

"And you really did go to UT?"

"Yes. I played on the national championship football team in 1914."

"Wow. My dad will want to hear all about that. Oh man, you're older than my father. I think I better sit down and yes, I will have a glass of wine." I moved to the couch.

Roger walked to a minibar and selected a bottle of New Zealand Sauvignon Blanc, a favorite of mine. I watched him uncork it with dexterity.

"I was thinking the other day about how pilots and others in the military say, 'Roger that.' Did you have anything to do with it?"

"*Roger* was the name used for the letter *R* in the military phonetic alphabet for radio communications as early as 1941. Now it's *Romeo*. But it stands for the *R* in 'Message Received.'" He smiled.

"Interesting. But it doesn't answer my question, though I was joking."

"I fought, and flew, in World War II."

"Were you also in Vietnam?"

"No, I'd already stalled in my thirties, and I was a Secret Service agent."

"For Nixon?"

"And Ford."

"Was he clumsy like they said?"

"Yes, and he never stopped cracking jokes. Great guy. Hell of a way to become president," he mused. "Would you like to eat?"

"I know there's something you're waiting to tell me." I took a bite of risotto with artichoke in creamy lemon sauce. "And it's weird to realize you were in DC when I was a kid. Wait a minute. Were Red Orbiters involved in Watergate?"

"Bite your tongue. We were not involved in the scandal. Or the coverup. Did you wear that red dress to torture me? Would you like more wine?"

"Sure, if you'll have a glass with me. You're too tense, and you didn't answer my question. Were you working as a Red Orbiter spy while you were in the Secret Service?"

Roger smiled and reached across the table to pour me more wine. "I'll take the Fifth on that one. You know we've been around forever, so isn't it logical some of us were involved in major historical events? Over time, you'll learn details, but Watergate's not what I invited you here to discuss. You're worse than Lois Lane, beautiful."

"Another Superman reference. Let's talk about that tattoo. Was it something you did on a dare?"

"I got it in the fifties. Tattoos were big then but not like they are today. Wow." Roger shook his head. "I've been around more than a century and can't remember ever feeling this…trepidation?"

"You couldn't just get a naked lady tat like all the other guys? And I already know your actual age, so why are you uptight? It turns out I didn't have to worry about you being too young for me, at least in mind and life experience. But the physical body thing is still unnerving, and overwhelming." I looked away from his all-knowing gaze.

"You're so concerned about physical appeal at your current age. Do you want to hear my theory on why so many human marriages fail?"

"Sure, have at it," I said, sipping my wine, happy he was letting his guard down.

"Most unions occur when people are young and initially drawn to each other, to the youthful versions of each other. This works well for procreation but doesn't always stand the test of time, because people evolve as they age. Which means change. The expanded version of a spouse isn't always appealing to someone who fell for twentysomething attributes."

"So you shouldn't choose a spouse solely for superficial reasons." I shrugged.

"True, but it's not that simple. It's about physical attraction and how big a role it plays."

"The bigger the role, the greater the risk?"

"Possibly."

"That means it's always been a huge risk for you," I said.

"You're very perceptive. Also, those of us who've been around for a while aren't as hung up on the human ideal of a youthful feminine form."

"Easy for you to say, Superman!"

"About that. It's part of my identity. Being who I am, this body is part necessity, part image. I developed myself to look this way because it complements my enhanced abilities."

"Enhanced abilities? Is this like leaping tall buildings in a single bound, being more powerful than a locomotive, stopping bullets?

Wait a minute." I put down my wine glass and leaned towards him. "Are you telling me you're Superman?"

Roger's bright-green eyes peered into mine and imprisoned my gaze as I held my breath.

"Yes," he said, but his lips didn't move. The word was inside my head. "I was the impetus for the comic book character," said Roger aloud. "I am an alien, after all, and there were people who witnessed my abilities if they were paying attention, as two guys were back in the thirties. Although I never had that black hair. I think they thought a headset we used was hair."

"You have got to be kidding me." I reached for my wine glass.

"I'm also Roger Ramjet, or the idea behind his creation. It's one of the reasons I started letting my hair bleach in the sun. Made me less recognizable, back in the day. But I never had a cape—or wings, until now." He chuckled.

I was flummoxed on many levels. "Did you just mind meld with me? And are you going to tell me you're Batman too?"

"No, that would be billionaire Octavius Wynne in all his effeminate glory. Or at least he was the idea for the comic character in his younger years. He stalled for a while in his thirties, like me, but is now aging due to his Vegas mogul status."

"Batman is gay?"

"What was your first clue? The whole Robin boy-wonder thing not enough for you?"

"Well, this is disappointing," I said.

Roger's eyes narrowed. "Do I want to know why?"

"As far as my bucket list goes, Superman was never in the running. But Batman definitely was."

Chapter 78

"You know what gets me?" I said as Roger and I lay on a blanket under the stars, deep in the desert where we could see the Milky Way.

"What's that, beautiful? Your skin is so soft."

"Leave it to Americans to create an alien character like Superman that exists only to protect us from our own stupidity, as if you have nothing better to do."

"Well, Red Orbiters *can* stop bullets. And I can block missiles," said Roger.

"It's either that, or aliens are all evil and out to destroy us. No middle ground, which doesn't reflect well on us. Have we evolved at all? I don't think so. The projection is pathetic. Wait. Did you say missiles?" I sat up and stared at him. "Like the one launched at the moon on my birthday?"

Roger smiled.

"You really are Superman. Do you have x-ray vision? Don't answer that. I can't handle much more."

"Sure you can, beautiful. You handled me just fine." He was looking at me with those electric-green eyes, and I heard the words in my head.

"How do you *do* that?" I said.

"It's kind of like x-ray vision. It can be useful at times, but most don't pay attention like you do. And I prefer to converse out loud."

"Do you put ideas in people's heads that way? Can all Red Orbiters do that?"

"Not all of us have this skill. Senator Rojas-Ortiz does. It has to do with our eyes. And it's not necessarily for putting ideas in anyone's head. It's useful for communicating when you don't want others present to hear."

"So your eyes do more than change color."

"Yes, and there's definitely more I'd like to do. Shall I put an idea in your head?" said Roger as his body rose up to cover mine and I kissed that Superman tattoo.

Hours later, I stretched and marveled at the lithe feel of my muscles. I should've been exhausted. "Who knew the ultimate superpower would be the ability to make a woman feel young again?"

"As long as it's in your mind, I can take care of your body," said Roger.

We were on a mountaintop in the Black Mountains, and the cooler crystalline air felt marvelous on my skin.

"Can I ask more questions, or are you too tired?"

Roger's chuckle was so deeply sensuous, I reveled in its vibrancy. "I shouldn't be surprised you're not too tired," he said. "Then again, I'm not done yet."

Holy super moly.

"Olivia Warnock's husband, your college buddy, Oggie. He's your age?" I asked.

"Yes, but once he married, he chose to begin aging with Olivia."

"Is that weird for you, watching people age while you stay the same?"

"Not really. Take Oz. He's always been a character—that hasn't gone away with aging. Most people become more interesting, even if their bodies change. And I haven't stayed the same except in my physical body."

"I know I can't ask too much about that," I pursed my lips. "So I'll change the subject. How did O.W. make all his money?"

"Diamond mines on Mars."

"So that really is a red diamond on his finger," I murmured.

"One more stop before I take you home. You ready?"

We flew through the air, my skin caressed by the night air and the feel of Roger's body against mine.

"Could you have let me put my dress on first?" I said as we touched down onto soft sand. "What if drones see us?"

Roger chuckled and continued to hold me close.

"I know you can't really see your favorite petroglyphs in the dark, but I thought you might enjoy being here without tourists."

I looked about at dark shapes of boulders surrounding us, inhaling the scent of sagebrush. The air felt denser, almost moist.

"We're on Mouse's Tank Trail, aren't we? Valley of Fire. My favorite spot."

"Yes, ma'am," he said, kissing me as I leaned against Aztec sandstone so very ancient and magnificent.

And I didn't even mind his calling me ma'am.

Nearing dawn, I was splayed on top of Roger's body, elbow resting on the Superman tattoo, my palm cupping my chin. "I heard voices," I said. "While we were...while I was, you know. Was it Red Orbiters at headquarters? It was so muted and strange."

"And it wasn't just sex," said Roger, but his lips weren't moving as I stared into his eyes, glinting green by the light of the moon.

"I didn't mean to—"

"It's okay, Rowan. I know this is new for you," Roger said aloud, stroking my face. "The voices weren't Red Orbiters nearby. You heard the ancient ones of the universe, spirits surrounding us in this sacred space."

"I always knew this place was special, but why haven't I heard them before?"

"You were completely open, receptive. No guards, no barriers. Engaging with abandon yet fiercely embracing every facet of your being, and sharing your own inner spirit."

Chapter 79

I slept in. Bodie still got his walk, four hours late. It was hot and sticky, and all I could think of was how wonderful that cool night air had felt caressing my skin, among other things.

Between cups of coffee I showered before checking out what was going on in the world. As usual all hell was breaking loose with breaking news.

"HOMELAND SECURITY SECRETARY RESIGNS"

"HOMELAND LEADERSHIP IN CHAOS AMID ANTI-ALIEN SCANDAL"

"AG KAHN INVESTIGATED FOR ABUSE OF POWER"

I called Tim Rider's private number.

"Hi, Rowan. It's crazy here, for sure. And unfortunately, before the secretary resigned along with the acting deputy director for cybersecurity, they fired Bart, claiming he was the whistleblower and leaker and anything else they could lob at his head."

"What will he do?"

"Fiction becomes truth. Bart's turned whistleblower and will testify before Congress next month."

"Are you going to be okay?"

"I am. I got a cat, and Maggie and I are getting a house together, so I'm staying in Vegas. I'm her plus-one for the Red Orbiter wedding in October, and my parents visit in November to meet her.

We're having Thanksgiving dinner at Galaxy Table, courtesy of Rose Bergin."

"I don't mean this to sound patronizing, but I'm proud of you, Tim, and so happy for you."

"And I'm in awe of you, Luna Moth Woman," he said.

I called my sister next, figuring she could bring me down to Earth. "Interesting development."

"What? They're not trying to get you to run for office, are they?"

I told her about Roger being the prototype for Superman.

"You know what this means, don't you? Luna Moth Woman really is Lois Lane!"

My fictional character *was* a journalist. "You're right," I said. "Truth once again tangles with fiction. But that's not all. He's Roger Ramjet too."

After she finished laughing, G said, "Leave it to my little sister to have found her own Arnold. You always were obsessed with his muscles."

"Remember how Mom wouldn't buy me that Pumping Iron calendar for my birthday when he was Mr. Universe? She said he was tacky. But I don't think she's going to find Roger tacky, though I'm worried what she might say to him when we're there for the wedding."

"About the wedding," said G. "Your mother is now the official flower consultant and helped Ophelia select her wedding shoes. But guess who gets to be sous chef for Rose Bergin?"

Chapter 80

Ophelia's wedding shoes weren't black, a surprise and a relief. Neither were the flowers, which were red and white. Not a carnation or gladiola in the bunch, thanks to Mom, who considered them funeral-arrangement fodder.

Red Orbiter weddings were not too different from ours. Ophelia wore white, and she and Bruce spoke vows to each other and bestowed rings, but without anyone officiating. Witnesses were all that was required, and there were plenty of those, including both sets of parents, not to mention mine. Mom shouted "Bravo!" after the ceremony was done.

Rauc's folks announced their decision to stall in their seventies so they might enjoy watching grandchildren grow up. Red Orbiter children were part of the vows Ophelia and Bruce had exchanged, including loving and living together, and helping each other grow into their individual gifts, along with their children.

I asked Rauc if Ophelia was already expecting, given the focus on procreation.

Rowdy overheard and said, "She's having triplets in the spring! Word has it one will be named after me!"

We were on a hillside overlooking a vineyard in Oregon wine country, the autumn air crisp with the scent of apples piled in bowls as part of the flower arrangements. Special red apples originally from Jupiter, aka Cumulus.

"Doodles, did you hear the news!" Mom called out from the winery's events room.

No, but all Red Orbiters present now had breaking news of my childhood nickname.

My dear friend George approached with the rest of my family, saying, "Phil is coming to work with us at OUTWARD, finding new technology and ideas for us to invest in!"

G said, "No telling how many wristwatches he'll end up with after this."

Mom said, "I just hope my son-in-law finds some good shoe stores! Doodles, do you need to shop for shoes while you're here?"

"Who's Doodles?" said Roger, striding up in an all-black tuxedo.

"Thanks, Mom." I glared at Roger because no way did he not already know my nickname.

"Sorry, Rowan. I forgot. But who is this?" Mom extended her hand to Roger. "I'm Audrey Layne, and I'm more *matooer* than I look, but it's important to stay with it, no matter what your age, don't you think?"

"Roger William Rogers, at your service. And you are a stunning woman in that black dress! As beautiful as your daughters." He looked from Mom to G when he said it, so my sister gripped my arm and emitted an eek.

"Breathe," I muttered to her under my own accelerated breath.

Dad reached out his hand to shake Roger's. "Gene Layne. William's also my middle name. Were you in the Navy?"

"Yes, sir. I was a pilot."

"He also played football for Texas," I told Dad.

"Did you ever play basketball?" asked G.

Before anyone could ask about golf, Mom said, "I would like to toast." She raised her glass of champagne. "To Red Arbitrators for coming into our Doodles' life and being so good to her! You are part of our family now too!"

"Thank you, Audrey. I hope you saved me a jitterbug because it sounds like the band's playing," said Rauc, looking extraordinarily fine in black tuxedo with red cummerbund.

"Watch out," said Phil. "Once you get my mother-in-law dancing, she won't stop. We might need to invest in Red Orbiter Audrey survival equipment."

As everyone headed inside the winery and I chuckled at watching Roger explain to Dad how he'd played football in 1914 and fought in World War II, a hand slipped around my waist, pulling me back outside.

"I'm enjoying ogling you in this dress now that I can enjoy it," said Win. "At the convention, I had too much to pay attention to."

I was in my teal-blue dress and shoes, and Kyle had cut and styled my hair and Mom's once I'd arrived in Portland via Rauc's orb. I'd had to do my own makeup, though my sister helped and talked Mom out of the false eyelashes she was pushing for.

"You look positively yummy yourself, Mr. Superspy. Genie wants to dance with you."

"I want to dance with you, among other things. But let's talk shop for a second," said Win, still hugging my waist.

"Always working," I said, shaking my head.

"Who, me? I wanted to tell you that when we met with your brother-in-law, we also spoke with your dad. He's curious about the technology we're working on. I told him he can visit our Washington State location or the new facility in Vegas anytime he wants."

"Win, you need to go easy on him. He's in his mid-eighties, you know."

"Bruce wants to help him understand his abilities. He isn't concerned about his age. His dad's also in his eighties and plays golf. I think it will be great for him."

"Okay, but if you get a wild hair and decide to hire Mom for fashion coordination, I'm moving to Scotland."

"Red would approve," said Win.

"Why? Does he now hate me so much, he wants me out of the country?"

"On the contrary. When I told him you'd studied comparative law in Scotland, he said he might just have to find a way to marry you."

"I'm surprised he's not at this wedding," I said, floundering for a response.

"He's in DC testifying against government officials who colluded with the Homeland secretary and others to wage war on aliens."

"It's all going down, isn't it? And in two weeks, we have an election."

"Yes, but there's something else going down that involves you, and that's what I need to talk to you about. I've received electronic messages. From Greens. They've been trying to reach out to you."

"Me?"

"Yes you. They want to meet, at Mount Charleston."

Chapter 81

I picked up Bodie and Morris at the local vet, where I'd boarded them for the wedding and a week spent visiting my family. I didn't have Oapule for home visits in Vegas, so I decided this was best and tried to convince myself it was harder on me than them.

Once home, Morris made a lot of crotchety noises and buried himself in my bed. Bodie wouldn't leave my side once we were in the house, which was surprising because Rauc was there.

"Look at this pic Ophelia just sent," said Rauc, handing me his phone.

Bruce and Ophelia on the banks of Loch Ness. They were in Scotland for their honeymoon, after which they were headed to the moonship for a post-wedding party with Owen and others who hadn't been able to make the nuptials.

"Hey, I just realized what with Ophelia being a marine biologist, she might know about Nessie. What do you know about it?"

Rauc laughed. "Don't you think we should leave something for the Red Orbiter book? You don't want to know everything all at once, do you?"

"Is that a rhetorical question? You sound like Roger, or Rowdy. Speaking of which, I'm not sure what was scarier at the wedding, Oz cutting in on you to dance with Mom or Rowdy dancing with her after that."

"I just remember how much I enjoyed dancing with you, Copper," said Rauc, pulling me close to two-step across my tiled floors while Bodie leapt alongside us.

The next afternoon my burner phone rang as Rauc was getting ready to leave for headquarters. I wasn't going because I had my own very important meeting.

I answered, and Win said, "I'll be there at five to get you, and they want you to bring Bodie."

"I thought they didn't like dogs."

Rauc's eyebrow rose as he watched me on the phone.

"I think they see it as a chance to better understand canines," said Win.

"I don't like you going there without Red Orbiter protection," said Rauc for the umpteenth time when I got off the call.

"We've discussed this." I laid my hand on his shoulder, giving him a peck on the cheek. "They asked Win to bring me. They're familiar with him from way back. It's not like you'll be far away. Plus, you know they're not a threat."

Rauc departed and I filled water bottles to take for Bodie, who at least would smell nice for his meet and greet, as he'd gotten a bath where he was boarded.

Win didn't need evasive driving up the mountain, but the road still gave me vertigo, so I tried to concentrate on shadows of Joshua trees. He handed me a bottled water, taking it away from me when I kept squeezing, making it crackle.

It was dark save for moonlight as we entered a clearing beyond a campsite, the Jeep heading into a wooded area, its headlights illuminating a cove of trees and the silhouettes of small gray figures. Win parked, and I grabbed Bodie's leash. He whimpered.

"We're going to make new friends, Bodie, and I'm nervous too. But it will be okay."

As we approached, figures stepped from the pine trees, appearing green by the light of the nearly full moon. One of them held a glowing saucer I soon realized was a fluorescent Frisbee likely left behind by campers. Bodie loved having one tossed to him in my big backyard in Yearntown.

My head filled like an incoming storm with clouds about to burst. "Canine. Play?" This time I could distinctly detect a question in the tone.

"I'm sure he would love to play. Just remember, he will only chase you if you run from him. And you'll need to move out of his way if he wants to leap on you to play, but he isn't trying to hurt you."

I let Bodie off his leash as three smaller Greens approached with the Frisbee, one tossing it across the clearing but not too far. Bodie yipped with joy, running in a streaked blur to fly through the air and catch it.

"He doesn't like to bring it back," I explained. "I'll get it from his mouth."

We stood and watched them play, and Win and I looked at each other, smiling. What were the odds we'd ever see "little green men" throwing a glowing flying saucer for my dog?

I poured water in a bowl for Bodie as two Greens approached and my head filled with wispy clouds.

"Talk. Now?"

"Yes, I am happy to talk with you, and I thank you for inviting me up here. My friend Win says this is one of your headquarters." I gripped Win's hand as I spoke, trying to relax and let my head fill with words as they came.

"You. Welcome. Here."

"Thank you!" I smiled. "I've wanted to visit Mount Charleston, as it's been years since I've been here. I'd like to come back in the daytime, and once we get snow."

I sensed an agitation or some sort of disturbance in my head.

"No. Welcome Earth."

I turned to Win. "They said I'm welcome here, and I thought they meant this mountain, but then they said no. They said, 'Welcome Earth.' I don't know what they mean, and I don't want to upset them."

One of the Greens stepped forward and reached out a hand with three very long fingers.

I looked at Win, and he nodded. I let go of his hand and reached out to take the hand of the small creature as my head filled with lighter, breezier clouds.

"Rowan. Welcome. Earth."

"I'm welcome on Earth?"

The alien squeezed my hand and nodded. "Win. Welcome."

"You're welcome too," I said to Win, beaming.

I was now surrounded by Greens coming forward like something momentous was about to occur. My head felt as if billowy clouds were drifting through.

"First. In. Time."

It was as if a great gust of wind was swirling around me as the revelation hit.

"Oh. My. Gosh. You. It was you. You were first in time on Earth? You're not aliens!"

I thought I might need to sit down, I felt so woozy. I looked at Win with Bodie leaning against his legs. He was grinning.

"I knew it," he said. "It makes so much sense when you think about it."

"So what do you call yourselves? Do you mind that we call you Greens? I was worried you might not like that," I said, still holding hands with this marvelous creature, its fingers laced with mine like we'd been pals for a thousand years.

"We. Earthlings," it said inside my head, and if they had mouths I knew it would be grinning.

As Win drove us back down the mountain, I said, "No way is the world ready to hear this first-in-time news. I'm glad it's their story to tell so I don't have to."

"As far as Greens and their existence, that's a no-brainer. They don't want to out themselves. It's a different story when it comes to the origins of humans, and that may be what Red Orbiters are aiming for in the book you're to write."

"Roger that," said Roger in my ear.

"Damn it, you made me spill my water!"

"Sorry, beautiful, just popping in to let you know we had a meeting to discuss Oz's big reveal on *60 Minutes*. The show airs next Sunday, right before the election."

Win asked, "Which Red Orbiter is horning in on my time with you?"

"Roger, of course. Rauc would never be so rude."

"Yeah, but that big jerk Rowdy would," said Rowdy.

"Okay, you two spooks, out of my ears! I will talk to you later about this big reveal! Maybe I'll have one of my own for you!"

Win said, "I think they already know about Greens, Rowan."

"No fair," I muttered. "A gal can't have any secrets."

Chapter 82

I was in Roger's suite, but we weren't alone. It was a watch party for Oz's appearance on *60 Minutes*. Rauc and Rowdy picked me up in a red orb for the occasion, and Genie and Maggie and Tim were also present, along with Win and Red and even O.W. and Rose Bergin, who'd prepared yummy finger food, and I learned pistachios were from Venus.

Win joined me on the couch, sitting too close, as usual, but I didn't mind.

"You look like you're lost in thought," he said. "You okay, sweet pea?"

"I'm great. I was thinking how far I've come since the last time I watched Oz on TV. It was a very lonely, difficult time, and here I am surrounded by friends, loving life in Las Vegas."

Win leaned forward and kissed me. It wasn't a passionate kiss, but tender and perhaps a tad possessive. "I'm always here for you," he said.

When the show began, I was on the couch between Rauc and Tim, another thing I would not have imagined six months ago.

"Careful," Rowdy snarked at me, nodding toward Tim. "Or we'll start calling you cougar."

"Zip it, Rowdy," said Rauc, but he and Tim and Maggie laughed.

"Everybody zip it because Ozymandias is speaking!" said O.W.

The interviewer opened by asking, "When we spoke last about Red Orbiters, you did not reveal that you are one. Can you explain why?"

"Yes, I am a Red Orbiter, head of our North American organization in fact, and getting ready to retire next month. At the time, it was decided each individual member of our species could decide when to reveal their identities. My nephew Rauc Wilde chose to reveal his when he announced a book to be written about us and what we do here on Earth."

"Was he a spy before he was an astronaut?" I whispered to Rauc. "Because he didn't really answer that question."

"You're retiring? What are your plans?" Oz was asked.

"My niece is having triplets in the spring, so I plan to enjoy being a great uncle and maybe doing a little flying here and there. Plus I'll be available to consult with Rowan Layne on the book about Red Orbiters."

"So are all Red Orbiters related, or will that be covered in this book?"

"We're all connected by DNA," answered Oz.

"Let's talk about DNA, since you mentioned it. A lot of folks are learning about, and grappling with, their alien DNA and—"

"You mean despite the president continuing to deny he has any?" interjected Oz.

"We'll get to that. Can you tell us where Red Orbiters came from and why they look so much like humans?"

"First, the traits you see as human are actually alien. The first humans to arrive on Earth came from a planet that no longer exists that was in that big gap you see between Mars and Jupiter. It was hit by an asteroid millions of years ago, so survivors had to find a new home, some coming to Earth. Those that stayed, along with visitors from other planets, moons, and stars in the galaxy, blended and evolved into what you see as humans today but are in fact hybrid aliens from all walks of life in the universe. Red Orbiters are from what you know as Jupiter, but we don't name planets after your concept of Greek gods." Oz shook his head.

The camera panned to the stunned interviewer before cutting to a commercial.

"Anybody checking Twitter?" said Rowdy.

"On it," said Win. "President tweeted five times that he is not a nasty alien and not from Uranus like those evil fairy bugs and that Oz guy is a liar and should be kicked out of the universe. All variations on that theme, plus he misspelled *universe*, *fairy*, and *Uranus*."

Back on the air, the interviewer recapped, "So you're saying human origins did not begin here but came from another planet? But why would we then have DNA identified as being from other countries on Earth?"

"It's simply DNA of your most recent ancestors," said Oz. "The last few hundred years out of millions. Had your great-great-great grandmother had her DNA tested, it would not necessarily have revealed her to be from whatever country she was living in at the time. It would have shown DNA of her ancestors, wherever they might be from. Just as no one's DNA in America identifies them as from the United States, because that's not how DNA works. It's not your DNA that makes you an American, or even a patriot."

"President rage-tweeting in all caps that real Americans are not nasty aliens and he or his ancestors never had sex with aliens. Misspelled *ancestors* and *Americans*," said Win.

"And we haven't even gotten to the good stuff yet," said Red.

They broke for a commercial before the interviewer returned asking for a much-anticipated explanation of why Earth's moon was a spaceship.

"The moon was destroyed by nuclear war among two feuding factions of aliens thousands of years ago. Red Orbiters built a spaceship to resemble the moon so that those on Earth would not live in fear of why their moon vanished. Survivors from the moon were invited to live in the moonship, and there are descendants living there today who did not take kindly to the US president launching a missile attack on their home, without provocation, and without reason. And also without following constitutional protocol of his own nation when it came to engaging in an act of war against them and all aliens."

"So you're saying aliens have nuclear capabilities?" said the *60 Minutes* interviewer.

"Nuclear weapons did not originate on Earth," said Oz.

"President tweeting it's fake news and we are the greatest nuclear power in the universe over which he has absolute power and anyone who says otherwise is a liar who must be annihilated. Misspelled pretty much everything," said Win.

Oz turned to face the camera, as if addressing all of us watching. "The president is no doubt right this minute tweeting and raging about fake news, when in fact the only thing truly fake, he has failed to recognize as so. You and your cronies, Mr. President, you claimed everything real was fake and all aliens were out to get you. So we gave you fake aliens out to attack America. You fell for it. You gave in to your hate and fear. You wanted an enemy. We gave you one. Wrapped up in a phony, bright, and shiny package."

Chapter 83

Three days after Election Day, Red Orbiters were also undergoing a change of command at their Valley of Fire headquarters.

I was seated as a guest of honor in the front row between Roger and Rowdy waiting for the ceremony to start, discussing the unprecedented election.

"That wanker lost by a landslide, didn't even win in his home state, and yet he still might have to be forcefully removed," said Rowdy. "What a putrid putz. Still claiming he has no alien DNA and that aliens can't hold office so he'll get to be president forever."

Roger looked at me and said, "We knew he would never resign like Nixon. But unlike Nixon, he will be prosecuted, along with his attorney general, as Nixon's was."

"They are both more dangerously corrupt than their predecessors," I said. "And I'm not sure I want to know how much you two were involved. Scratch that. I want to know everything."

My phone pinged with a text from Mom. "That jackass deserves to be in jail!!! He can't handle it that we will finally have a woman president!!! Bravo for us!!! Your father and I also send congratulations to Rock!!! I made reservations for you at Seven Gables and dinner too!!! Enjoy your special Thanksgiving!!!

374

(clapping hands, kissy face, turkey, table place setting, face with stars for eyes emoji)

Rowdy said, "Rowan, surely you haven't forgotten our theory of low matter? As in, those we deem greatly lacking in brain matter don't matter in terms of our time, so we don't intervene?"

"Yes, but you do intervene if someone crosses a line. You told me so."

"The president crossed that line," said Rowdy sounding serious, which was beyond weird.

Roger snorted. "That's the greatest understatement of all time."

"The problem is," I said, "his cult members are going to get worse. Their rage will explode against a woman president and an otherworldly vice president. It's like we've taken a giant step forward only to go three steps backward."

"Red Orbiter work is never done," said Rauc in my ear. "Don't worry, Copper. We've got this." He was walking onto the stage.

We all got to our feet and cheered the new head of the Red Orbiter organization for North America.

Rauc thanked everyone for coming and Oz for his introduction, saying how much the former astronaut would be missed at headquarters but knowing we'd all be safer with him patrolling the skies in their newest spacecraft, for which he gave kudos to OUTWARD.

I turned in my seat and smiled at the group sitting behind me, including my sister and her hubby, Phil, and George, Win, and Red. Maggie and Tim were there too, and of course Genie, O.W., and Rose Bergin. Bruce and Ophelia and Owen the Marine were still in the moonship but were watching via satellite.

I whispered to G, "Is Rauc taking me to Monterey for Thanksgiving? Did you know?"

"Did Mom spill the beans? She can't keep a secret!" said G.

I turned back around as Rauc was coming to my favorite portion of his speech, which I'd helped him write.

"Earth has always enjoyed the protection of our planet's magnetic force, that powerful gravity nudging dangerous comets away. But its inhabitants have never known how much Red Orbiters have protected them as a people from those who would seek to destroy them and what they have created, the very freedoms they stand for. Under my leadership, Earth's species will learn more about us as we continue to nudge those dangers aside and work together to allow this planet, this continent, this nation to be the safe harbor it has always been for so many species in the galaxy."

At the party that followed, Rauc pulled me aside. We were outside on the Red Orbiter flight deck, currently chock-full of flying saucers, orbs, and pistachio crafts. So many had arrived within a short time span that voluminous clouds were created so as not to alarm park visitors. Greens even got involved with dust devils on the ground to distract tourists.

I chuckled at the thought of it.

"What's got you grinning, Copper?" said Rauc, wrapping his arms around me from behind and nipping my earlobe next to my shooting-star earring.

"I just realized how ironic it is the Air Force claimed the Roswell crash was a weather balloon." I turned and grinned at him. "And were you going to tell me about your Thanksgiving plans, or just swoop in and abduct me like Greens or an evil giant bug?"

"I confess, I told your parents I wanted to take you back to Monterey, though I did want it to be a surprise I was going to reveal today." Rauc looked sheepish, but deliciously handsome.

"Mom blabbed. Is that what you brought me outside for?"

"Partly, and to get you alone for a few minutes. We haven't really had a chance to discuss what this new role I'm taking on means for us." He pulled me into his arms.

"I know you'll be busier than ever, but I'm thrilled for you. I'm tickled about going back to Monterey too."

"But, Copper, it means so much more than that. I will be busy, but I'll be right here most of the time. I won't be flying every day and hour with Rowdy, traveling the region."

"Are you going to miss flying?"

"Sometimes, but I can still fly whenever I want—it just doesn't have to be as an observer. And when I do fly, it can be with you, for the book. I'm going to have a chance to answer your questions, to share with you what I know, and who I am."

I could hear music from the party inside the conference center.

"They're playing our song from *Hope Floats*," said Rauc, moving my body with his to a two-step. "I want to make you feel my love, Copper. I know this song has a line about not having made your mind up, but I'm willing to give us time."

"Okay, but I hear this growing-old stuff is not for sissies. Are you going to call me Silver instead of Copper if I stop dyeing my hair?"

Rauc laughed and kissed me, swatting my butt.

"This Red Orbiter leader of North America title's going to your head, isn't it? No more passive nice guy? Should I call you Romulus and treat you like a Roman god?"

"Interesting thought. Too bad I can't carry you off to my chariot in the sky right now so we could explore that proposition thoroughly."

Rowdy called out, "Hey you two lovebugs, Oz is ready to make a toast!" just as fluffy clouds filled my frontal lobe.

"Rowan. Be. Happy."

Later, I had a chance to sneak away for a chat with my sister.

"I've got aliens in my ears, in my head, and in my bed. What on earth happens next?"

Lightning Source UK Ltd.
Milton Keynes UK
UKHW020643290920
370728UK00013B/1069